"Rose, you are putting words in my mouth."

"And are you saying that even if I asked you, we no longer have the wood because you returned it to the carpenter without asking my permission?"

"Rose, please, you aren't letting me—"

"Oh, and even if we did have the wood, 'twould be better used building a wharf for Peter Walters, whose plan it is to use my river frontage to dock his ships and run his family's business from my land?"

Peter swiped his fingers through his hair. God in heaven, what had he done? How had he gotten into this? A few simple words, and she had taken them beyond the moon. He had no idea how to work his way back.

"Now see here, Rose," he began. Her mouth opened to argue with him once more, and his control snapped. He seized her arm and brought her up against him. Her eyes widened. But instead of picking her up as he'd done just days ago, he merely brought her against him, her body pressed all along the length of his. He had time to register how good that felt, just barely, before he brought his lips down on hers.

And then they were truly beyond the moon, sailing somewhere amid the stars. He hadn't expected to feel such a shock of recognition, as if this had just been waiting for them both to acknowledge it. He strove to keep the kiss light and not punishing, but there was too much temper between them. The anger that turned so neatly into passion, however, stunned him. This was a new, unwelcome dimension to the challenge that occurred daily between him and Rose . . .

Dear Romance Reader,

In July last year, we launched the Ballad line with four new series, and each month we'll present both new and continuing stories set everywhere from medieval England to the American West—the kind of passionate, romantic stories you love best, written by the most gifted authors. At the back of each book, we'll tell you when you can find subsequent books in the series that have captured your heart.

Debuting this month with a fabulous new series called *The Rock Creek Six*, Lori Handeland offers **Reese.** The first hero in a series of six written alternately by Lori and Linda Devlin, Reese is haunted by the war—and more than a bit skeptical that a spirited schoolteacher can heal his wounded heart. If you liked the movie *The Magnificent Seven*, this is the series for you! Next, critical favorite Corinne Everett continues the *Daughters of Liberty* series with **Fair Rose,** as a British beauty bent on independence in America discovers that partnership is tempting—especially with the right man.

Alice Duncan whisks us back to turn-of-the-century California, and the early days of silent films, with the next *Dream Maker* title, **The Miner's Daughter.** A stubborn young woman hanging onto her father's copper mine by the skin of her teeth has no place in a movie—or so she believes, until one of the film's investor's decides she's the right woman for the role, and for him. Finally, the fourth book in the *Hope Chest* series, Laura Hayden's **Stolen Hearts,** joins a modern-day cat burglar with an innocent nineteenth-century beauty who holds the key to his family's lost legacy—and to his heart.

Kate Duffy
Editorial Director

Daughters of Liberty

FAIR ROSE

Corinne Everett

ZEBRA BOOKS
KENSINGTON PUBLISHING CORP.

http://www.zebrabooks.com

*For Christopher and Colin, the world's greatest sons.
Thanks for eating all that pizza so I could finish this!*

Chapter One

I would be married, but I'd have no wife,
I would be married to a single life.
—Richard Cranshaw, *On Marriage*, 1646

Peter Walters walked up the steps of his sister's riverfront home, shading his eyes against the dimness of the gallery where Lily Pearson sat sketching floral designs for an upcoming wedding. Disentangling his legs from his twin nephews' exuberant embrace of his knees, he took off his wide-brimmed planter's hat to wipe the sweat from his brow, because even the river's breeze could not cool the August morning of Tidewater Virginia.

"Lily, do you remember the Earl of Lansdale's riverfront property that I offered for last year?" he said, a faint tinge of distaste in his voice for the English title. "You recall the Earl agreed, but then Adam's London barrister learned that Lansdale had died? I've just had a letter from someone there—Lansdale's family name is Fairchild. One of them is coming to look over the estate. The new heir, I believe."

Peter waved away the milk and sweet biscuits his nephews offered him, surprised that their sister Violet—who considered herself a triplet, although she was a full year younger than the twins—wasn't arguing over the division of food. She must be taking one of her rare naps.

"Thank you, boys, but no," he said, as they held out the plate in their grubby hands. "You eat them."

"Peter, sit, won't you?" Lily waved him toward a seat in one of the rockers.

He shook his head. "No, no, I wouldn't feel right if I needlessly dirtied your verandah, Lily." With a glance at the eight-year-olds, Adam and Arthur, who had turned back to their task of sorting the James River's choicest—and muddiest—rocks at her feet, she laughingly tried to persuade him that a little more dirt wasn't a major concern of hers.

Again Peter resisted. She would only try to get him to talk, he thought. He had always adored his older sister, but her well-meaning efforts to help him out of his self-imposed isolation these last two years weren't helping. Ashamed at his own churlishness, Peter pointed to the sweat-damp kerchief tied round his neck and his old tunic and stuck with his "I'm dirty" excuse.

"We're working in the south orchard. I should get back."

He slapped his hat against his thigh, thinking how good it would be to finally build a dock of their own, not realizing that he'd spoken aloud. Lily leaned forward, as if to put aside her work. Peter caught her movement from a corner of his eye and reflexively retreated a step. Lily frowned.

"Peter, Will and Adam and the workers are doing well enough. You needn't spend so much time in the orchards," Lily said. "I know you're itching to do other work." From his sister's slightly melancholy smile, he knew that his step back hadn't offended her, but she would have liked him to talk about his instinctive need to distance himself.

Peter just wished he'd kept his mouth shut. Despite her three children, busy floral business, and the expansion of the Pearson-Walters business from flowers to fruit and ornamental trees, Lily still had far too much time to worry about him, as far as he was concerned.

"You know I don't mind it, Lily. I'm happy to lend a hand wherever I'm most needed. After all, my ships and our own landing won't do Tidewater Nurseries any good without the products to transport, now will they?" He mustered a smile, and that was all the social grace he had for the day. Dirt, sweat, and good honest labor were preferable to sitting around thinking—much less talking—about his own life.

"Be good for your mother, you scapegraces," he said to the boys. "And kiss your sister for me." At the look of horror filling their eyes at the thought—kiss a girl! worse, kiss Violet!—he did smile. Then he replaced the woven straw hat on his head before turning to go. He waved at Lily.

Hoping it didn't look too much like a strategic

retreat—if he kissed Lily or let her get up, she would start trying to keep him here—he refused to consider that his behavior could be at all similar to that of his nephews. After all, he didn't run away from girls, and he quite liked kissing them. Or he had, until Joanna. After her, nothing seemed open or honest or easy anymore.

Lost in his own thoughts, he didn't see Lily's furrowed brow as she stared after him, or hear the twins' raucously noisy farewell.

A sleepy Violet stumbled out of the house a few moments later, too late to see the visitor. "Was that Unca Peter?" she asked her mother. Lily, who still gazed after Peter's distant figure, nodded absently. Violet took the plate of cookies while her brothers weren't looking. They were busy fighting over who had found the smooth green stone that they declared to be "marble." Only another trip to the river would satisfy Arthur that Adam hadn't gained a permanent advantage and made his collection of treasures better than his brother's, so off they ran.

Violet seemed for once content to sit with her mother and not insist on following the boys. "Why is Unca Peter sad, Mama?" she asked, swallowing her biscuit properly before speaking.

Maybe Violet wouldn't be a complete hoyden after all, Lily thought, more impressed by her daughter's manners than her insight. Violet's intuition was startling, but Lily had grown used to her small daughter's keen observations. She looked like a miniature of her father, with her thick dark hair and aquamarine eyes, while the boys looked more like Peter and Lily with the Walters tawny hair and eyes. Her husband Adam looked at the world with extraordinary blue-green eyes that analyzed everything; it seemed their daughter already did the same.

"Do you think he's sad, sweetling?" Lily asked. Peter looked just as handsome as when he'd studied law at the College of William and Mary ten years before. But the war for America's independence had changed him. The sunny lad who'd been her heart's delight, the boy she had raised alone after their parents' untimely death, had grown up.

She'd expected that, of course. What she had not expected was war's effect on him. The United States were free now—Cornwallis's surrender at Yorktown had seen to that in '81—but Peter, late of America's small navy, had been a prisoner of war then, and was not released until two years later, when the Treaty of Paris, ending the war, had been signed.

Peter had never spoken of the prison camp where he'd been held in New York, but she did not think that was the problem, nor had he been ill-treated. She'd received a few letters about a lass he'd met, then called her his fiancée in one letter before he'd been taken prisoner. After that, although his letters had been few and far between, he had never mentioned her again. When he came home, she learned that Joanna and her family had moved, but nothing more than that. Peter would no longer even speak her name.

The bitter edge to Peter's warm voice, the cold fire in his eyes when he spoke of the British, troubled Lily. Fortunately, Peter bore her husband

Adam no ill will, although Adam was British. Or had been British. Adam had converted to the Patriot cause unbeknownst to his commanding officer, who had ordered him to infiltrate the Patriot Sons of Liberty group. Adam had also single-handedly rescued Peter after his capture by Redcoats. He had risked his own life again and again for the Patriot cause, and for her family.

Knowing Adam, for one, why had Peter's feelings about the British changed? Even Lily no longer hated or resented the British, now that war was done and America was free. And America's freedom had never been about despising the British, anyway, only what their King and government had done to restrain Americans' rights. After over a hundred years here, Britain had persisted in treating the colonists as children, not as adults with rights acquired in the work they had put in to make America the strong, free, rich land that it had become.

Lily noticed her daughter was unusually still at her side. "You really think he's sad, not just, ah, tired?"

"I don't know, Mama," Violet said. "He's not exac'ly sad. Sometimes I think he's mad, but I don't know who at, and sometimes I just think he needs to be more like you when you're with Papa."

"What do you mean?"

"Unca Peter needs a lady who makes him happy."

"I think you're right, darling. Well, it doesn't have to be a lady, but yes, Uncle Peter needs to be happier."

Violet wrinkled her tiny, patrician nose, a minia-

ture of her father's. "If it's not a lady, then what?
An ol' ship?"

Lily laughed. "It doesn't seem exciting to you,
I know, but we do want our own ships, and Uncle
Peter was in the navy. If we build our own landing,
we won't have to wait for the shipmaster at Harrison's Landing to sail and risk losing any of the
plants we send to England. Dried tobacco can wait
around in a warehouse for the right time and tide,
but not some of our plants."

This was getting too complicated for Violet. She
looked around, not seeing her brothers nearby as
usual. "I wanna find the boys. Where did they go?"

"They're at the river looking for more green
stones. Arthur thinks his rock is marble," Lily said,
knowing a warning against digging in the mud at
river's edge would be useless. She knew the prospect of getting dirty didn't bother her daughter in
the least. Violet would like nothing better than to
muck about in breeches like her brothers, but Lily
drew the line at being "triplets" there.

"Marbul? I bet it came here all the way from
Italy." She scrambled to her feet and ran off before
Lily could explain that marble had to be quarried
and didn't float across the ocean on its own.

Lily looked at her lap, not seeing the floral
designs spread out there. Maybe progress on the
project that was to be Peter's distinctive contribu-
tion to the family business would help his mood.
Adam's idea to ship live plants had given them
an edge in dealing with the fussy connoisseurs of
Europe. But shipping live plants required short
deadlines, quick shipping, and the most careful
handling imaginable.

Thus had been born Peter's idea to establish

their own landing—one under their own control, and with their own ships. No longer would they need to pay their neighbors for cargo space, or risk losing the precious perishable cargo in case a captain in someone else's pay had to hold off sailing until the hold was full.

But Peter needed better river frontage for that than they had: deep water for ships and a broad swath of riverside land to build greenhouses near the wharf. Oak Grove had a landing for the family's regular travel—everyone traveled by boat on the river—but it was located on a small inlet off the James. They needed to be directly on the river, the way Willow Oaks was.

Peter had found the perfect river frontage at a neighboring estate that was ideally situated. There was room to dock as many as three sailing vessels, room even to build greenhouses at water's edge, something that could not be done at Harrison's Landing. Now all he had to do was acquire it.

And there was the rub. An English family owned this ideal property, and they had fled before the Revolution. Not to Canada as many Royalists had, but back to England.

Peter was too honest to claim the land was abandoned, and therefore could be confiscated. It probably could be and few would blink an eye, Lily knew. But Virginia planters along the James were a conservative lot, despite having been Patriots, and weren't likely to look favorably on confiscating property, even though such land had belonged to a Tory. Peter might not yet be able to put loathing for the British behind him, but most of their neighbors had.

From a practical standpoint, they'd had no

choice. Continental currency was weak and growing weaker. Trade was critical for the hard currency needed by the new American nation, and that meant, inescapably, England. There'd been no confiscations of British property along the river, nor would there be. No one wanted to risk the ire of potential trading partners.

Lily had learned that many remembered the Lansdale family fondly—the Earl, if not his Countess—and the children had played with the Byrd and Harrison children when they were small. Peter and Lily had been living in Williamsburg when war broke out and knew nothing of the Fairchild family, but from their neighbors, Peter had learned the direction of the Earl in England. Some months ago, he had begun a correspondence to inquire whether the Earl was willing to sell, as it did not appear that he would return with his family.

Peter had worked hard alongside Lily and her husband Adam to add more ornamental trees—exotic fruit trees that were highly popular among connoisseurs in England and the Continent—to their flower export business. With his naval background, he had proposed that their Tidewater Nurseries, an outgrowth of Lily's original flower-arranging business, carry out the shipping themselves. Adam, a colonel who had returned from war in 1781 blessedly unscathed, had supported the idea. Peter had planned for Oak Grove Landing to carry the freight of their business to Europe. He planned to captain the ships himself.

But he would not set foot on British soil now or ever, he had sworn. The lessons he had learned at British hands were too painful, he had said once, just once, before refusing to ever talk about it again.

Lily didn't know if his reticence and bitterness were related to Joanna.

She did know that his best friend Ethan, who had left Williamsburg and enlisted in the navy with him, had died in the same prison camp, but not through torture or ill treatment. They had all eaten poorly and been cold in winter, Peter had said, and Ethan's wound had never properly healed. They had both been in a field hospital when taken prisoner, although Peter had been less seriously wounded.

Lily suspected Ethan's death and Joanna's departure all formed part of the bitterness that still plagued Peter, but she did not see how the events or the people were related, or how it all factored into his adamant dislike for the British. For the hundredth time, she wished she could draw him out of his shell, but he would not discuss that period of his life with either her or Adam.

Lily sighed, then rose. She needed to go find the children. They had lessons and she judged that the impromptu trip to the river should curb their natural restlessness for a couple of hours. If only Peter's restlessness could be mended so easily. It wasn't that he didn't like the nursery business, just that his heart wasn't in it.

His heart wasn't in anything. And as her daughter had already figured out, that was the core problem.

Rose Fairchild, daughter of the late Earl of Lansdale, could hardly contain her excitement. She was going to America! The latest letter burned a hole in her pocket where it was tied at her waist, but she didn't feel guilty or ashamed for what she'd done, not yet anyway. A man named Peter Walters wanted her family's land in Virginia.

She had decided to go there to discuss it with him as the family's representative—that was what she had called herself in the letter she'd sent some time ago. Peter Walters didn't need to know that she had no authority and no idea of her brother's plans, mired as he was somewhere deep in India where it might take a year or more before he could come home to inherit the title he'd never expected.

Even though her beloved father and less-than-beloved older brother had died—the only reason this was possible—at last she had the chance to return to the land of her birth. Virginia was the place she'd always considered her true home, even if her Loyalist mother had managed to wipe her own memory clear of "those wretched years in the Colonies," as she liked to put it in her usual melodramatic style.

If only Papa were still alive. He wouldn't have forced her to marry against her will as Mama was doing, and might even have backed her return to America. Well, not really, that was doing it a bit too brown. Ralph would have been the one with the right to go to America, to dispose of the plantation, to do what he wished with the land along the wide, blue James River.

And Ralph would have sold it to pay his debts. After all, if he hadn't spent his inheritance in the months since Papa died, gone a-wenching one too many times, gotten caught in the wrong bed, and then killed in a duel, none of them would be in this position.

Thoughts of her father brought tears, which she fought back. They had been out of mourning for such a little time when Ralph had died. She did not feel like mourning for Ralph, the wastrel, and she would not take mourning clothes with her. Impatiently tugging her unruly red hair back, she pulled the portmanteau from beneath the bed.

Her maid Eunice burst into the room just then, breathless as usual, and carrying a pile of freshly pressed and folded linens.

"Oh no, Miss Rose," she squealed. "You aren't really going to defy your ma, are you? You're that bold."

"By the time Mama finds out what I've done, I shall be long gone." Yes, Rose thought, starting to go through the linens, the Lansdales' ugly duckling daughter would be out of sight and she hoped out of mind. Mama couldn't force her to marry that old man, the Marquess of Chilters, just to keep herself in wigs and shoe buckles. Once away from here, Rose wouldn't have to forever compare her own unfashionable looks to England's reigning beauties.

"I shall become a gloriously happy spinster, leading a quiet life in Virginia running a plantation that makes enough money for Mama to be happy and for Bertram to leave me alone. I can hardly wait."

"But your brother Bertram in India is the heir now, ain't he? Now that Master Ralph is passed on?" Eunice asked unnecessarily.

"Yes, he's in India, far, far away. Bertram wanted to get away from all this and have a life of his own, remember? I can't imagine why he would care that I'm going to America, so long as he makes money from it. He won't miss me. You know how horrid he was to me the last few years before he left."

Eunice looked dubious, but began dutifully to pull items out of Rose's chifferobe for the portmanteau. And won't the American be surprised, Rose thought. He probably assumed they were just another Royalist refugee family from the former Colonies, and that they would be only too happy to rid themselves of the reminder of a past they'd put behind them.

Not Rose. All her life she'd remembered the wide, flowing James River, the mild Virginia air, the beauty of waving spring branches in full flower. Rose had been a free, happy child until forced to return. England was too cold and too confining, and it would hold her no longer. She felt giddy enough to spin in circles.

"Miss Rose, don't go please. What will I do here alone?" Eunice asked in entreaty. "Your ma will turn me out without references if I let you run away like this."

"Eunice, I regret to say this of my own mother, but Mama will turn you off anyway once she finds I'm gone, even if she knows you had no part in it. She will have to find someone to blame and it will be you. So you might as well come with me. You shall be a proper chaperone so I am not traveling alone, and just think of the life you will have in America."

She should probably add something about men, Rose thought, knowing that Eunice was rather obsessed with the notion that at the advanced age of twenty-two, she might not find a husband. Rose herself was twenty-three, but did she care? No indeed! She had three failed Seasons behind her, with the prospect of never having to face another one. She couldn't be happier.

America was the land of opportunity, was it not? If that audacious people could overthrow a King, surely a chambermaid could find a sturdy man to marry? And an ugly duckling could find a suitable pond.

Chapter Two

Oh wrangling schools . . .
                              —John Donne, *A Fever, Songs*
                                        and Sonnets, 1609

Over the last few months, Peter had taken to riding or boating over to Willow Oaks occasionally to see that all was in order. He'd never been inside the house, but the exterior had been maintained and he thought the inside would be no different. The house had not fallen into disrepair; someone had maintained it after a fashion. Now that he'd contacted the land agent about purchasing the property, however, the man must have hired a crew to clean it up. The outbuildings had been reopened, the oval driveway cleared of weeds and trash. Peter had begun to feel rather proprietary toward Willow Oaks, yet he had missed all this. Of course, the land agent was under no obligation to contact him about cleaning up the premises. They weren't Peter's, not yet, at any rate.

What Peter didn't understand as he tied his skiff up at the dock today were the signs of sudden activity that he saw. He'd not been by for more than a week, having been hard at work with his brother-in-law Adam and the Oak Grove workers to begin preparing the orchards for fall. Had Sam Gannon, the land agent, received word that the Earl of Lansdale was ready to sell? Was all this activity prefatory to a contract?

Peter's steps quickened. A woman burst out of the kitchen building, berating a hapless servant carrying a covered tray. "What do you mean you can't cook in the house? Why is everything out here, so far away?" she asked. Peter started to smile, then stiffened as he recognized the accent. Not only was the short, mousy woman a stranger, as her ignorant question about the cookhouse showed, but he recognized the English accent.

They hadn't noticed him as he trod the dirt path well behind them, but their voices carried in the afternoon air, blown toward him by the breeze off the river. It was cool for late September—but still the woman was overdressed for the weather. Another sign of a Brit; their cold and chilly isle ill prepared them for the mild climate of the Virginia Tidewater.

He hardly needed to hear the servant's answer, from a local girl who looked vaguely familiar. Kitchens were always placed well away from the main house due to the terrible risk of fire. But who was the British woman, a servant from the looks of her?

He'd as yet had no opportunity to declare himself when the back door of Willow Oaks that looked out onto the gardens and outbuildings was flung open. "Eunice, come see," a lovely but thoroughly English voice cried. "The furniture that stood in the nursery when Bertram, Ralph, and I were small is still here. Mama must have thought the pieces too mean to take back with us. The portraits and china are all gone, but there's a rocking horse, a chest that still has toys, and . . ."

She broke off, clearly having seen past the women to Peter. "Are you with Mr. Gannon, sir?" she called. "If so, I must thank you for the lovely care you have taken of my home. I had feared it to have fallen into disarray, but I see 'tis not the case."

The servants had turned to gaze at Peter. Peter himself was flummoxed. Who were these women? Why did they talk as if they lived here? Had Gannon, the land agent, found another buyer? But surely not so quickly, especially not when Gannon knew of Peter's interest.

"I am not who you think," he began, then waited until the servants entered, passing the woman in the doorway, who nodded at them as they went by. He wondered who she was. She had fiery red hair and a surprising lack of freckles on a flawlessly straight nose. She was tall for a woman but her head would only touch his shoulder, he noted as he came to stand before her.

"Well, if you are not Mr. Gannon, then who are you?" she asked briskly, but not impolitely.

"I should like to ask the same," he said, wincing

slightly at his own formality, but unable to help his stiffness. It was the accent. That crisp, upper-class sound reminded him of Joanna, and bitterness never failed to rise in his throat.

"It has been pleasant, Peter, but only a diversion. Surely you understand that." Peter, who had stood with a ring of gold growing heavy in his pocket, had not understood. Not at all. Not then. Only much later had he understood it all.

"My family owns Willow Oaks," she said, pride evident in her tone. "And you, sir, might be . . . ?"

"Peter Walters, at your service," he said, anger growing inside him. "The would-be purchaser of Willow Oaks." He had drawn level with her now and she stepped back inside the house as he came forward.

"Oh," she said, falling back a bit more. "I wasn't ready to . . . I mean, I thought you . . ." The woman's fair skin had flushed and she looked unaccountably flustered.

"Are you the new Earl's lady wife? Is he here?" Peter asked. "I would like to speak with him."

Peter moved deeper into the long wide hallway. The back door stood in a straight line with the front door, which looked out onto the river. The main door stood open and he followed her gaze. Like hers, it was drawn to the river sparkling at a distance, but he turned toward her again.

Tall for a woman, yet graceful, she reminded him of Joanna. But where Joanna had been all cream and porcelain, this well-built young woman was fire and light. She wore no ring, but was not a servant, not with that accent. She couldn't be the Earl's daughter, because what on earth would she be doing here? Why would a fair English flower leave her cultivated garden?

Rose was growing tired of Peter Walters's skeptical gaze. All right, she hadn't told him yet who she was and why she was here, but how could he dislike her when he didn't even yet know she meant to thwart his plans? From the moment she'd first spoken, his pleasant expression had turned dark. His eyes had somehow changed to a wintry evergreen and his voice held a chilly note that hadn't been there a moment before.

Rose gave herself a little shake. Her next words were going to be a problem anyway—once he found out she wasn't here to sell the land—so she had best get on with it.

"There is little business possible between us, I fear, Mr. Walters," she said. "I am here on my . . . brother's behalf, and it is my—his—intention that I run the plantation for the family." She stood in the wide front hallway, aware that she had never been so bold in all her life, feeling suddenly frightened. Just then, the breeze from the river entering the house ruffled her hair, and she felt a sense of exhilaration, one she'd never before known. She was free to say and be whatever, whomever she liked, far from her mother and the narrow-minded conventions of English society.

He emitted a strangled sound, pinning her with a look from those eyes that seemed to sense her lie. "You can't mean that," he said with no finesse whatsoever. Rose's soaring feeling evaporated. This was more familiar ground—someone trying to tell her what to do. She folded her arms, wondering how someone so handsome could look so forbidding. Peter Walters was tall, taller than either of her brothers, with dark golden hair that waved back from his high, intelligent forehead. His eyes seemed to be a variable green.

"Let's not discuss this in the hallway, although why I owe you more than the courtesy of a good morrow, I do not know," she said, letting her annoyance show in her voice.

"We who live here along the James are a close-knit group of planters," he replied, following her into the sitting room, where the furniture still bore muslin covers.

"Yes, my father was well known and well respected, I am told, although all ties were severed by our departure and the war." And her mother, she thought, but did not say so. "We left when I was but ten. You were not here then. Where are you from?" She had not been trying to sound haughty, but she could tell from his look of mild disdain that he was taking it that way.

"Ten years ago, my sister and I lived in Williamsburg. I joined the American Navy during the war for independence while Lily moved to Oak Grove, the neighboring plantation, after her marriage."

"She did not marry that old man, what was his name?" Rose burst out, then clapped a hand over her mouth, so appalled was she at her own impropriety. She dropped her hand and tried to pretend she hadn't committed a terrible faux pas. "We, ah, visited there very rarely."

For the first time he smiled at her. It was a bit dazzling. "I can assure you my sister did not marry an old man. Her husband Adam won Oak Grove in a card game."

"In a card game?" Rose was slightly scandalized.

He folded his arms. "Aye. A common practice among the aristocracy, no?"

"My brother had . . . has rather too great a fondness for cards." She wasn't going to explain that Ralph was dead and she had no idea whether Bertram even knew he was the heir yet. "So your sister married someone with a similar fondness?"

Peter looked annoyed briefly, and then gave a snort of laughter. "Hardly. But that is a story for another time and place. My only interest at this moment is with you."

Had he not looked so forbidding, Rose might have sighed. Wouldn't it be just her luck to meet someone so breath-stealing and have him declare his interest was only in her property? He was so tall, with a frame thrillingly well-muscled, broad-shouldered, and lean-hipped. His hair was thick and full, a butternut color that complemented his golden skin and moss green eyes.

What a shame Mama couldn't have found someone like this to marry her off to provide for the family. But then, Rose doubted that there were any English lords so strong or bold as this, at least not among Mama's circle. And if by chance there had been one, he would not have been interested in her. Unfortunately Peter Walters wasn't interested in her either, he wanted to buy her land—which would provide for the family—but would leave her with nothing, no livelihood, no sense of purpose.

Mama might like the situation, but not Rose. She would not be a brood mare. Nor would she sell this land. And she would do everything she could to keep Mama or Bertram from learning of this offer, so she had intercepted the letters after Papa died. It hadn't been hard; Mama had been interested only in London gossip, not what came in the post.

Rose pulled a bell and Eunice hurried in. "Eunice, perhaps Mr. Walters would like some . . ." She nearly said **tea,** but did not want to see that look of contempt on his face again. She knew about the boycott America had staged years ago. She looked at him. "Ah , . . what would you like, sir?"

"Tea would suit me very well," he said with such a bland expression she could have sworn he was trying to vex her.

"Tea then," Rose said, and Eunice hurried out.

"How long do you plan to stay?" Peter asked, with a carefully neutral expression.

"Forever," Rose said with such unguarded longing that she knew she had revealed too much.

He raised one golden eyebrow at her emphatic tone but did not comment. "How is it that you have come here?" he asked.

"My father . . ." she stopped, momentarily at a loss for words. Being here had brought back so many memories, and suddenly, they threatened to overwhelm her. She had been so happy here, before they'd returned to England and Papa had become ill. Dear Papa. They should never have left Virginia, where the warmer climate had been healthier, she was sure, than England's chilly dampness. Papa's lungs had only grown weaker.

"I'd had a letter that there was a new heir. That must be your brother. I am sorry for the loss of your father," he added gently.

"Thank you." Eunice arrived with the tea just

then, so there was the usual fuss, which gave her time to regain control of herself.

Peter waited with no evident impatience, though she was acutely aware of his scrutiny. Finally, with tea poured and cakes served, she met his gaze squarely but remained silent. The initiative was his. She would wait for him to speak again.

"Is your brother arriving soon? Or perhaps you brought his proxy," he said.

"No, Mr. Walters, I am in control of the property and I intend to remain." From there the conversation deteriorated. Rose did not want Peter Walters to pry too deeply into her status, so she simply refused to provide him with more information than she had already given. She'd had no practice at being obstinate, but thought she had managed to refrain from rudeness.

Somehow she didn't think that he would agree about her manners. He gulped his tea—burning his mouth, she was certain—he was in such haste to leave after it became clear that she had no more to say. He was angry, too. Watching the broad set of his shoulders as he left, he did not have to tell her this wasn't over for her to know of his determination.

Ah, well. She hadn't thought it would be easy, and obviously it wasn't going to be.

Peter was too irritated by the encounter with Rose Fairchild to be around Lily and her brood, so he took himself off to Williamsburg instead. This meeting was to have been the culmination of months of work and planning, and in less than ten minutes he had been sized up by that chit and dismissed. He intended to drink himself into a stupor and take his ease with a tavern wench— both actions totally unlike him. He hoisted many a pint at Chowning's Tavern but, in the end, did nothing more than that. He hadn't even picked out a wench.

The Lansdale woman, damn her, was too much on his mind, with her snapping eyes and generous curves. She was nothing like Joanna, with her cool blond looks. This English Rose was spirited rather than contained, lively rather than cool, gloriously red-haired where Joanna's locks had been the fashionably correct shade of blond. Rose's complexion looked like cream, smooth and rich—not the pale and translucent porcelain that had characterized Joanna's. Even more unusual for a redhead, she had no freckles. If that came from being indoors in England, that was likely to change in the hot Virginia climate.

But he absolutely couldn't be attracted to her: he wouldn't allow himself to be. Peter wasn't ready to deal with another Englishwoman, not after Joanna's betrayal.

Yet this Rose, Countess of Lansdale, had come to America, although for what purpose he couldn't imagine. Perhaps she'd wanted to survey her dowry? That had to be it, he decided. After all, what else could she want here?

He discounted her words totally. Of course she didn't intend to stay here. What Englishwoman would? She was too refined, too spoiled, and too British.

He recited the list of requirements in his mind. He would get the land; he would build the dock; and they would expand the business. And he'd do it with or without the fiery English rose he'd met today.

From what he heard the next couple of days in town, she might not last long at all. All the merchants were a-buzz. No one knew what sort of crops she intended to plant, but her supply order was nothing short of bizarre. Sugar, salt, flour, fine— those were expected and necessary staples until the plantation could begin to produce them on its own. But she'd also ordered wood palings, vast quantities of them. Surely she couldn't mean to . . . was her brother a fool, or had he given her a ridiculously free hand?

By the end of the day, he'd formed a plan. Then he headed home from Williamsburg.

Chapter Three

My hand delights to trace unusual things,
And deviates from the known and common
way.

— Anne Finch, *The Spleen*, 1701

Here he came again. Rose wiped her hands on
her apron—her mama would have been scandalized by the lowly garment—and reached to smooth
her hair back. In truth, she wasn't all that unhappy
to see Peter Walters tie up his horse at the hitching
post, unless he meant to mock her. Her efforts so
far to create planters among the servants hadn't
been especially effective. But then her servants
were all house servants. They were the only kind
she knew, the only kind among whom Eunice had

made contacts. Rose hadn't wanted any more contact with Mr. Gannon than was necessary, fearing
too many questions.

With Peter, she had less to hide—more to prove,
but less to hide. Surely he could recommend hired
help or offer advice. Seeing the grim look on his
face as he advanced on her, however, she wondered
if it was a foolish thought that he would help her.

"Hail the conquering army," she said brightly,
then watched him pause momentarily in confusion. "What I meant was that you look like you
intend to crush me beneath your feet," she added
in explanation. His face cleared, but the look of
determination never left it.

"What are you trying to do?" he asked with no
preamble.

"Please come in," Rose said, hoping he didn't
hear her pounding heart as he brushed by her.
She'd had furniture brought from Williamsburg
but only what the woodworker had on hand. The
rest of the work was on commission and would take
some weeks. She'd have to rely on credit for some
time to come, but memories of her father and his
good reputation would help her there.

"Why did you order wood? Or perhaps more to
the point, why did you order so much of it?"

"To fence the land," she said, trying to sound
as confident as she could.

He laughed. Blast him, he laughed. Tipped back
his head so she saw the strong muscles in his neck
work, gleaming beneath the open collar of his shirt,
burnished with sweat. If she had been Eunice, she
probably would have swooned. But she was Rose,
and she sternly told herself to remain immune.

"Come with me," he said when he'd finished

laughing. Peter took her arm, leading her out the door and toward the outbuildings. "Let's ride out, I want to show you something." They entered the stables, where with comfortable expertise he quickly saddled two horses. His assistance in mounting was impersonal. He kept his silence as they rode, until the house disappeared behind them and they approached the fields. No one had cultivated tobacco here since her father's time, but the ground cover could be cleared with a little work. And some field hands, which so far, she didn't have.

Finally Peter began to speak, and while his voice lacked condescension, its authority seemed to brook no dissent. "You don't fence this kind of land. This isn't England, with its plots divided among heirs, or Scotland, where they fenced the Highlands after Culloden to drive the poor Jacobin bastards out. Here there is enough—more than enough—land for all."

He looked around, and then settled his gaze on her once more. "You haven't the least idea what you're doing, do you?"

"Oh, I know what I want to do," she said, stroking the neck of the chestnut mare, one of three horses she had purchased from the livery stables in Williamsburg.

"I know you want to live here. I shan't question you, Countess . . ."

Oh, she wanted to react to his tone of voice even more than the incorrect form of address, but she caught herself. He'd really think her a snob if she said he could call her Lady Rose. Her involuntary reaction didn't escape his notice, but he said nothing, and Rose remained silent.

Peter continued. "Many such poor and disenfranchised came to America for the chance to remake their lives. Why you came back from England"—he didn't say "you the rich and privileged," but she heard it nonetheless—"I neither know nor care. But I do care about this land and what happens to it. You've not the least idea how to grow tobacco, do you?" he asked, his voice soft but quite inflexible.

There was no point hiding it. "True enough. And I suppose you want to teach me?"

He smiled, a dimple flaring briefly in one cheek. "Now why would I want to do that?"

"Oh, I see. You want to hasten my departure, not lengthen my stay. You want me to fail." She should be angry, but truth be told, something in her relished the challenge.

"That won't be my fault," he said, deftly turning the horse's head. Rose turned her own mount to follow.

"Of course not." But the proud set of her shoulders slumped a little. His self-loathing grew. He didn't want to ruin her, after all, just discourage her.

"Look, what is normally grown here is tobacco. It's what everyone does."

"I'm not everyone."

"That is most certainly true," he said, his expression neutral, as best she could tell through the sunlight that picked out his thick bright hair, making it gleam brighter.

"Your family doesn't grow tobacco," she pointed out.

"That is true. My family cultivates flowers and now flowering trees for America and for export to . . . England. But 'tis a difficult business, and one that takes time. Years, in fact."

"Years? For flowers?"

"That depends on what is planted," he allowed. "Flowers, of course, do not take so long as flowering trees. Your land is part of our plan to improve our export abilities, because your river frontage is ideal for a large dock and for greenhouses to shelter the tender plants before shipping."

He had developed such a plan without consulting her? Perhaps the two of them were at war after all. Although she had always denied that she had the legendary temper of a redhead, she found herself so furious that she could barely speak. She clenched her fists on the reins, relaxing them when her horse sensed her distress and became restive. "Your plans are all laid, I see," she said in a tone that left no doubt what she thought of his plan.

"Aye, then *you* came," he said, frustration leaking through his tightly controlled voice. Well, that was his problem, wasn't it, not hers? Still, she was intrigued by his plans. She had heard a few things about his family from the gossip Eunice had gleaned, chatting with the new servants. The Walters had been staunchly Patriot, both brother and sister involved with the clandestine Sons of Liberty. A brave family. She thought she might like this Lily—if she wasn't like Peter, disposed to dislike her at first sight.

But it must be she, Rose, not Britons that he didn't like, because his sister was married to a former British officer and a nobleman. The thought that his dislike might be personal gave her no comfort at all.

They had turned back from the fields when the

woods rose before them. As they rode and the land
curved around the river, the house came into sight
again. With its warm red brick framed against the
river, and the meadow's sweep in front of them,
it was an impressive sight.

"Well, Mr. Walters, what are we to do?" Rose
asked. "You have plans for my land, and I will
admit they are a bit better formed than my own."

"That is kind of you, Countess," Peter began.

"Please, call me Rose. I dislike titles."

Thick golden eyebrows rose at that, but no caus-
tic comment came, although she was sure she could
see one forming inside that stubborn head.

"You have said that you intend to stay. I would
prefer that you sell the property to me."

She began to wonder if he was coming to enjoy
this sparring, because he had to know what she
would answer. "And as you already know, Master
Walters, I do intend to remain." She waited.

This wasn't his preferred strategy, but really what
choice had he at the moment? Hostility would just
strengthen her resolve. Best to play along, then
she would realize she was in over her head, and
give in. He heaved a deep sigh, as if reluctant—
which indeed he was.

"Countess . . . Rose," he amended quickly as he
bypassed the stables and turned toward the remnants of the formal gardens. "Let's walk here a
moment, shall we?" She had a fine carriage, he
had to give her that. She sat her horse elegantly
and rode with style. Her dismount was neat as well.

Her style wouldn't help her run a plantation if
she didn't know how to grow a crop. But a man
could admire something without having a use for
it, couldn't he?

Rose was tall enough to dismount without his assistance, but she placed her hand on his arm as they began to walk, as naturally as if he were taking her in to dinner at a ball. That reminded him of Joanna, and then of who she was, and he stiffened despite himself.

She felt it, and dropped her hand. Coming to a patch of wildflowers that had sprung up far from any previously planted bed, he stopped, then knelt to pluck a daisy. "The land is like this," he said, "beautiful, wild, untamed. To make it better, to make it livable, we must cultivate it. But unlike in England and Europe where every plot is old and tired, and has been endlessly divided, the land is fresh and fertile. It needs only to be coaxed and nurtured to blossom." He spun a flower between his hands, caressing the petals.

A spurt of warmth started deep within Rose as she stared in fascination at his strong, capable hands. What would those hands feel like on her? she wondered. Would he caress her skin so gently? Would she rise to his warmth, would his touch be velvet on her skin?

He caught her looking at his hands, and when he looked up and met her gaze, an almost visible spark passed between them. His green eyes were deep, intense, compelling. She knew her skin had flushed, and felt the heat rise into her throat, past the fichu at her neckline.

His hand rose toward her cheek. She held her breath. Then, just before his knuckles would have grazed her cheek, she saw his awareness of who she was, and that mysterious dislike crept back into his eyes. She didn't know why he didn't like her—

other than that she had thwarted his plans for her property—but he didn't.

He turned to point out something in another direction and the moment was lost. She didn't know what to expect, or why she was so disappointed—after all, how much unfriendlier could a neighbor be?—but she was. It would have been nice to have a friend here, but maybe that was too much to expect from a man, any man. Bertram and Ralph had never been her friends; and in her last Season she had spent most of her time dodging rich old men who were willing to overlook her poor dowry if they could fondle her body. Of the men in her life, only her father had ever treated her with genuine affection and tenderness, and she certainly didn't think of Peter Walters in a fatherly way. No indeed.

She also didn't need to stand around calf-eyed gaping at him. Her land offered plenty of spectacle for the eye to gaze upon. She needed him only in a practical sense, because she had to talk to someone knowledgeable about cultivation. Growing fruit trees seemed like a dauntingly lengthy enterprise. She needed income and something to show after this year's growing season. This year, not five years from now.

"Are there any crops that can be grown more quickly?" she asked.

"You are in need of a cash crop?"

"Since I intend to earn my living from the plantation, yes," she said stiffly.

"As a Countess, surely such matters are irrelevant to you?" he countered.

Her temper finally erupted at that. "Mr. Walters, cease insulting me or leave this property. I am not rich, stupid, spoiled, or incompetent. Managing a plantation is a major enterprise, one that you should realize was not part of the upbringing of an English gentlewoman. As a neighborly courtesy, I would willingly listen to your greater experience—indeed, even ask you for it—but if you use the opportunity only to point out how inadequate I am, then I will thank you to leave me in peace."

She strode toward the copse where they had left the horses. Retrieving the reins, she swung herself up to mount. Peter's hand was at the bridle before she could signal her mount to depart. He gripped her boot with one hand, forcing her to look down at him.

"You don't belong here," he said intently but without malice.

"I do," she said, then tucked her heels into her mount's side. She knew the way back. He let her go. It was some time before she realized she was shaking. Anger, of course. What else could it be? How presumptuous he was.

"Peter, do you mean to say that the heir to Willow Oaks is here and you haven't told me about this poor man or invited him to dinner?" Lily was scandalized. He, Adam, and Lily sat in the elegant sitting room after dinner. Lily insisted that even if they worked like field hands during the day, they were not to look like it at night. No one wore wigs or extravagant clothes, but Lily maintained standards and especially wanted to set a good example for the children.

Peter groaned inwardly. He deserved this. If he weren't so tired, he would have seen this coming and been better prepared. He'd been so irritated by Rose's behavior that he'd decided not to discuss Willow Oaks and its new owner. Lily's ingrained sense of hospitality was far too fine to allow her to ignore a fellow neighbor, however.

What he was about to say next wouldn't help his case with his sister either. Well, there was no help for it. He'd survive Lily's chastisement; he certainly had before.

"Not a poor man," he muttered. Adam raised a dark eyebrow but said nothing. Lily poured the coffee they usually drank after dinner. When it was just family, the men smoked at table if they wanted a puff from the long, thin pipes that were commonly used.

Neither he nor Adam really smoked, except when there was a houseful of company. It was more of a social ritual, nothing more. Peter didn't particularly care for it, but living in Virginia made tobacco impossible to avoid. It was the basis of their economy, after all. Even at Oak Grove, they grew tobacco as a cash crop against a time when the weather might be especially harsh to the flowers or trees.

"I don't care whether the Earl is rich or not," Lily was saying. "In fact, I assume he must need to get the plantation going again to come himself, since our hostilities with England ended not so very long ago. Some Royalists have come back, but not many, I think, have they?" She looked at Adam, who nodded.

"Not a man, Lily," Peter muttered again. When had he started talking with a clenched jaw that made him nearly unintelligible? Worse, when had he come to find conversation so objectionable an experience—he, who had been used to talking for hours with Lily when their family had consisted of just the two of them alone?

His manners were getting to be worse than those of his niece and nephews, and they had the excuse of extreme youth. What was his excuse? He had none.

"You don't think he's a man? That's rather unkind of you, Peter. Did he reject your offer again?" The twins scampered through just then, laughing. Violet was hard on their heels, clearly furious. Violet had her mouth open, to protest the boys' treatment of her, she was sure.

Lily put a finger to her lips in a shushing gesture, and her daughter closed her mouth mutinously. But Violet redoubled her steps after the retreating boys. They looked back, saw her gaining on them, her piquant face set with determination, and swerved. With the sound of muffled thunder, the children all raced up the wide stairway toward the upper floors.

Peter let his eyes follow the exuberant progress of his nephews and niece. Unfortunately, Lily had already turned back to pursue their conversation. She was concentrating too closely on Peter to notice the twins' jeopardy. She heard him say, "It's a she," however, because she glared at him in a manner reminiscent of Mistress Rose Lansdale in a temper.

Like her daughter with her scapegrace brothers, Lily was upset with him. "Peter, unless that poor woman is accompanied by her mother, grand-mother, and a host of retainers—in which case I feel certain I would have heard about it—then you have some explaining to do. I won't have the hospitality of Oak Grove go unextended to a neighbor."

"She's hardly been friendly herself," he said defensively. "I had a letter clearly indicating the Earl had changed his mind and was interested in selling. The last letter from Adam's barrister indicated no change in position after the Earl died. I'd expected the next ship to bring a contract. Then she showed up here, taking up residence as if she means to stay."

"Alone?" Lily's topaz eyes had begun to glow, and Peter's heart sank. Why hadn't he thought of Lily's possible reaction before? He realized Lily might actually approve of the bold actions undertaken by the Earl's daughter. After all, Lily had launched herself as Williamsburg's first florist with nothing but hope and stubborn determination. She might even admire Mistress Lansdale or Lady Lansdale or whatever her correct title was.

"She says she has her brother's proxy, and why?" Lily tapped a foot. Clearly, she was expecting more information.

"I suppose because her brother is posted to India. At least that is what she said," he added grudgingly.

"Everything sounds normal enough to me," Lily pronounced. Adam gave Peter a look that essentially said, "Give up, friend, she's got the bit between her teeth." And who knew Lily better than Adam?

"Perhaps 'tis a bit unusual that she has come the way she has," Lily continued, "but India is a dreadfully long way. He probably gave the proxy to her when leaving England after their father's funeral.'' Peter knew Lily would stop at nothing to meet this resourceful Rose now.

He saw the moment on her expressive face when she remembered her original indignation at him for being so uncommunicative. Adam winked at Peter, and squeezed Lily on the shoulder in encouragement.

"We must have her to dinner, Peter. At once.''

Peter rubbed the back of his neck, almost disarranging his stock. He deserved this, no doubt. Why had he been so discourteous to Rose? Oh yes, she irritated him, but dislike for her position about the estate that belonged to her family really was no excuse for poor manners. Lily had certainly raised him better.

Out here on the river, where people often lived miles away from each other on their plantations, hospitality was an absolute. Even during the war, families had taken in combatants on both sides, dispensing hospitality and bandages equally for the most part. It had enabled more than one plantation to avoid burning. Indeed, it was a sign of high respect for Rose's father that no one had confiscated Willow Oaks—or burned it.

But the daughter was here and what had he done? Chastised her, argued with her, told her she was foolish, and never once offered a speck of assistance. Lily was correct. He was little better than a boor and a cad. It was one thing to be unhappy with himself, but he had no right to spread it around. Not in front of Lily and Adam, not in front of his nieces and nephews, and certainly not in front of strangers.

"You are correct, Lily,'' he said, his hand reaching for the habitual kerchief around his neck that he wore against the heat. Then he remembered that he was dressed for dinner, and stopped. Of course, it wasn't there; he was wearing a clean stock. "I've no excuse for my manners. Do you want me to invite her to dinner?"

"No, matters have gone past that now," Lily said ominously. Adam hid a smile at Lily's words, his gaze telling Peter that while Adam might sympathize, he wasn't about to interfere.

Lily's smile reassured Peter, however, that she was now finished with lecturing. "Bring around the boat tomorrow morning, won't you, Peter? We're going downriver."

The next morning, Lily commandeered the remaining bread and biscuits, added a ham cured in their own smokehouse, found some jars of clover honey and jam, and had their housekeeper, Mistress Steele, make up a big basket. Peter had come in from the orchards by then, propelled by a laughing Adam, who had advised him not to wait until the sun was high or Lily would have yet more time to think about her brother's sins.

So here he stood feeling foolish and out of sorts. She turned and he knew from the look in her eyes what was going to come next.

"Peter, get cleaned up. You look ah, disheveled."

She was being surprisingly polite. What she really meant was that he was dirty. Remembering that he had left Willow Oaks the last time looking just like this, he flushed.

Lily cast a critical eye at him. "Good, at least you aren't so far gone that you've forgotten shame. Take off that kerchief and get some toweling to clean yourself up with. Or wait, better yet, I think you should—"

Peter clapped a hand over Lily's mouth moments before she could call for the tub, for he knew that was what she was about to order. And Mistress Steele, who had been Adam's housekeeper since he first came to Oak Grove, and had known Peter since he was a stripling student, would no doubt be happy to fetch it.

"That's enough, Lily. I do not bathe in the kitchen or at your pleasure anymore, sweet sister. There's naught to be ashamed of in good honest sweat."

Lily batted his hand aside. "Naught to be ashamed of perhaps, out in a farmyard. But also naught to gain," Lily retorted. "Or is she fifty and unlovely?"

If possible, memories of Rose's unconventional beauty sent his color higher. Damn, why did Lily have the power still to make him feel like an untried and somewhat boorish boy?

"Oho, I see," Lily said. "She's fair, then."

She had not teased him about a woman since Joanna. His face went stony at the thought.

Lily looked exasperated. "Come, Peter, life goes on. She did you some ill, I gather, but in the end 'twas providential, was it not? Suppose you had wed and then she wanted to go to England?"

But he wasn't ready to be cajoled, not about this. There was so much Lily didn't know. And God willing, she never would.

The old pain flared again, and with it the anger that needed an outlet. Good humor and civility fled. He could not see the Englishwoman, not this morning. Forgetting all his self-reproach of the previous night, knowing only that he needed to abuse a hoe rather than the sensibilities of anyone he knew, he turned abruptly on his heel and left, leaving Lily to perform the errand on her own.

And God knew she would carry it out with far more graciousness than he would have anyway, even under the best of circumstances.

Adam met him outside as he strode away from the door and returned with him to the fields. God bless his brother-in-law, because he asked no questions. Even Adam didn't know what Joanna had done, and Peter had no plans to tell him either. But reminders of his past were what he was trying to avoid, so he made some inane remark about the condition of the soil. In the blessedly silent tradition of male camaraderie, Adam replied and asked no further questions. With undemanding company present, Peter felt no need to unburden himself.

Chapter Four

A ministering angel shall my sister be.
—William Shakespeare, *Hamlet*, 1601

Rose cast a glance around the elegant front hall as she stepped inside Oak Grove for the first time. Like her house, Oak Grove gleamed with polished wood floors. Unlike her single curving stair, a double staircase descended from either side of the top hall to a central landing, then split into two wings again to reach the foyer.

On a semicircular table before her, she spotted a massive flower arrangement, beautiful enough for a painting. Except that the colors were even more vibrant than any painting she'd ever seen in England. The arrangement contained carnations and day lilies, softly scented stock, tall gladioli, and pale blue rosemary blossoms, as well as a few flowers she didn't recognize.

Just then, a handsome, elegantly dressed man stepped forward from a side room with a gesture of welcome. "Adam Pearson, my lady," he said, bowing low over her hand. "My family and I welcome you to Oak Grove." He straightened and Rose caught a glimpse of the most extraordinary blue-green eyes she'd ever seen.

Then she saw the petite woman she had met that morning descending the stairs. Lily came forward to welcome her. Before she reached Rose, however, Adam turned and placed an arm around his wife's waist. She placed a quick kiss on her upturned smiling lips, and Rose felt a sudden pang of envy.

That intimate gesture of affection she had just witnessed would have been most unusual back in England, in her family's home. Her mother would probably have said her father was "pawing" her had he dared try something so unfashionable as displaying fondness for his wife in public.

Then her wistfulness vanished as Peter Walters strode into the foyer. At once the air seemed both charged and uncomfortable, although Peter did nothing more than salute Adam and kiss his sister's cheek.

He turned and executed a gesture almost identical to Adam's, though his leg wasn't as deeply bent and his kiss hovered in the air well above her hand. But when he straightened and looked into her eyes, her breath caught. His hair was pulled back in a queue that was smooth for once, the golden butternut color a rich contrast to his tanned face. Laugh lines near his eyes made it plain that he hadn't always been so grim-faced and serious, and his mouth, relaxed now, looked like he had once smiled often.

"Welcome, Mistress Lansdale," he said, his voice and manner more composed than she had ever heard. Was this for his sister's benefit? Mistress Pearson had been so polite this morning. She should be the Countess of Dalby, but had already told Rose that her husband was an American through and through, even though he retained his title as the only living son. She didn't want to be called Lady Lansdale, she had said.

Peter's eyes sparkled though his expression did not change as he leaned toward her. "Don't look so alarmed, my lady, I don't bite," he said in a low voice that only she could hear.

"Did your sister make you behave?" she couldn't stop herself from asking. She smiled to show she was funning, but he had dropped his gaze from her face.

He frowned and released her hand, but as soon as he began to step away, Lily moved forward. "His bark truly is worse than his bite, my lady," Lily said, placing a hand on Peter's arm with a warning look.

"Please, call me Rose." Adam raised a dark-winged eyebrow at that as if in surprise, but he let Lily set the tone.

" 'Tis Rose then, as you wish," Lily said with a smile. "Because we are all planters here and rise early, we have an early dinner hour. But I would like to introduce the children to you before they go to bed. Will you indulge me?" she asked, her pretty amber eyes alight with pride.

"Of course," Rose said instantly, liking the petite, vivacious woman more and more. She'd been afraid when Lily Pearson had first appeared this morning that she would be as dour as her brother. Instead, Lily had told her of the years after their parents had died when she had supported the two of them, and later, how she had struggled with creating and running her own business in order to pay for Peter's education.

Rose had the impression that Lily would have no bad impressions or negative feelings about a self-made woman, since she was one herself. That thought had cheered her all day.

Then she had turned up here to find Peter neither scowling nor scolding, and his good looks had struck her anew. With both Peter and Adam in conservative but well-cut and flawlessly tailored evening clothes, she almost felt like she was back home. But these strong men were far handsomer than their sallow, foppish counterparts in England.

Lily beckoned Rose to follow and led her up the staircase, while the men drifted out of sight to the sitting room for what she assumed was a predinner glass of spirits. This, too, was most unfashionable, seeing the children in this manner, but Rose found herself looking forward to meeting them. Two boys and a girl, like she and her own brothers had once been.

Bertram and Ralph had been better companions when they were small, before the awareness of Ralph's status as heir affected his behavior and then that of Bertram, his eternal follower. But they had never been her friends, as Lily and Peter seemed to have been. Rose couldn't help the unkind thought that her brothers had inherited their maliciousness from their mother, while she had been fortunate enough to possess her father's temperament.

Violet informed her that she and her brothers were triplets, which had astonished Rose. Lily waited until they were on their way downstairs again to correct that bit of misinformation. Rose wondered privately why it was so important to Violet that she should make such a fantastic claim, but she was too polite to ask. It was probably just the vivid imagination of a child. Certainly, Violet was a lively and intelligent child, as were her brothers.

"Your daughter looks remarkably like you," she told Adam later over dinner. "She has those wonderful eyes and lifts her eyebrow in just the same way." She turned to Lily, who smiled and nodded. Rose knew this was far too familiar a topic for a dinner in England, but the warm atmosphere here seemed to encourage confidences. And it had been quite some time since she'd had wine. Perhaps there was warmth from that, too.

Peter had not been quite so charming as the Earl of Dalby—Adam, she really must get out of the English habit of thinking in titles—but his conversation had been noticeably more polite than before. She supposed she had Lily to thank for that. Because she was still a bit skittish of Peter after their encounters at Willow Oaks, she hardly noticed when Adam began to ask her about her plans for the plantation.

"What does your brother plan to do with Willow Oaks?" Adam asked, toying with his empty wineglass, but not calling for more, as Ralph would have done.

She almost gave herself away by saying "I," then remembered what she'd told Peter. "Bertram remembered how much I had loved it here, and . . . since I'm considered on the shelf, he . . . ah, he allowed me to come. I really would like to stay here."

"On the shelf? Not here," Lily assured her. "There were always more male than female colonists, and after the war, I doubt that ratio has changed. You will be quite in demand."

Adam saw the look of surprise on her face. "We are rather more direct here than in England, and I hope you will consider us friends as well as neighbors," Adam said by way of explanation of Lily's statement. No doubt he remembered how polite and limited social discourse traditionally was in England. "Do you mind, then, if I ask what crops you intend to plant? May I assume tobacco?"

Business wasn't discussed among the upper classes, either, but Adam's conversational foray was far less personal than Lily's assurances that she would not be considered a spinster here. Rose didn't mind either subject, and was not at all offended by Lily's speech, but she had nothing to say about her personal life or lack of one. Whereas she was, of course, vitally interested in business matters. Pushing the thought of her mother's vocal disapproval of either strand of conversation out of her mind, she turned to Adam with some eagerness.

"I know that's what everyone plants, but my father had formed an . . . attraction to tobacco that my mother found unpleasant." The Countess of Lansdale hadn't noticed, but Rose thought the tobacco might somehow have been involved, because the matter her papa had coughed up from his lungs at the end had been as brown as the tobacco he used to put in his long clay pipe.

Adam's face assumed an intent look and he shot a swift, unreadable glance at Peter. "Is it possible that you might be open to suggestions, my lady, if you are not thinking of planting tobacco?"

Goodness, if only Peter had been this polite, they'd have been on a far better footing.

She didn't realize she'd spoken aloud until Lily's unaffected laughter rang through the room, while Adam seemed to be struggling to contain his own. Peter's handsome face flushed but instead of rising and storming away as Rose half expected, he tugged at his carefully tied stock, and managed a slightly apologetic look.

Lily gave Rose a conspiratorial smile as if to say "Men," and Rose smiled hesitantly in return. "Let me tell you about Oak Grove," she said. "I began arranging flowers fifteen years ago to support myself and Peter after our parents died. We expanded the work after Adam and I married and moved to Oak Grove. In addition to the arranging of cut flowers, which I do alone, we also grow American flowers and plants that are eagerly sought after in London and on the Continent."

Casting her husband a warm glance, Lily continued as the servants brought in bowls of fresh fruit—blackberries and cream, topped with sprigs of mint. "We've been able to transport bulbs by using ships from our neighbor's landing at Berkeley Hundred. But we cannot always tell which bulbs will reproduce well, and our well-born purchasers are often in such a frenzy of competition with each other that they can scarcely wait for them to grow."

Rose nodded. She had heard of the hysteria over

hyacinths that had gripped Holland fifty years ago. That event had been surprising, since the Netherlands had undergone a far worse panic in the previous century over tulips. Although her countrymen had taken that lesson to heart, and flowers did not drive the English economy, still flowers and botanical novelties, especially from America, were highly sought after and could be outrageously expensive. The Royal Botanic Garden at Kew near London, and the voyages of the explorer Captain Cook, were famed for their work in discovering and analyzing new species of flora brought to England.

By the end of the evening, Adam and Lily had convinced Rose to cast her lot with Tidewater Nurseries. The Pearsons had bulbs that could be divided and transferred to her, to plant in her own fields. And Peter, his diffidence forgotten for once as he warmed to his subject, explained their audacious idea to ship living plants and flowers, possibly even trees.

Their clients would have the upper hand in their own competitions with fellow horticulturalists, Peter and the Pearsons explained, because they would have the pleasure of the blossoms without the waiting period. And Tidewater Nurseries' skills at growing the plants, plus their arrival in good condition gave the assurance that the imports from America were of good quality.

It wasn't until Adam escorted her to her room for the night—it was customary here, as with house parties in England, to stay overnight and avoid any perils on the road or river—that Rose realized no one had mentioned Peter's designs on the land in general, or her waterfront area in particular.

Feeling warmed by the first real hospitality she'd

had since arriving, she didn't want to spoil the general mood. So she said nothing. Perhaps through his brother-in-law and sister's good offices, Peter might be induced to be more polite, and they could all work together.

The thought made her downcast, however, for reasons she could not well articulate. She supposed she had hoped that Peter would be willing to help her, not compete with her, and that he would do so for reasons of his own, not his family's. But he hadn't mentioned his ambitions, which meant, she thought, that he had not abandoned his goal, just that he had not mentioned it in front of his sister and her husband.

This fantasy that he'd relinquished his designs was probably born of her inexplicable attraction to him, and her desire to be seen as attractive in return.

A faint hope. And one, she reminded herself, that she didn't need. She hadn't come here for love. Nevertheless, despite the somber thoughts that closed her evening, the atmosphere of Oak Grove was still warm and welcoming enough that Rose slept without the usual turmoil she had experienced ever since meeting Peter Walters.

The next morning, Rose accepted the offer to stay a little longer amid the welcoming provided by Oak Grove and its inhabitants, a place whose way of life had already proven to be so different from her life at home. She was curious about the years she had missed since her family left, and about the Walters' activities as Patriots.

Lily was happy to oblige by filling in the history.

She had played a unique role among the Sons of Liberty, using her flowers to pass messages.

"Peter was most unhappy with me when I offered to help convey messages between the Sons of Liberty and Adam," she confided.

"Why?" Rose asked. "Wasn't Adam their leader?"

Lily offered Rose more biscuits and jam. Only the two of them were left at table, the children having accompanied Adam and Peter to the stables for a riding lesson before the men rode out to the fields. "The Sons of Liberty were a clandestine group and Adam was sent from Boston to train them in military tactics. Because he had been a British Army officer before converting to our cause, he was in hiding. No one here was supposed to know who he was or see his face. That way, there would be no one to betray him if he were to be captured by the British. Peter thought it was all too dangerous and wanted me to have no part in it."

Rose thought it sounded tremendously exciting, but said nothing.

"They needed me, and so I told them," Lily continued. "I believed in the Patriot cause and wasn't about to be put off by an overprotective younger brother. Or by my future husband."

"You didn't know that at the time, though, did you?" Rose asked.

"That he was my future husband? Oh, of course not. But I knew his voice did odd things to my stomach and my presence of mind. I think I fell in love with his voice before I ever saw him face to face."

Lily's warm laugh had a lovely sound. No wonder

the Earl of Dalby had fallen in love with this bright, vivacious woman.

"Tell me about your flower vocabulary," Rose said after a moment. "Where did the meanings come from?"

"You would be surprised at how many you already know. Let me fetch my vocabulary. I'll be back in a moment. Please have some more tea." Lily left the breakfast room but returned quickly with a sheaf of papers tidily rolled and tied with ribbon.

"What did you mean, I would already know some of the meanings?" Rose asked when Lily reseated herself.

"What does it mean when a man gives a woman roses?"

"Well, love, I should think. Certainly that is why a man gives them at home, to a woman. Red roses, that is. But yellow, that is different." Rose paused.

"And yellow means . . ." Lily prompted.

"Friendship . . . or jealousy," Rose answered automatically. "Oh, I see what you mean. How do I know that?"

"Yes, how do you know that?" Lily echoed. "Common usage that has evolved over time, for one. Sometimes meanings are given in the Bible. Then there are legends from classical antiquity. Don't forget poets. Shakespeare was a great one for using flowers to convey thoughts or feelings, for example. Do you recall Ophelia's sad little speech after she has gone mad—'There's rosemary, that's for remembrance, pray you love, remember'?"

Rose nodded in agreement.

Lily pointed to an entry on one page. "Here,

this was our signal that a message awaited Adam in Raleigh Tavern.''

"An iris?" Rose asked.

"Yes. The flower was named for Iris, the goddess of the rainbow. She was the messenger of Hera and Zeus to mortals. The ancient Greeks often planted iris on women's graves as a token of the goddess's role in ushering souls to the next world along a bridge made of rainbows. So you see how Iris's role as a messenger goddess became associated with the flower that was named after her, and how that led to its meaning?''

"Why, that's fascinating," Rose said, delighted. "Do tell me more." Not until the children came running back in did Rose recollect that she had responsibilities of her own, and that she should leave Lily to hers.

She accepted Will Evans's company on the ride back downriver and lent him a horse to return. Once at home, however, she found her mind was full of Lily's explanations all day. Without minimizing the very real dangers they all had risked when war had broken out, she could not help but think what an exciting time that had been!

She doubted anything half so exciting would ever happen to her, even though she was now in America herself. Times were different now; the world had shifted, then settled back into its usual course. She shrugged; she had already experienced adventure that most women of her age and station would never know. Just coming here had been the boldest action she had ever undertaken in her life; meeting Peter shouldn't mean that her life suddenly counted for nothing, just because she yearned for something she would never have.

Chapter Five

LEAR: So young, and so untender?
CORDELIA: So young, my lord, and true.
— William Shakespeare, *King Lear*, 1605

"Here," Peter said unceremoniously. He had turned up unexpectedly a few days after her visit to Oak Grove. Now he stood in the room that had been her father's study and receiving room for visitors, and she watched as he dumped a pile of heavy ledgers on to the desk. More furniture had arrived, so the room didn't look quite so vacant.

"What's all this?" Rose said, looking up from her mending. She was wearing out clothes faster than she could mend them. She'd have to go into Williamsburg soon for cloth because the gowns she had brought with her were suitable only for ladies' morning and afternoon dresses—the most practical she'd had at home but highly impractical here.

Wouldn't it be just like Peter Walters to think she was doing lace or embroidery or some useless feminine task? If only she could figure out whether he disliked her in particular, women in general, or just women living on the land he had come to think of as his. But he'd never actually *said* anything—it was all in his eyes.

"These are the records of our early years at Oak Grove. They may be of some assistance to you in planning for what you need and in what quantities." The incident of the fence posts still amused him, she was sure.

"What I need, sir, is someone to help me plant a crop that will earn me some cash against my credit, which is accumulating rapidly." She expected dislike to show on his handsome face, but for once she saw only approval, which mystified her.

"True enough. We can look at these at night." That warm feeling flooded her again at his unexpected words. My, but he was a fine-looking man, when those green eyes of his were clear and not stormy.

She gave herself a little shake. "At night?" Had her voice squeaked? Oh dear.

"You can't work outside past dark." Well, that was true enough. Why did he always make her feel like a fool?

"Why have you suddenly become helpful?" His eyes narrowed at her suspicious tone but Rose was not to be deterred. "A few days ago you wanted only to be rid of me."

" 'Tis not my place to drive you out of your own home. Let me propose the assistance of Oak Grove in getting you set up."

Oh, but these were important words indeed. She rose to face him, refusing to give him the advantage of height. "Was it your idea about the flowers?" she asked.

"No, that was Lily," he admitted.

"Is it then your idea to help me?" she said, toying with a bow on her bodice.

"We would like to help you." She noticed his eyes were drawn to her hand. She dropped hers.

"And you?" Rose persisted.

"The assistance of my family is not sufficient for you?" he answered, but somewhat testily, she thought.

She was irritating him. Well, frankly she was glad. She'd rather have his honest anger than this polite carefulness. Not that the exchanges between the two of them had been particularly pleasant, but she knew where she stood with the angry Peter Walters, rather than with this one wearing the mask of careful politeness.

"I don't want assistance if your true goal is to get rid of me," she said. There, now she would see if he would be honest with her.

"If we help you, we help you. None of us will go back on our word." Damn him for still sounding so remote.

She had heard enough references to his family. Rose laid down her mending, realizing she still clutched it in her other hand. "Peter Walters," she said, "what do you want from me?"

He smiled briefly. "My lady, I want your property, but since it seems you are determined to hold on to it, at least for now, then I will offer you my services."

At last he had chosen to speak about himself, even if only a few words. There was some story here, some hidden hurt that kept him from stating what he truly wanted. But she didn't see that they were destined to be friends, so Rose did not pursue his moving from "we" to "I."

She also didn't like the "at least for now," but she couldn't fail to take him up on his offer. If he really would help her, she needed his assistance. She might want to do it all on her own, but she knew enough now to realize that she was not equipped for the task she'd set herself. This weakness had been difficult to admit to herself; therefore, she had no intention of admitting it to him.

He might think his offer was a way to convince her of her inadequacies, but she would just prove to him that this wasn't the case. She would make a go of Willow Oaks. Moreover, she would provide for her family, live in this beautiful land again, and please herself in the process.

If only Peter Walters were fifty years old and had the gout. He seemed no more attracted to her than she had been to the man her mama had chosen for her to marry, but that didn't mean her body was going to cooperate. Oh, but she had no interest in him—no, none at all, she told herself firmly— and this thumping heart and racing pulse were naught but the products of exertion and her determination to end this uncomfortable conversation.

"My lady," he said, frowning slightly at the words that had come so easily from his brother-in-law's tongue. "I will bring servants from Oak Grove and together we will help you plant your crop. You are certain in this choice of flowers over tobacco?"

"Oh, yes," she said. "Come look." As she walked past Peter, her skirts brushed his leg and she could not have said which of them started more. This . . . connection between them was most uncomfortable.

"These are lovely, Rose. Who did them?" he said, looking at the sketches she had laid out on the secretary. Some were watercolors and some were pencil, but they were all of flowers.

"I draw a little. I did these," she answered, watching him study her sketches. Some were of the flowers Lily had spoken of, but others she had gleaned from the notes Lily had given her, flowers or plants whose meanings had captivated her imagination.

She had drawn ivy for fidelity—it made good ground cover but she knew that it had to be watched lest it take over everything in its path; tall columbine, which in its purple color meant resolution; bachelor's buttons, which stood for refusal to marry or desire to remain a bachelor— or spinster, in her case; dogwoods, which grew wild here but were popular in England, a symbol of endurance; the dianthus family that included carnations, pinks, and the wildly popular sweet william. She had drawn white carnations to represent talent, and sketched, then painted, pinks for boldness. Finally, she'd chosen lavender for success.

She had laid out before him a litany of her intentions, but she did not think he noticed. Rose wondered how much he even remembered of the flower meanings, although he had known them once, according to Lily. Peter glanced up from the drawings to her again, and that unsettling frisson of awareness shivered through her once again.

Peter was struck by the quality of the drawings. Her botanical detail was superb—she drew far better than Lily, who was herself quite good—and the watercolors were delicately shaded. She must have wonderful powers of intuition since most of these flowers would not appear until next spring, and some of them were not that well-known in England outside the jealously guarded homes and conservatories of a devoted set of horticulturalists.

"Did you do these all from descriptions? Many of these are spring blooms that are not present in our gardens just now."

"Did I render the colors correctly?" As if you had been born to paint them, Peter thought. But he did not say so aloud, only nodded wordlessly.

His gaze met hers and he was rocked with sudden awareness of her as a woman. Pleasure had softened her face and erased the lines of worry and strain that he had probably helped put there. Her pride in her work was evident, but he would ignore the uncertainty he saw in her deep blue eyes. He sincerely hoped it wasn't there because she thought he was about to disdain her efforts.

"Truly, you have a fine hand," he said, gently sifting through the drawings until he had seen them all. He held her gaze for only a moment more before they both looked away as if embarrassed.

In Peter's case, he did not want to be too interested in her as a woman. As for what Rose felt, he did not know. He had been so rude to her that she could not possibly have conceived an interest in him. And if she had, she would only be disappointed.

"We haven't many servants to spare," he said, "but if you are willing to work, I am willing to help." And he would test her mettle. He did not think for one moment that a rose as fair as she— tall and well built though God had made her— would be suited to or able to sustain the kind of interest and work necessary to get a crop of bulbs planted before the season grew too late. He did not plan and he would not try to make anything harder for her; he simply thought she would be unable to do the work that lay ahead.

When she realized that, she would go home, and he would soon have a contract for Willow Oaks. He was sure he could buy out her brother's interest in the land. After all, the Earl had not even come himself. How interested could he be?

Peter extended a hand to Rose. After a moment's hesitation, she reached to grasp it.

"Then we have a plan, Lady Fairchild?" She frowned slightly. He knew it wasn't her proper address, but told himself he didn't care. "Countess" was too formal and "Rose" seemed too familiar.

"Do I have it wrong?" he asked.

"Yes, but 'tis of no import."

"No, tell me," he said.

She looked anywhere but at him. "As the daughter of an Earl, I am addressed as Lady Rose, and use the address 'The Lady Rose Fairchild' only in formal correspondence, or 'Rose Fairchild' in social correspondence."

He shrugged. "I just thought Lady Rose might have been too familiar. How was I to know that I was actually correct?" He smiled.

"And yes, we do have a bargain," she said. After

all that, the union of their hands was brief. Peter was seized with an unaccountable urge to kiss her hand, but he refrained. Let him observe such pleasantries at home, with Lily and Adam around. Here they were cooperating on a business venture, and businesslike he would be.

If she had not trusted that Peter Walters was at heart a fair and honest man, Rose would have considered accusing him of scheming to make the tasks more difficult. She had spent several days with Lily, dividing bulbs, digging them up carefully and shaking dirt off the roots gently before dividing them. Peter had taken care of the larger root balls, and cut dozens of branches for grafting.

But Lily was too busy at home to come herself, and Rose was not going to let Peter Walters take over her plans for her plantation, so it was just the two of them amid the servants. Rose had also determined that she would not spare herself. She had to take control of her own land and her own life, and if it meant working shoulder to shoulder with a man who both irritated and attracted her, so be it.

Although the days were growing shorter as summer drew to its inexorable close, the weather was still unpleasantly hot and humid. Nevertheless, it was not the weather but the exertion that felled her first. The first day she did too much. She had felt no more than pleasantly tired at the end of the day, and thus was completely unprepared for how sore she was the next morning.

But she was absolutely determined not to show it. Rose put a plain apron on over her dress, and out she went to the planting beds again. There she found that Peter had arrived with the dawn.

Each day her aches and pains grew worse, no matter how hot the water she asked Eunice to draw for the hip bath. The fourth morning she hobbled out, feeling like an old woman. Peter, already hard at work with the half-dozen workers from Oak Grove that came daily, turned to watch her.

If he showed even one sign of amusement, Rose swore to herself as she approached, she just might take the spade to him. He did not; if anything, he studied her more closely than was his wont.

"Good morrow, mistress," he said with careful formality. "How do you fare this morning?"

"Quite well, and you?" she replied blithely. But those piercing green eyes assessed her and she was sure he knew that she lied.

By midmorning, she was in agony. Her knees ached with bending in the dirt; her arms were tired from the constant sowing motions, and her back was stiff, although her hands were spared somewhat by gardener's gloves. When she stood to fetch another group of bulbs from the basket left at the end of the last row, she gave a little groan.

She hurried away as fast as she was able, but was conscious of Peter's eyes on her the entire distance. When she returned, he was leaning on his hoe, watching her.

He held out a hand. "Give me the basket, Lady Rose."

She did, barely holding back a sigh of relief as she gave the heavy basket over to him. He hefted it expertly, then put it down.

"Shall I repeat the morning's question?"

"No. Why is it necessary?"

"Because it is your last chance to answer me honestly before I toss you over my shoulder and carry you to the house." He laid the hoe aside. He looked prepared to do exactly as he had said.

"I am not your niece or one of your nephews to be carried about," she answered hotly.

His gaze swept her form. Ruefully, he grinned. "No, you certainly are not. Nevertheless, you are acting like one of them."

Rose couldn't help it. She took a step toward him, so incensed was she. "What do you mean to say such a thing, Peter Walters?"

He took her hands, pulling off her heavy gloves and his own. Her hands were red and tender, and as he gently squeezed, she realized they hurt, too. Never taking his intent gaze from her face, he moved up her arms, gently pressing. The winces and little sounds she couldn't help emitting proved that she certainly was not fine, and his eyes turned stormy.

He took her shoulders—gently, perhaps, but she couldn't tell—and at the cry of pain she couldn't suppress, ruddiness swept even his golden tanned face.

"That's it," he said. Without warning, he half bent to seize her under the knees with one arm, while his other slipped down her back to hold her secure.

He swung her up against his chest and turned toward the house.

"Peter, you can't do this. 'Tis . . . 'tis most unseemly," she spluttered.

"Act like a child, be treated like one," he muttered but did not break stride.

"Put me down," she said, but could not even

raise her arms to try to pull herself away from him. Appalled at this evidence of her own weakness, she subsided momentarily.

"You can't do this," she protested again.

"So you said." His face was set in implacable lines. "But I am."

"I am too heavy for you," she said, remembering how Mama had always complained that she was too tall and too big. She'd been made to half-stoop during dances if one of the gentlemen proved to be too much shorter than she. Oh, how she had hated it.

"You are heavier than my nephews and nieces," he acknowledged, "but not so heavy as all that." He looked directly down into her furious, upturned face, and grinned.

The impact of that unforced smile was so devastating that Rose mused on it the rest of the way to the house and did not utter another complaint. She suspected he hadn't even been trying to charm her.

She'd never be able to resist the deliberate application of his charm in that case, not for a moment. It was as well, then, that he had never tried.

Chapter Six

Who loves a garden loves a greenhouse too.
Unconscious of a less propitious clime,
There blooms exotic beauty, warm and snug.
　　　—William Cowper, *The Task*, 1785

Peter rapped sharply at the door of Willow Oaks with his foot. Rose muttered something about his boots dirtying the door, but he didn't stop to point out that was why a wide strip of hammered brass guarded its lower edge. Besides, his arms were full of Rose, and he had no intention of putting her down until it was on something soft or in something hot such as the well-deserved bath she needed. And despite his denial of her weight, she really was a good armful, and he couldn't afford to spare an arm to reach out and knock.

Conceding to her grumbling, however, he did not kick again. "Rose, reach up and use the knocker, please," he said, turning.

She complied but the unwilling groan she gave only told him how overdue this lesson about her physical limits was.

Eunice opened the door and gasped at the sight of Peter holding Rose in his arms. "Your mistress is well, Eunice, but in sore need of a hot bath and liniment," Peter said quickly, as the little maid looked like she might faint from surprise or concern.

"Would you heat water, please, and bring it to Lady Rose's chamber." Rose nodded wanly to confirm the request, and Eunice was off like a shot. Peter turned to walk up the curving staircase without another word, Rose still in his arms.

He had known Rose was getting sore—she had to be, coming from her soft life in England—but his inclination to help her had only gone so far at first. Uncharitably he had thought that the sooner she gave up, the better it would be for everyone. Unfortunately—or fortunately—he wasn't a complete brute, because seeing the obvious pain she was in this morning had moved him, and he had reproached himself for allowing her to overwork herself into this condition.

"Which room?" he asked curtly, becoming all too aware with each passing minute that Rose was not only a handful to deal with, but also had abundant physical charms. Her form was curved, generously so in all the right places, and even her soiled apron and sturdy shoes couldn't disguise the lush feminine beauty of this English rose.

"There." She pointed to the room at the top of the stairs to the left, which overlooked the river. Peter carried her into the room, gently lowering her to the bed. Immediately she rolled from her back to her side away from him.

"Rose, don't be embarrassed," he said. "You have overtired yourself, and are suffering the predictable consequences." He deliberately made his voice brusque. "I'll go help Eunice carry the water from the kitchen." He didn't look at her again, didn't want to see her sinking into the down counterpane, its billowing arms embracing her soft curves.

He needn't have worried. When he and Eunice returned with the water for the hip bath that stood in one corner of the room, Rose was sound asleep, and he could think of her again as but a wayward child, not so very different from Violet. Eunice was able to get her clothes off, and she helped rouse Rose enough to get her into the tub.

Peter had gone in search of liniment by then, and when he returned, he sat down on one stair while waiting for Eunice to finish helping Rose with her bath. Eunice came out of the room a few minutes later to empty water buckets.

"Master Walters," she said, doing her best to look scandalized rather than avidly interested, "you can go now."

"No, I need to rub her muscles, or that bath won't help her feel better for more than a few minutes."

"You can't do that, master," she said.

"I must. She's taken baths all week, hasn't she?" he asked.

Eunice looked genuinely scandalized this time. "How would you be knowing that, sir, I'd like to ask?" Peter took the buckets of water from her and preceded her down the stairs.

"Because she's been sore every night, hasn't she?" he asked.

The plain little maid nodded.

"Then you can tell for yourself that 'tis not sufficient. Just like a horse after a long run, an unconditioned person needs to have the muscles and tendons loosened that have tightened up. Your mistress is the same."

"Well, she's not no horse to rub down," Eunice asserted in indignant tones.

"I know that. Does she have a wrapper?" At Eunice's look, he chuckled. "Come, miss, I was raised by my sister Lily, so I have well and good an idea of what a woman's garments are. We needn't rely on an excess of modesty. Wrap your mistress in a robe and I shall be up in a moment. If she's sleeping, then 'tis all the better, as I will be less likely to disturb her. She may even think that I am you and stay quite relaxed."

By the time Peter finished emptying the buckets, Rose had been wrapped and tucked in the bed so securely that he could hardly see her, and she was fast asleep again. He almost thought to leave her as she was, in peace, but she rolled to one side. A tiny, piteous sound of pain issued from her that moved him so much, he knew he could not leave her.

"Eunice, would you prepare your mistress some chamomile tea? And have Cook fetch biscuits or

some other refreshment for her. She'll be starved,
I've no wonder, when she wakes."

The little maid squinted briefly at him, but when
she saw the jar of liniment in his hands, his businesslike expression, and the length of toweling he
held, her suspicions seemed relieved, and she went
off to do his bidding.

"Ah, Rose," he said softly as he approached the
bed. "You needn't try so hard." He gently rolled
her to her stomach after lifting off the confining
counterpane. He pulled the wrapper up to her
knees and began to gently knead her calves. The
liniment went on smoothly and made his hands
slippery so that they slid up and down her calves
more easily. The tight knots of her muscles began
to loosen.

He stopped at her knees, though. There was no
good way to rub her back through the wrapper
because he could not use the lotion. She still
seemed fast asleep, so he quietly worked her arms
out of the sleeves, and peeled back the wrapper
from around her shoulders. As her arms rolled
back slightly when he took off the wrapper, she
groaned, and her upper body lifted slightly from
the bed.

Peter caught the merest glimpse of her breasts
before she sank back to the bedding. His body
tightened in a rush and he cursed himself for not
doing this with Eunice in the room to help. All
he'd thought at the time was that the little maid
chattered like a sparrow, and he hadn't wanted
Rose to wake up.

Well, that was one question answered at least.
Long celibacy had not meant his ability to feel
desire had disappeared. He told himself to banish

those thoughts—this was not the time or place, and certainly not the woman—and went to work. The muscles in her back were just as knotted as those in her calves had been. He moved to her arms to work on them from time to time, finding them taut as well. She had to be exhausted not to have woken, because he knew from her whimpers that she felt what he was doing.

Would she whimper with delight if it were her breasts he was kneading this way, slowly, and with great care? Would he feel her ribs just under her breasts, and thus be able to savor and delight in the contrasts beneath her smooth skin? How would it feel if he leaned forward and took one rosy nipple into his mouth and . . .

He hardened more, if that was possible, and he swore under his breath. But try as he might, he could not think of her with detachment again. Moving his hands to her shoulders, he pulled the toweling over Rose's smoothly curved back.

He wished now that Eunice would return, because his arousal had not eased. His imagination rendered him helpless: now he wondered about Rose's hair, which he had moved out of the way to work on her neck. Her hair was thick and vibrant. How would it feel to plunge his hands through that mass, sifting the strands, spreading them gently across her breasts?

Abruptly Peter stopped rubbing her shoulders. This was madness. He rose and went to the window, looking out broodingly at the fields. He saw the patch of earth near the house where Rose had prepared a bed. A kitchen garden, he supposed, although the kitchen building was some distance away as well as behind the house.

This area was to one side of the house, not far from the river; pretty, perhaps, but useless from a cultivation standpoint as the land was neither large enough nor situated near any other plants or flowers that they had planted. Peter wondered when she'd had time to work on that ill-chosen location, and this time he was glad to feel his anger rising, as it blocked out other, less welcome sensations.

So Rose had also been spending her time on this? Little fool. She would work herself to death at this rate and he would not be responsible. He would not. He'd offered to help her but that didn't mean she should waste her strength this way. She was best suited for a lady's life, playing the violoncello, sewing with tiny stitches, married to some equally soft lord back in the chilly land of her birth. The sooner she was gone, the better.

He took the pottery jar containing the liniment with him as he went downstairs, and met Eunice coming in the back door with a tray. "Tell her to stay in bed the rest of the day," he growled, thrusting the jar at the surprised Eunice. "If she comes out, tell her I'll carry her back the same way. So I advise her to stay put. In fact, I don't want to see her out again until she is recovered. Do you understand?"

The maid bobbed and nodded, managing not to upset the tea tray. "Go on, then, take care of her," he said, still in a foul mood. "She needs someone to look after her, since she isn't taking care of herself. Bloody hell," he said, then stalked off, aware that Eunice's brown eyes had gone round with surprise or shock.

To the devil with both of them, he thought, as he stepped outside, wanting to slam the door, but knowing even in his anger what a childish thing that would be to do. He wasn't made to play a lady's servant, that was all. Especially not an English lady's.

When Rose awoke hours later, she found a tray set beside her bed containing a pot of tea gone cold, and a selection of both sweet and savory biscuits. She was also undressed and wearing a wrapper she could not remember putting on, had a smell about her that distinctly reminded her of the stables, and despite the strange circumstances, had to own that her sore body felt more relaxed than it had been in days. The story related by Eunice about how she had come to be in this position was hard to believe, but someone had certainly worked out the knots in her muscles and she doubted Eunice had the strength or skill.

Rose didn't waste any of her energy being outraged. Although she didn't remember much of what had transpired, she was absolutely certain she would have remembered Peter Walters kissing her or taking some other liberties with her person. How could she not, when it sometimes seemed she was attuned to the blasted man's every breath, whether she wanted to be or not?

And wasn't it just her luck to have slept through all his ministrations, chaste though they had been? Still, she minded the warning passed on to her through Eunice and stayed in bed the rest of the day.

Rising the next morning to dress and go outside wasn't the easiest thing she had ever done, but neither was it the torture to her aching body that she had come to dread.

Rose came out the next morning, but had chosen to work near the house, Peter observed. He had asked Eunice and it seemed that Rose had chosen to plant some of the flowers in her sketches in the special plot. As he had observed yesterday, she had chosen a site that overlooked the river, near a tall willow oak but not in its shade. The curve of the land kept it near the house, although it was visible only from the side of the house where her bedroom was located. In short, a lovely place for a bit of privacy and perhaps to showcase a special grouping of flowers, for someone who had the time and energy for a task that was purely ornamental.

To have Rose working nearby but out of sight was fine with Peter, as he couldn't decide whether he wanted to kiss her or shake her. So it was better that Rose wasn't within his line of vision. That way, he didn't have to choose. But he did notice that she seemed to move about more easily, and he relaxed somewhat.

She worked for three solid days putting in the bulbs and plants in the area she'd chosen. She seemed to be creating a formal knot garden, arranging plants in a circle composed of quarters like pie slices, but there was a large opening in the center. He hoped she didn't want a fountain or some other folly only an Englishman could conceive of.

But when he asked her the purpose of her garden's center, she hesitated a good long time before speaking. Plain-spoken, forthright Rose? Peter folded his arms and waited, knowing which of them was more patient. And sure enough, she soon began to speak. Her voice held a pleading note he hadn't heard from the proud Miss Fairchild before. "Lily showed me the gazebo at Oak Grove, when I was there helping her divide bulbs. I thought a gazebo here might be nice."

"What do I want with a gazebo?" Peter said without even thinking about his choice of words.

He saw her shoulders tense. "Isn't the question, 'What do *you* want with a gazebo?' " she asked in a soft voice that should have warned him he was heading into trouble.

"Isn't that what I said?"

"Not amusing, Peter," Rose warned.

Peter wasn't feeling amused. If this was a pleasure garden she was planting, then he had no interest in it. She could do what she wanted, of course, for as long as she was here. But in the end, it would only go to waste, and he didn't want to spend time on a caprice.

But he supposed that he could be more tactful; clearly this project meant something to her. "Ah, do you think that planting a pleasure garden is the best way to spend your time?" he countered.

"Perhaps not," she admitted, but refused to drop her gaze. "Nevertheless, 'tis what I wish. This garden is special to me."

Peter tried, and failed, to recall what had been in the drawings she'd shown him. They had been pretty and well executed. He had been surprised at her skill. But he couldn't remember a single specific flower in those paintings and sketches.

Once more, he tried to reason with her. "We don't really have time to spend on such indulgences." He really was out of practice at talking to women; he could practically see her fume.

"Aren't these flowers as good as any others planted in rows?" Rose asked.

"Well, yes," he acknowledged, "but your plan to build a greenhouse in the center . . ."

"Gazebo," she corrected.

"Yes, gazebo. That is of even less use than a greenhouse, which I'd planned to put in nearer the water, close by the dock."

"Ah, yes, your wharf, your greenhouse."

" 'Twill profit us all," he said in what he thought was a reasonable tone. "A gazebo is just . . . just for pleasure. And the wood you will need, well . . ." He rubbed the back of his neck.

"What about the palings I ordered for the fencing you told me I did not need? Where are they? I had thought to use those."

"I returned the wood to the vendor, with credit to you."

She'd begun tapping her foot, probably not a good sign. "How thoughtful of you, Master Walters."

He sensed he was heading into danger, but not exactly why or how. "There's actually little enough wood used in a conservatory. A glazier is more important, but we may have to send to New York or Philadelphia for proper glass. We haven't even made any glass at Oak Grove yet, and we've been established for many more years than you." She nodded, still looking impatient.

Peter tried to explain further. "But greenhouses are important, you see, Rose, for they will allow us to make flowers bloom out of season. If they can be sustained under glass jars during a ship voyage, we will have the ability to deliver to customers flowers that are already in bloom rather than dull brown bulbs.''

Rose's fair skin had flushed. Peter looked at her, wondering what lay behind her furrowed brow. He already knew he didn't understand women, and after Joanna, had never again been inclined to try. He almost wanted to make that effort with Rose, but what would be the point? She would leave, and soon. Thus, there was no point in that particular challenge. It never occurred to him that he might not win it.

In any event, he thought he had better concentrate on the moment at hand. Something about the way she was looking at him made him think she was on the verge of blistering his ears.

It turned out that he was correct, at least about that.

"Sooo, you are saying that my desire to plant a garden with flowers that are meaningful to me is a foolish idea.''

"Rose, I didn't say that.''

"Next, you are saying that you don't want to build a gazebo in the center of this plot. Did I ask you to build me any such thing?''

"Rose, you are putting words in my mouth.''

"And are you saying that even if I asked you, we no longer have the wood because you returned it to the carpenter without asking my permission or consent?''

"Rose, please, you aren't letting me . . .''

"Oh, and even if we did have the wood, 'twould be better used building a wharf for Peter Walters, whose plan it is to use my river frontage to dock his ships and run his family's business from my land."

Peter swiped his fingers through his hair. God in heaven, what had he done? How had he gotten into this? A few simple words, and she had taken them beyond the moon. He had no idea how to work his way back.

"Now see here, Rose," he began. Her mouth opened to argue with him once more, and his control snapped. He seized her arm and brought her up against him. Her eyes widened. But instead of picking her up as he had that time when she had worked beyond her body's resources, he merely brought her against him, her body pressed all along the length of his. He had time to register how good that felt, just barely, before he brought his lips down on hers.

And then they truly were beyond the moon, sailing somewhere amid the stars. He hadn't expected to feel such a shock of recognition, as if this had been just waiting for them both to acknowledge it. He strove to keep the kiss light and not punishing, but there was too much temper between them. The anger that turned so neatly into passion, however, stunned him. This was a new, unwelcome dimension to the challenge that occurred daily between him and Rose.

Her lips were soft and yielding beneath his, a sound almost like a hum emerging from deep in her throat. He shifted to align the fit between their lips, each pressure better, more perfect than the last, each yielding on her part met by an advance on his own, until there was no more retreat and challenge, only a continuous melding in which each gave and each took, and neither could have said where one ended and the other began.

Peter found his hands smoothing down her back to her trim waist. Her hands had fisted in his hair, which was disheveled and missing his queue ribbon. He had meant to calm, not frighten her, but he was the one frightened. Of the depth of feeling that flowed between them, of the sense that each of them needed this, needed the other.

Need? Never. He wasn't ready for this and neither was she. He lifted his lips from hers reluctantly, feeling lost before the contact even ended. He had to clear his head, uncloud his senses. Sweet heaven, this could not be. It could not.

She wasn't much happier, he could tell. In the pause after they had parted and stepped back, they glared at each other. The spark of initial irritation had soared well beyond any acceptable bounds into flames.

The kiss they had just shared had stirred the flames of an unwanted, exquisite passion, as precious and as volatile as the flame markings that had striped the priceless tulips of a hundred years ago. The flame tulips had been so costly because no one was ever certain the pattern could be repeated, not until it bloomed.

God help them both, if they succumbed to this . . . this uncertain lust. Whatever it was, it was something that neither of them wanted. The passion for those one-of-a-kind tulips had nearly bankrupted the Dutch, who had lived only for the moment when they would be able to possess the matchless flower.

They did not need this complication. Still breathing hard, Peter lowered his gaze from her flushed, confused countenance. He opened his mouth to speak, closed it, then turned and walked away.

He stopped a few feet away, turned back. She was standing frozen in place, much as he had been. "I don't want this," he said in a low voice.

"Neither do I," she said, wiping her hand across her mouth as if no one had ever kissed her before.

"Good," he said.

"Good," she echoed faintly. She spun on her heel, and he turned to go. This time he did not look back. He doubted she did either, because he heard the heavy oak door of Willow Grove close firmly behind Rose as she went inside.

Once he was alone, Peter swore savagely in a low voice, neither Rose nor servants around to hear him. How could he risk his life's plans for a moment's desire? For the passion of a woman, which he knew firsthand was easily roused but as easily quenched?

All he could do was go back to work and hope that her resistance to desire remained as strong as his. He refused to consider that there might be feelings involved for them both, something that went beyond a moment's pleasure. If there were, she wanted them no more than he. For once, he thanked God for her stubbornness, and that her thinking was the same as his.

Why he didn't feel better about that, he didn't know. But he also wasn't going to waste time thinking about it.

Chapter Seven

> We must take them [our children] and love
> them as God gives them to us.
> — Johann Wolfgang von Goethe
> *Hermann and Dorothea,* 1797

Rose didn't know what to do with herself after
what had transpired between her and Peter, so she
took Lily up on her invitation and went to visit Oak
Grove. She had been drawn to Lily's lively children,
who seemed so happy, so unlike her own childhood
after they had left Virginia. Rose thought that she
did better paintings of nature than of people, but
it was a convenient excuse and she planned later
to give Lily the charcoal drawings of the children
that she'd said she wanted to do just for practice.

Getting three healthy children used to having the run of the plantation to sit still to be sketched was almost impossible. But it took her mind off Peter, so she was pleased with the challenge. They were lively and entertaining and she couldn't help but laugh at their antics, especially Violet's constant efforts to keep up with her older brothers.

Rose didn't want to follow the children around too much in case she should run into Peter, but Lily told her that he had gone into Williamsburg for "supplies." Rose could tell from Lily's worried look that it was something Peter did when he wanted to escape from everything around him, but she figured he was a strong, grown man who would survive a round or two with a jug of ale. He hadn't shown any signs toward excessive drinking like her brother Ralph. And if for some reason he got into trouble, Adam could always go after him. Rose thought Lily was being a little overprotective— Peter would be thirty soon, according to Lily—but didn't want to be rude by saying so.

Rose gave up trying to draw the children as if they were sitting for portraits. One of them invariably pulled the hair of the other, stole a treasure from someone's pocket, or committed some other prank that led to mock wrestling, rolling on the floor, an extended chase through the house or grounds, or a challenge to race that seemed to be an outlet for their astonishingly high spirits. Violet gave as good as she got, and the boys seemed to treat her no differently from the way they treated each other, for the most part.

Two days after her arrival, she sat with Lily on the shaded veranda watching the children chase butterflies around the bushes. Violet got too close, not to a butterfly but a bee, and was stung. Although her little face screwed up with the desire to cry, she said nothing as she came toward Lily. Lily rose to go to her, but swayed suddenly and sat back down.

"Lily, are you all right?" Rose asked. "Do you feel faint?"

Lily nodded and bent over her lap to counteract the dizziness. "I'm fine. Would you ask Humphrey to fetch some ice from the blockhouse and put it in a towel for Violet?"

"Certainly, but I think you had best lie down."

"No, no, I'm fine."

Violet had reached them by now. Rose saw the angry-looking bee sting on her arm just below her sleeve and her obvious puzzlement at her mother's behavior.

Rose rushed down the steps. "Come with me, Violet. Your mother says we need to go put ice on your sting."

"What's wrong with Mama?" Violet said, her own lip starting to tremble. The boys were still chasing butterflies among the flowers and didn't appear to notice that Violet had left them.

"Your mama's feeling a bit faint, dear. Do you know where her smelling salts are?"

Violet stared. "She doesn't have any."

Rose thought all older women had them. She tried to think of something else, as she and Violet went through the house and out through the back on the way to the kitchen. The way that bite was swelling, she didn't want to wait for the servant to find them.

"This not having kitchens in the house is such foolishness," she muttered.

"No, it isn't," Violet countered, distracted from her pain. "Lots of houses burn down when their kitchens catch fire. It's a, it's a percussion, a . . . a . . . precushion . . ."

"A precaution, I imagine your father said," Rose said. Violet started to bob her head, then a fresh flood of tears welled up in her eyes at the pain.

"Come on, little love, we're almost there." Rose felt foolish. Of course Adam was right, and she should have remembered that herself and ignored Eunice's complaints. Fire was a real and common danger in these parts. Besides, now that Willow Oaks had a cook, Eunice didn't have to fetch trays very often anymore.

Rose was amazed that Violet still hadn't cried. As soon as they saw the little girl and her arm, all the kitchen servants rushed forward to help. Offers to put lard and other kinds of grease on Violet's arm came from all sides, but Rose only allowed the ice.

One of the cooks produced a mug of something to drink called mobby, which turned out to be fresh peach juice. Violet accepted it eagerly. Rose agreed to try it, finding, to her surprise, that it was about the most refreshing drink she had ever tasted.

The kitchen door was suddenly pulled open and Peter rushed in with an accusing look at Rose. "My sister has nearly fainted on the veranda, and you are sitting here doing what, making the servants give you a cool drink for your pleasure?" Violet was seated beside her on a bench, which Rose's full skirts and petticoats concealed.

Rose knew Peter hadn't seen Violet, but she was

offended nonetheless. Why did he immediately have to assume the worst about her?

"I was about to ask for smelling salts to be sent out to Lily," she started to say.

"About to? When you'd had a glass or two of juice? Why didn't you go back there yourself?" Peter continued in the same accusatory vein.

"Unca Peter, don't be mean to Aunt Rose," Violet piped up.

"Princess? What are you doing in here?" Peter said in a completely different tone of voice.

"Miss Rose brought me in here 'cause I got a bee sting out chasing flutterbys with the boys," she said in a pitiful voice.

Rose realized Violet still hadn't cried. "And she's been very brave, too. She hasn't cried one little bit," she said, kissing the top of Violet's dark head.

Rose stood, gathering her skirts. "Violet, I'm going to go back and see to your mama while Uncle Peter helps you with the ice. The swelling should go down very soon, although I think he should take you upstairs to lie down for a little while, all right? I'm going to ask your mama to do the same thing."

Peter had the grace to look abashed as she swept by him, but he was fully occupied with Violet, who looked as if she was about to finally give in to her tears. Rose quickly asked one of the kitchen servants to fetch Mistress Steele to see to Violet, and she ran back through the house with eucalyptus leaves and some hastily picked mint from the kitchen garden, remembering the strong scent both had. Perhaps these would work as well as her mother's smelling salts.

By the time she reached the veranda, Lily was

sitting up again, but she was leaning against the cushion behind her, and her face looked pale. The boys were nowhere in sight. She smiled wanly at Rose and told her the leaves were just the right kind, as their aroma was strong. She asked Rose to crush them in a square of linen, and then to hold them to her nose.

After a few deep inhalations, Lily laid the packet of crushed leaves in her lap and asked anxiously about Violet.

"She will be fine, I'm certain," Rose said. "Peter came in just as we were applying the ice and . . ." She closed her mouth before any bitter words could emerge, such as "and your brother thinks I'm an idiot because he accused me of taking my leisure in the kitchen while you were fainting out here."

"He wasn't harsh with you, was he?" Lily asked, bringing the scented packet to her nose again and inhaling deeply with her eyes closed.

She opened her eyes when there was no answer forthcoming from Rose. "Oh blast, he was, wasn't he?"

Rose wasn't shocked by Lily's vigorous language, but she didn't want her to become agitated about anything, so she tried to brush it off.

" 'Tis all right, Rose, I know my brother isn't a paragon," Lily said, her voice somewhat muffled by the impromptu smelling salts. "He cares for you, though, or else he wouldn't be so ill-tempered. I know that seems odd, but trust me, men can be such perverse creatures."

Rose couldn't help the little pang of envy that Lily could speak so knowledgeably about men. Would she ever be able to do that herself one day? "I haven't much experience with men, but that wasn't one of the reactions I've ever heard about," Rose said.

"I'm serious. You are the first woman he's shown any interest in at all since Joanna, and he doesn't know how to behave."

"Lily, we don't have to talk about this, truly. How are you feeling?"

"Much better, thanks. 'Tis true," Lily insisted, not to be put off the topic. "Peter was affianced to a woman he met in New York while the American Navy was battling the British. I don't know exactly how their relationship ended. Peter was injured on a ship that sank; he was taken prisoner, he and his friend from Williamsburg, Ethan Holt."

She sighed. "Poor Ethan died of his wounds, but Peter was held for almost two years, and by the time he was released, the girl and her family had moved. I believe they went back to England, but Peter won't discuss the circumstances. I don't know if that is how their betrothal ended, or if 'twas already over by that time."

"Is that why he doesn't like the British?" Rose asked, observing Lily closely at the same time. As interested as she was in the conversation, her principal reason for talking was to distract Lily and then to see if she was feeling better. Rose noticed that some of the color seemed to be coming back into Lily's face, so her concern began to ease.

"I've often wondered myself since he returned home how he came to dislike the British. I simply do not see how the war can be the only reason. After all, I don't hate the British; I'm married to an Englishman. But Peter will not talk about his imprisonment, and the key is there, somewhere." She took another deep breath of the aromatic leaves, keeping her head tilted back and her eyes closed.

"I don't think 'twas because Peter was mistreated," she continued. "Other than the wounds that had long since healed, he never mentioned any ill treatment or showed signs of it that I could detect. Do you know, he had even been captured by redcoats once before, in Williamsburg? Peter was held for only a few days before Adam rescued him, thank goodness." Lily stopped speaking for a minute, but kept her eyes closed.

I don't know what to do about him," Lily resumed, with frustration coloring her voice. "He used to tell me everything before. But since he came home two years ago, he's been a changed man. When he visited during the times he could snatch during the war or when he had shore leave, there was none of this moodiness or sense of distrust. So there are only two things I can think of that it could possibly be: Joanna or being a prisoner of war. Perhaps the two are somehow related, although to be honest, I can't think how."

Rose was about to suggest that she fetch some cooling cloths, when Lily held up a hand. "And now I think it's time for me to tell you my news, so you won't worry about why I was suddenly faint."

She smiled. "I am expecting another child."

"You are? How wonderful." And Rose leaned forward and hugged Lily before remembering that it was a very forward thing to do.

"Oh, I'm sorry, I shouldn't have . . ."

"Nonsense," Lily said strongly. "You're in America now. You are our neighbor and my friend, and we don't stand on ceremony."

"Does the Earl know?"

Lily frowned a little at the use of the title. "Adam suspects, but is waiting for me to tell him, I believe. Peter doesn't know yet. He's been so focused on the work at your plantation and he has hardly been here."

"Peter doesn't know what?" came a suspicious voice and Peter emerged onto the veranda from the house. He held a tray with three glasses on it. Mistress Steele followed him, carrying gingerbread cakes on a platter. She had been torn between rushing to Lily's side and taking care of Violet, but it seemed Peter had persuaded her to help with Violet while Rose had gone after Lily.

"Something I'm not about to tell you before I tell Adam, or we will both be in serious trouble," Lily said teasingly. She smiled, apparently feeling restored and in good humor, so Peter's face cleared. He shot a puzzled look at Rose, but she didn't want to spoil Lily's secret, so she kept her face blank.

Peter sat down in a rocking chair next to Lily, pulling up a wooden bench and placing the tray of drinks on it. "Violet has fallen sound asleep in her room, worn out by the bee sting and the aftermath. The ice brought the swelling down considerably," he said, nodding in Rose's direction. "Rose did the right thing. Violet will be fine," he finished, patting Lily's hand.

He offered a glass of mobby to Lily, and then turned to Rose. "You hadn't finished your drink so I brought it out to you," he said.

Rose thought that gesture and what he'd just said were probably as close to an apology as she would ever get, so she nodded and took the glass from the tray.

"I will go on upstairs to lie down now, I think," Lily said and refused both Rose's and Peter's offers to help see her to her room. She sternly warned Peter not to call in Adam from the fields, saying she would talk to him at dinner.

Rose and Peter looked at each other. "I think she's fine," Rose said, then realized she should say no more.

Peter still looked concerned. "I have no idea what's wrong with her, but I've no doubt Adam will get it out of her. She can't refuse him anything." He felt somewhat baffled by the vagaries of love, then shrugged. He had no doubt that Adam was fully equal to the task of both taking care of Lily, and of getting the information out of her about what had made her ill this afternoon.

"I'm not sure, though, whether I shouldn't go fetch Adam," he said as he began to stand up.

"Lily said not to," Rose reminded him, placing a restraining hand on his arm.

"I know, but if something's really wrong, he'll have my hide that I didn't ride out to tell him."

Rose pondered for a moment. "I don't know what is wrong with your sister," she said carefully, "but my mother used to feel faint quite often. She never seemed any the worse for wear from these episodes. I think she actually used to enjoy the attention she got."

Peter frowned. "Lily would never fake being ill." Rose opened her mouth, but he held up a hand. "No, I don't mean to say your mother would either. It's just something that seems to happen to fashionable ladies a lot, don't you think?" Joanna hadn't been above employing the tactic to win attention, he remembered.

Deliberately he shut down the thought. "Sometimes I think women are encouraged to feel helpless," he said. Rose nodded thoughtfully. "But Lily isn't like that, so something must have been troubling her this afternoon."

And he let it go at that. He didn't want to gossip about Lily, and didn't want the children to come in and hear him speculating about their mother, since that would be sure to upset them. Adam would deal with this when he came in from the fields. Rose didn't seem inclined to argue or dispute with him for once, so they finished their afternoon refreshment in companionable silence.

And that was something else he hadn't expected to find with a woman, he thought, as they went off to their rooms to dress for dinner. Companionable silence. In fact, he'd come to think the two were mutually exclusive in the feminine gender. But Rose kept surprising him, as she'd done with her level head and sensible treatment of Violet this afternoon.

Peter's suspense about Lily's condition didn't last long. Rose and Peter were in the parlor before dinner when Lily came in on Adam's arm. The children had been allowed to come down for a glass of lemonade before bed and the boys were making much of Violet over the fact that she hadn't cried once during her ordeal that afternoon.

Lily was glowing, and the love Adam felt for his wife was clearly visible in his unusual blue-green eyes. Rose and Peter exchanged glances once, almost as if to say, "Wouldn't it be wonderful to be loved that way," but they quickly looked away from each other's too-revealing faces.

"Peter, Rose," Lily said, coming forward to take one of each of their hands. "I wanted to tell you this afternoon, but since I hadn't yet spoken to Adam, it wouldn't have been fair." She winked at Rose. Rose smiled back, thrilled but uncertain why Lily would have picked a veritable stranger to tell her news to first, as she had that afternoon.

"What is it, Mama? What is it?" little Adam and Arthur said, while Violet watched with a knowing expression, as if she had already guessed what none of the rest of them knew.

"We're going to have an addition to the family," Lily said, Adam's arm tightening around her waist. "I was fairly certain already, but the fainting spell and nausea confirmed it. The same thing happened with the twins and Violet."

"You're going to have a baby brother for us to play with?" young Adam asked, jumping up with excitement.

"Baby sister," Violet said smugly.

"You don't know that," the twins said in unison, rounding on their sister.

"Don' I? Just wait," she said, folding her arms and looking superior. The twins would have started a tussle then and there, but Adam reminded them that it was a special treat to be in the parlor at all, and that meant they had to be on their best behavior.

So the twins merely stuck out their tongues at Violet, who did not deign to return the gesture for once. She just smiled, watching her mother from those uncanny eyes that looked so like her father's.

"When do you go get it?" Arthur asked. Peter

hid a smile behind his hand, while Adam looked faintly uncomfortable. "You were too young to remember when Violet was born, son," Adam said. "And I was at war. But you don't actually go anywhere to get a baby. The baby, ah . . ." He cast a look at Lily, whose amber eyes were sparkling, but she was clearly not going to help him out. She shook her head, smiling with suppressed mirth.

"The baby will come from, ah, inside your mama. Her stomach will get bigger and bigger until the baby is ready to be born. And we will all be here for this birth. Your brother or sister will be born upstairs," Adam finished, desperate to get away from a topic that might require discussion of the actual mechanics of birth.

"If you don' go someplace to get it, then how do you pick out the one you want?" little Adam asked, still confused.

"It's not like going to the pumpkin patch to pick out the biggest or the best one," Adam said, trying not to roll his eyes. Rose was surprised at the frank speech, which would never have been allowed in polite society in England. But then, this wasn't society, and she was only incidentally included as part of the family because she was staying here.

In fact, Rose realized that she probably shouldn't even be here at all. These were private matters for this family, no matter how friendly they had been to her as a stranger.

She turned, as if to walk into the dining room and leave the family to finish their conversation, but Lily wouldn't let her. "Rose, no, please don't go. If we had wanted to have this talk alone, we would have told the children up in the nursery. But you were here this afternoon when I took briefly ill, and you are our neighbor and friend. We wanted to include you." Peter put his hand out to stop her and smiled when Rose looked up at him, startled.

He was always relaxed and unforced around his niece and nephews, she recalled, and she knew he adored his sister. So this was probably the real Peter Walters, beneath the layers of hurt and anger and whatever else had happened to him between the time he went to war and had come back.

She took this Peter Walters's arm to go into dinner, and had the pleasure of watching him and participating in the easy banter that characterized the dinner, under which lay the solid core of love that spread from Adam and Lily to include all those around them. She had felt awkward at first. Her mother would no doubt have found it one more crude Colonial trait to discuss something so delicate in public and over dinner. But by the end of the evening, she felt almost like an aunt, the term Violet had used that afternoon with the innocent affection of childhood.

Soon the boys started using the same form of address. Peter watched her with those clear green eyes, a faint smile playing about his mouth from time to time. She could find no fault in his manners or conversation all evening, but when she went to bed, she dreamed of him kissing her in the gazebo that stood among the rosebushes behind Oak Grove.

His kisses were daring, but her response was just as ardent. Her imagination quickly outpaced her knowledge, however, so the dream ended in a blur once Peter's hands and lips ventured beyond the woefully few places she had ever been touched.

She woke toward morning, feeling flushed, her

breasts and belly heavy with unsatisfied warmth. Even though she didn't know exactly what it meant to feel as she did in those regions, she instinctively knew that the only one who could satisfy her curiosity would be Peter.

Chapter Eight

Let us give Nature a chance . . .
     —Michel de Montaigne, *Essays,* 1580

When Rose went home the next morning, it was with the greatest sense of contentment she had felt in years. She remembered the radiant glow around Lily and began a watercolor of her, surrounded by a twining border of flowers whose symbols she took from Lily's vocabulary. At the top, above Lily's head, she painted white Madonna lilies, associated with the Virgin Mary, the very symbol of motherhood. She put in ranunculus with its various bright colors for radiant charms; white heather for protection and its other meaning, "wishes will come true."

Among the border blooms, she scattered purple and yellow pansies for thoughts, and violets for their meaning of constancy in love as well as for sweet little Violet; added bouvardia blossoms for enthusiasm to represent the twins, then twined honeysuckle through all the flowers around the oval framing Lily's face to represent the bonds of love and devotion; with ivy for fidelity in marriage to tie it all together.

She planned to present it to Lily for Christmas, along with a series of charcoal sketches she had done of the children. Their verve and vitality were particularly suited to the quick, bold strokes of charcoal, as she had long ago given up on getting them to sit still for her.

Working on the painting and the sketches, thinking about the baby to come, feeling a part of their happiness, even just as an outsider and neighbor, still felt as special as anything that had ever happened to her in her life.

Except for Peter's kiss, which she would never forget—and given his hot and cold behavior, probably never understand.

Rose watched Peter carefully from the corner of her eye for the next few days, wondering what she would do if he approached her and that frightening flame of passion burned between them again. She dared not look too closely within herself, though, afraid of her own answer. She wasn't sure why he had kissed her. She only knew that it had been dangerous—dangerous to her peace of mind—but judging from the startled look on his face, it had been equally dangerous to his.

But could she ever really regret such a kiss? If not, she'd never have known that it could be so wondrous. A couple of stolen kisses from boys, then later, from the old men her mother had allowed to court her—that was all she'd ever known. Without that kiss from Peter, she would never have experienced a moment in which two minds, two hearts, met in a place where there was no time and where only pleasure existed.

And if he knew that he could turn her mind to mush so easily, wouldn't he use it to his advantage in this contest of wills in which they were engaged? It should not have happened, but it had, and since she was determined to be a spinster and this might be all she would ever know of passion between men and women, she wouldn't regret it. But neither would she let it happen again.

Despite her resolve not to let him get close to her again, he almost trod on her as she planted the ivy border in her knot garden. And wasn't that a fine view, she thought, looking up, hoping her face didn't show her appreciation. Peter Walters had as fine a leg as she could ever have imagined and she knew he didn't pad his stockings like some of the macaronis at home.

She forced her eyes past his manly legs, lean hips, and broad shoulders, up to a face set in the same polite lines she hoped she had adopted.

"Yes?" she asked in what she hoped was a neutral voice.

"Have you forgotten about tonight?" Peter said, shading his eyes as he looked down at her.

"Tonight?" Her heart gave a quick little thrill. It chilled the sweat that was even now dripping down her back beneath her cotton dress.

"Lily's harvest festival?" he said.

"Oh, yes. I had forgotten." Her hand went to

her head, where her curls tumbled out over the
crownless rim of her straw hat. She was sure she'd
developed freckles in the Indian summer heat of
this September week, but Lily had promised her
the use of a cream that would keep her complexion
smooth. She glanced at Peter, thinking resentfully
that *he* looked just fine tousled and sun-kissed.

"We had best clean up and take ourselves
upriver," Peter said, holding out his hand to her.
She pulled herself up with his assistance, groaning
a little when her knee joints popped audibly. Peter
smiled briefly as they turned toward the house, but
he did not offer her his arm. For her peace of
mind, she didn't need him any closer, so she was
not offended.

This wouldn't be the usual harvest festival—not
that Rose knew what one was like—that concentrated on crops harvested, but one that celebrated
the specialized "crops" Tidewater Nurseries produced.

Lily and Adam had told her that when they
moved from florists' flowers to ornamental trees
and shrubs, they had learned to concentrate on
the fruits that were difficult to grow such as apricot,
pomegranate, plums, and pears. "Everyone has
apples," Adam had said, "and most of them have
peaches, too." Many gentlemen gardeners were
convinced that European species were superior
and ordered only from suppliers carrying these
varieties, or sent for them from England. Tidewater
Nurseries had devoted themselves to producing
hybrids that combined the best features of both
old and new.

Many landowners used their orchards only to
feed their livestock, but the Pearsons had created

the region's first specialty nursery and sold their connoisseur's fruit trees and scions to ornamental gardeners up and down the Tidewater, including George Washington and Thomas Jefferson. Prominent local landowners like Jefferson, John Hartwell Cocke, and William Byrd, whose interest in horticulture ran deep, delighting in propagating American varieties and their frequent correspondence with each other and abroad had led to much greater interest in American native and hybrid plants.

Rose had been looking forward to it. In a few short years, her plantings would yield some of these same fruits. Americans had made an astonishing variety of drinks and products from their fruits. In addition to pure juices, there were ciders and brandies made from them—liqueurs that would surely be frowned upon by society at home accustomed to rich French brandies. She could hardly wait.

Later that night, Rose was glad that Peter had remembered the festivities, for she would not have missed this for the world. All the neighbors were friendly, for the most part. They seemed not to hold against her personally the late hostilities with Britain, the way Peter did. People asked after her father, and it eased her heart rather than made it sadder that she had memories to share, and that the planters were eager to recount their recollections of her father.

There were many more varieties of pear, pomegranate, raspberry, and plum than she would ever have guessed, and Adam and Lily grew many varie-

ties of each. She had already tasted peach juice—
now she had also tasted pear juice. Both fruits were
commonly made into brandies, and apart from the
delicious juices, the ripe fruits had been made into
a wonderful array of tarts, cakes, jellies, and sauces
for meats.

There had been much discussion of grafting and
budding, scions and rootstocks, more information
than she could absorb in a week. The business of
fruit trees was much more complicated than she
had realized, and she knew she was lucky that the
Pearsons and Peter had provided not only their
stock and their labor, but also their expertise. She
had a great deal to learn.

Rose had little to contribute to the conversations
around her, but she listened carefully, smiling as
some of the more intense discussions centered on
such things as who had the better method of propa-
gation. It bothered her not at all that the Americans
mixed business with pleasure, although she knew
her mother would have been horrified.

The Pearson children had been put to bed,
strictly forbidden to stay up, but she had seen them
peek around one corner or another twice already.
Peter had rounded them up each time before their
parents noticed. She wondered if he'd been sterner
the second time because she had not seen them
in some time.

Once the musicians had set up, there had been
dancing. A few dances, like the quadrille, she had
recognized. But she had no experience with the
vigorous American dances, which she decided
wasn't going to stop her. She quickly learned the
favorite dance, the Virginia reel. She was flushed

and out of breath from it, but had felt wondrously invigorated.

Adam came up to Rose after her dance partner had declared himself exhausted and laughingly retired from the field. "Would you like to take a walk to cool down, Lady Rose?" he asked.

"What about Lily? Is she . . ."

"She is a bit put out that I won't let her dance the reel, and is not happy about having to put her feet up," he said, smiling. "Why don't we go find her and take a walk? She'll be glad of a little activity, and Peter can act the host for a while," he said.

With a lady on each arm, Adam gallantly walked them out to the gazebo. Unlike the one Rose wanted to build at Willow Oaks, this gazebo was behind the house, set between the extensive rose gardens behind Oak Grove, and the rows upon rows of florists' flowers that Lily and Adam had planted after their marriage for her business. The white-painted structure glinted in the moonlight, and Rose heard a happy little sigh from Lily.

"Since you were here last, Rose," she said, "Adam has put up wooden shutters around the gazebo that can be lowered if the weather turns inclement. I have always conceived many of my designs—"

"Plots," Adam interjected.

"—conceived many of my best ideas in a gazebo," Lily said with great dignity, although Rose heard the smile in her voice. Adam opened the door and ushered the women in ahead of him.

"Lily had a gazebo in the center of her garden in Williamsburg," Adam said. "When we married and moved here, I built her another."

Rose had admired the elegant structure from the

first moment she had seen it. She didn't know how to tell them she had planned one at Willow Oaks, too, without introducing her disagreement with Peter over it. Moreover, her recent dream about Peter kissing her in the gazebo embarrassed her, so she said nothing. But she was fascinated by Lily's story about how she had first offered her services for the Patriot cause while meeting in the Williamsburg gazebo with Adam and Peter.

They talked for a while, until Rose noticed that she could barely even see the gleam of her companions' eyes in the darkness. A breeze had sprung up that cooled her, but now it came on suddenly stronger.

Adam noticed it, too. He swore softly. "That's a September storm, the kind that comes up with no warning. Lily, I want you indoors," he said, and Rose heard the steel of command in his voice. "There'll be lightning with this one, make no mistake." He hustled Lily onto her feet, although Lily protested that there was plenty of time.

Now Rose caught the cool, swift scent of rain on a gust of wind, and she agreed with Adam. "Go ahead with Lily, I'll get back on my own," she said, knowing Adam's first concern would be with his pregnant wife.

"Thank you, my lady," Adam said in his rich, deep voice. "I'll send Peter out to help you get in safely." And he was gone too quickly for Rose to protest in her turn that she needed no help. Certainly not from Peter.

But the dangerous appeal of the approaching storm caught and held her, and she remained on the cushioned bench, transfixed. Adam and Lily had disappeared into the sudden dark, so that not even a glimmer of Lily's yellow silk dress showed. The moon was extinguished as if it had never been, while a cool, wet wind scented with honeysuckle and the fruit that had been crushed that afternoon for fresh juice also poured over her.

Thunder boomed in a long, slow roll. Lightning flashed in tiny, frequent bursts that lit the sky, the orchards, and the river. Rain was imminent, but Rose still hadn't moved. The scent in the air and the wind blowing leaves past the summerhouse were part of the spell holding her in place.

Until Peter burst in, disrupting the entire wild beauty of the atmosphere. "What the devil are you still doing here?" he demanded.

At that moment, the heavens opened and any reply Rose might have made was drowned out by the enormous thunderclap that announced the storm's arrival over their heads.

Peter reached for her. " 'Tis all right, Rose. You'll be safe with me," he shouted.

The peal of thunder stopped and into the sudden silence came the rush of the initial downpour. Cool, wet air blew through the gazebo. Rose laughed and pushed his proffered hand away, remaining seated. "I'm fine, Peter. This is splendid. Enjoy this with me."

During the next lightning flash, she saw a look of puzzlement on his strong, clean features, but with a shrug, he sat down. For long minutes neither of them spoke, and Rose found the silence between them perhaps the most comfortable she had been around Peter Walters since first meeting him.

The rain hammered down and stray gusts blew sprays of rain through the shutters occasionally, but none of it bothered her. Every breath was clear and clean and wonderful, and she loved it. She had never been this close to a storm in her entire life.

When Peter spoke, she was so caught up in feeling the storm with all her senses that, for a moment, she had actually forgotten he was there. "What is it about this that you like?" he asked, his voice low, just reaching her above the rain.

"The scents, the sounds ..." She gestured around her, although she doubted he could see. "This, all this, and perhaps for the first time ever, that I feel free. I *am* free. What I do, what I think, what I say ... there is no one to tell me I may not or I must not ..." She cast a glance at the shadowed darkness next to her where he sat.

"Except you, perhaps," Rose said.

For once, he didn't react stiffly. He only stretched his legs farther out in front of him, and stacked his hands behind his head. "As if what I say makes much difference to you," he muttered, but she heard the humor in it and laughed.

"Oh, what you say matters, I assure you. But following it, that is something else again." She pleated a fold of her skirt, nervous suddenly in case he should be offended by her sally.

"Had you not already wounded my heart to the quick, lady, that should surely be the final blow," he said in tones of mock tragedy. She breathed a quick sigh of relief, praying his lightened mood would last.

"Have you ever heard of St. Elmo's fire?" he asked. She shook her head, and then realized he couldn't see her.

"No," she said. "What is it?"

" 'Tis a form of lightning. We used to see it at

sea sometimes. Sailors are a superstitious lot, always afraid of what they don't understand. It plays around the masts of ships; maybe it's attracted to it. You've heard of Benjamin Franklin's experiments with electricity?"

She had, actually, and Peter emitted one of those typically male grunts of approval that needed no words. Her father had kept up with the activities of the infamous American Patriots, and he had always been interested in the various scientific experiments of Franklin and Jefferson.

"St. Elmo's fire looks like a ball of flame. It turns odd colors, blue and green, and looks like it dances sometimes. Whole ships have been driven into panic by it; many think it a harbinger of doom. That never happened on any ship I was on that sighted it, but out at sea, many a strange sight takes on new meaning."

After the initial drenching, the rain had slowed, and now it tapered off significantly. The moon came out and cast enough light to gleam off Peter's thick bright hair.

He turned toward her. "About what you said a moment ago. Truly, Rose, I do not mean to vex you."

"I know. Or at least, I think I know. But you do make it difficult sometimes. Why is that?" She dared to ask, since the confines of the summer-house seemed to have broken down certain barriers between them. Peter was acting much more relaxed than usual. She hated to break the mood, but she also wanted to know why he seemed so opposed to everything she did.

"Surely you have accepted by now that I am staying," she continued. "It has been nearly two months, and look at all that has been accomplished so far."

"Let's not spoil our enjoyment of this evening," he said in a voice as cool as the night air that surrounded them. "The things that divide us will do so soon enough."

"What are those things?" Her heart was really in her throat now but she'd gone too far to turn back.

"Rose, nothing has been accomplished as yet," he said in a weary voice. "We've made a good start, but there are difficulties in growing any crop. I don't mind helping you but it takes time away from my work at Oak Grove, from my family's business, from the plans we have for our future."

"And as your neighbor and not a member of your family, I am not a part of these plans. Only your family." God help her, she was as angry as the first day he had come to call, expecting to find a man, a property owner, someone who could affect the course of his life and his plans—and finding only Rose Fairchild. Peter was still looking, apparently, and the pain of that hurt was like lightning lancing into a tree, sharp and frightening in its intensity.

She bent over for a moment, holding her stomach as if the pain were physical, but he did not see her movement. She thanked God for that. She needed to hold on to the anger he'd provoked because otherwise the pain would kill her, and she had to get out of here before she ever let him see how much power he had to hurt her.

"Rose, I don't want to say this. We've had a pleasant evening thus far."

"Condescending to me or treating me like a

child won't help. Just say what you want to say,"
she said tightly.

"All right then, blast it, I will. You won't be here
long enough for any of this to matter. That is why
I haven't taken you into account in my plans."

"What?" She stood up, too furious to sit in the
cool, fragrant darkness any longer.

She saw from the brief glitter of moonlight on
the silver buttons of his waistcoat that he had risen
as well. "I do not say this to anger you. 'Tis merely
how things will happen in the end," he concluded.

"Why? Because you think I have no abilities, no
skills, is that it? You think I cannot plant good
crops, hire good workers, or supervise servants?"
she retorted.

"You are out of your element here, Rose. I don't
know what you left behind in England, but it will
catch up with you sooner or later, and then you
will go home." She stalked out of the gazebo at
those words, uncaring now that the wet lawn was
ruining her slippers.

Peter followed her, keeping his voice low, but
she heard every word nonetheless. "If you do not
have the authority over Willow Oaks that you claim,
your brother may undo everything we have done.
He is likely to want to plant tobacco, for instance.
It is relatively quick to grow, it serves in the place
of currency in these parts, and it exhausts the land
like no other crop I have ever seen. Nevertheless,
a man who only wants money will choose it every
time."

Rose's steps had slowed and Peter caught her
arm. He kept a grip on it—as if she could outdis-
tance him if she tried—and continued inexorably.
"Your choices will take time to bear fruit—literally

in the case of the ornamentals, less so for the flower crop that will be up in the spring—but running a plantation requires years of effort, and even then, debt will dog you as it does every planter whose livelihood depends upon and can be destroyed by such vagaries as weather, drought, and pests. You are not a planter. You are a fine, sheltered English lady playing at something that interests you for the moment.''

They had reached the wide circle of driveway that bordered the land entrance to the house. Everything around them was quiet, indicating that the guests were at the dock on the river side of the house on their way home, or that anyone who was staying the night had already retired for the evening.

The crushed shell and gravel path was hard on Rose's feet in her silk slippers, but at least it wasn't wet. If only Peter hadn't crushed her heart in the same grinding way. Slowly, relentlessly, he was sapping her will, and the only thing keeping her from screaming ''stop it'' at him and running away was her determination not to live up to the role of helpless female in which he had cast her.

She stopped, turned toward him, and he nearly ran into her.

Chapter Nine

Oh, what a dear ravishing thing is the
beginning of an Amour!
    —Aphra Benn, *The Emperor*
      of the Moon, 1687

Then the moon sailed out from behind a cloud
and she saw him plainly. "Peter Walters, listen to
me. I am not stupid. I know I have much to learn,
but I will learn. I may be ignorant of many things
about this nursery business, perhaps, but I am neither spoiled nor stupid." And out of sheer frustration, she stamped her foot. Gravel poked into her
shoe and she gave a little yelp.

His raised eyebrow told her just what she had
done. At her chagrined, answering epithet, he

laughed. She smiled back, her rancor suddenly forgotten. Even though it had been at her expense, part of her didn't mind, because she liked hearing Peter's laughter. She far preferred it to his wintry mood—the one that usually followed the occasional moment of lightness.

"I will retract nothing of what I said. But if anyone can make a go of this, Rose, I believe you have a chance. You have courage, heart, and determination, qualities lacking in many men. Moreover, there is not one among them that I would want to do this to . . ."

"What?" she said stupidly, flummoxed at his change of mood from light to dark and back to light again.

"This," he said, opening his arms as if he expected her to walk into them. Which she did, as her brain was not functioning at all. Peter's waistcoat and shirt were soaked, but the surprise of his embrace and the heat of his lean masculine body somehow felt utterly natural.

And for the last time that night she tasted fruit as his lips came down on hers. The taste of the fermented pear and the rain on his face mingled with his own distinctive masculine scent, tantalizing her so that she opened her mouth in order to taste him better. Completely oblivious to the fact that his shirtsleeves were now getting the back of her dress wet where he clasped her against him, she met his tongue's gentler invasion with her own return riposte. There was heat pooling at the juncture of her thighs, and when Peter slid one hand down her back to tuck her more firmly against him, she felt the answering heat and the thick, unfamiliar ridge of him against her.

"Rose, we shouldn't be doing this. You are too tempting," Peter muttered against her neck where he had taken to directing kisses there and across her exposed throat. Rose, who couldn't think of a single reason why they should stop, tilted her head back within the cradle of his arms and let him press those tender, urgent kisses everywhere. Until her knees buckled when one hand rose to trace the outline of her gown, his fingertips disappearing teasingly every few inches or so. And every few inches Rose drowned in the sensation of those light caresses, wanting more.

His hand strayed deeper, to the upper curve of one breast, and reason returned to Rose in a blinding rush.

"What am I doing?" she said, putting her hands against Peter's chest to halt him. "You have insulted me, my intelligence, my intentions, everything about me, and we stand here *kissing.*"

"I have never insulted your beauty," Peter said, but his hand slipped back up to caress her shoulders.

Since she was no beauty, she knew now that this was all some plan of Peter's to help drive her away. "Don't try to sway me again with your lies," she warned. "You just want me to give you this land and have me hie myself back to England. Well, pretending you are attracted to me won't work."

"And what the devil was going on between us just now?" he demanded.

"As soon as you mentioned my 'beauty,' I knew you lied."

"What?" Peter said in an incredulous tone of voice. "I have never lied to you."

"Then why are you attempting to seduce me?"

"I am not trying to seduce you, Rose. If I were, we'd be back on that gazebo with you under me on a cushioned bench, not standing here on sharp oyster shells, soaking wet from this blasted rain. A gazebo like that is made for romance."

She blinked once, twice, but wasn't going to be deterred. "Then what were you doing?"

"Seems pretty damn clear to me I was kissing you."

"And that's not seduction?"

"My God, are you really that innocent? We are standing here practically in public view and I was kissing you. That should make it clear that I didn't plan this—a key element of seduction is intent—and in fact never thought to kiss you at all until . . . until . . ."

"Until what?"

"Until I couldn't stand it any longer." Peter sounded more frustrated than angry, but she couldn't let up.

"I suppose I am too sheltered to know the difference then?"

He caught her arm to hold her when she would have turned to go, and then brought his other hand to cup her face. His touch was surprisingly gentle.

"Make no mistake about it, Rose. When I seduce you, you will know exactly what I am doing."

When, not if? Had he really said that?

He was still talking. "There will be no misunderstandings between me and the woman I finally marry. But when I do marry, it won't be a spoiled Englishwoman who expects an offer of marriage from a simple kiss."

"How can you take words I haven't even spoken

and twist them so?" Rose cried in outrage. "I don't want to marry you. In fact, I don't even want to kiss you. Well, maybe I don't mind that part," she said. Since he had boasted of never having told her a lie, she could hardly do the same.

"But I have neither time nor interest in either seduction or marriage," she went on. "This is my land . . . my family's land, and I intend to run it for the profit and benefit of my family. I don't need help from you or any other man and I will not marry you just so you can have it." It wasn't hers to give, but he didn't need to know that right now. Not telling him might be a sin of omission but it wasn't an outright lie.

They glared at each other, neither willing to look away. The contest of wills ended when Adam emerged from the house with a lantern and called to them.

"Are you all right? I didn't know whether Peter had gotten to you in time."

Rose forced a smile. "We enjoyed the storm from inside the gazebo instead."

As he ushered them inside, Adam thought he had never seen anyone look less happy than those two. What had happened in there since he and Lily left? A look at Peter's set face and he knew he'd learn nothing from his brother-in-law.

But as Lily whispered to him on retiring, there had to be strong feelings between Rose and Peter or the two younger adults would not look so unhappy. Adam had to agree. Remembering some of his struggles with Lily during their exceedingly unorthodox courtship—he had kidnapped her at one point—Adam conceded his wife's point. What else besides love could make two people so happy—and unhappy—and all sometimes within the space of mere minutes?

Peter came late to Willow Oaks the next morning, determined to break the habit of having a morning cup of tea with Rose before they each set about their tasks for the day. Rose was nowhere to be found outside and he was determined not to go into the house. This attraction to her was becoming addictive, but he would not let himself get accustomed to it. He'd been right the night before— her interest wouldn't last. She would return home. He was sure of it.

But Eunice came out and called him in. Rose had the account books spread around her that he had brought her weeks ago, as well as her own.

"Master Walters," she began formally. "You have asked about building a dock."

Peter kept his hands in his pockets, deliberately nonchalant. If she were playing a game, he wouldn't give her the satisfaction of a hopeful reaction, not if she was planning to crush his hopes. Then he was disgusted with himself for his thoughts. Why was he so distrustful of any woman who was not his sister? Damn Joanna. This woman, this beautiful, vivacious woman had proved her strength and determination several times over.

"I think we should reach an agreement for you to build the dock." She gestured around her. "The need for supplies is endless; the household expenses add up. You know all these things, I know. But I need to . . . have something to show my . . . my brother for my time here, not just credit locally."

"I understand," Peter said slowly, wondering if he did. Had her brother asked for some results so soon? If so, he was a terribly impatient man. Endeavors like these took years to come to fruition. He'd thought the old rumors that had brought the first colonists here two centuries ago in search of El Dorado had been long since vanquished. The New World was rich and lush, but jewels didn't lie on the ground for the picking. Even tobacco, called "brown gold," had to be successfully grown and cured into a sufficiently mellow product for a man to want to smoke it. Didn't the new Earl understand any of this?

But he mentioned none of these things aloud. "I'll have papers drawn up, and—"

"No," Rose interrupted. "I would prefer we have a gentlemen's agreement."

"A gentleman's agreement that you're selling me the land? It's far too important a transaction for that." Peter stopped leaning against the wall nonchalantly and dropped into a chair next to Rose.

"I'm not selling you the land," she replied at once. "I am agreeing only to your building your dock on my property, for which you will pay me, and you will pay a use fee for it once built."

Peter started to argue, then realized this was actually a fair deal and probably the best one he would get until she cashed in her chips on this solo venture and returned home. Perhaps her brother would come in person to see what was going on here, and Peter could make another appeal for outright purchase then. Or perhaps he'd write and see if the new Earl approved. This wasn't the first time he'd wondered if Rose was really doing this without her brother's backing.

But no, he couldn't imagine any English noblewoman doing something so audacious. Not even Rose.

And he wouldn't do that to her. No matter what his doubts were, he would give her the benefit of them, and treat what she told him at face value. He'd become ashamed of his behavior where Rose was concerned. Joanna's betrayal shouldn't color his every interaction with women. He had come to respect Rose. There was no time like the present to show her his trust.

"All right, Rose," he said, stepping forward. "I agree. Let's shake on it, shall we?"

They did, and Peter was proud that he maintained his control. Their kiss of the night before had left him only wanting more, but he didn't think sealing this deal with a kiss would prove anything but troublesome. Whatever he felt for Rose should be dealt with at another time, another place. He needed to keep his business interests separate from his personal life.

Perhaps it was time he thought about having a personal life again. All in all, he felt considerably more pleased leaving the house than he had entering it.

Later it occurred to him that he'd be spending more mornings having tea with Rose in order to accomplish the planning for the dock. But he was halfway to his goal of acquiring Willow Oaks, so what was a little tea? Surely he could keep himself under control, especially if Rose stopped being so argumentative.

* * *

Just when Rose thought she was inured to every pain, blister, and backache that the adventure of her new life in America could throw at her, something unexpected—worse, frightening—occurred. The area where she'd planted her special beds, hoping for the gazebo in the center, had bordered an area covered with grasses and weeds. Since her confrontation with Peter over his views of the stupidity of her plans for that area, she'd been working on it alone. She had finished up just the day before, then that morning she had noticed an odd rash on her arms. By midday, it had spread to her face and neck. It burned and itched, itched and burned, and she had finally gone to bed.

Eunice, terrified, had sent for Peter, despite Rose's vehement opposition. She didn't want to endure a lecture about how this was all her fault, which she was sure would be forthcoming.

"I don't want him in here," Rose said. "I don't want him to lecture me, Eunice, and I really don't want him to see what I look like."

For once Eunice dared to argue with her mistress. "But he maybe knows what to do for what's ailing you."

"Why couldn't it be Lily instead?" Rose asked, and then answered herself. "She's probably busy with her family, plus she has her new pregnancy. I certainly don't want to risk Lily developing anything, if what I have is contagious."

Peter had tired of doing it Rose's way, so as Eunice moved toward the door, he simply shouldered his way inside.

He hadn't known exactly what to expect, but he

actually breathed a sigh of relief. Rose's face was swollen, her arms covered with red rashes and welts, but not the spots of smallpox or some other infectious disease.

He gave Eunice instructions, then moved toward Rose, who had turned her head away.

"Rose, listen," he said, sitting on the bed. "It's all right."

"How would you know?" she said, her voice muffled by the pillow.

"Because I've seen this before. You've acquired a rash from poison oak or poison ivy. My sister Lily's children have had it countless times."

"They haven't died, so I guess that means I shan't either." Still, she would not turn her head.

"Rose, look at me."

"No," she said.

"All right. The more you rub against things like your bedding, the more you transmit the rash. It gets on you, your linen, and everything you touch."

She snapped forward and sat upright, although she still would not look at him.

"That's a good girl," he said soothingly. I've asked Eunice to bring up cool water and chamomile leaves. Crushed, they'll make a compress to cover the worst of your rash while I get some salve from Lily. The most important thing you can do is not to touch any of these spots or red marks. Do not scratch, though you will feel tempted by the Devil himself to do so. Do nothing. They are likely to itch ferociously, but you must not touch them. Do you understand?"

"Yes," she said in a small voice.

"Are you frightened?" It had not occurred to

him until just that moment, but her tone of voice had been most unlike Rose.

"N-n-no. I know little of this affliction, that is all." She drew in a breath, then was silent. But he was attuned to her very breath, it seemed, because he knew there was more she wanted to say.

"What else, Rose. Do you want to ask me something?" he said in his most encouraging tone.

"Will . . . will this leave marks . . . or scars on me?" she asked in a small voice.

Sweet Rose. She pretended not to care about feminine ways, but it warmed his heart strangely to know that she did. And she was beautiful; he couldn't understand why she didn't realize that.

"Look at me, Rose," he said gently.

"Can't you simply answer my question?" she asked.

He reached out a hand and captured her chin. "Rose, come on now, look at me," he whispered. He turned her face toward him.

She had welts on her cheeks and her eyelids were puffy and reddened. He thought that might be from crying rather than the plant's effects, but he scrutinized her carefully.

Her face crumpled. " 'Tis bad, then?"

"Have you wiped or rubbed your eyes since the itching took you?" he asked.

"N-no, I don't think so."

"I don't think so either, or your eyes would be swollen shut. I think the redness is from crying. Be very careful not to touch your eyes or your mouth."

She gave a shaky smile. "So this will pass?"

"Yes, 'twill pass. When Eunice gets here, we will put cool water on your eyes, and then compresses."

"Shouldn't you stop touching me?" she asked. "I don't want to risk you in any way."

"Have no fear, fair Rose. I haven't touched any of your sores, and they would have to be weeping for me to contract it from you."

"Then 'tis contagious?" Her expression grew panicked. "What about Eunice? Have I . . . ?"

He moved his finger from her chin to her lips. "Hush. 'Tis most common to contract a case of poison ivy from the plant itself, not from the person who has been affected by it. Unless, as I said, your sores were open or extensive, and even then, I would have to be very close to you indeed." His eyebrows waggled in a mock leer as he spoke, and when he saw her reluctant smile, he knew he had successfully diverted some of her concern.

"Lie back, and we will have you taken care of in a bit. Just resist any urge to scratch. You may wear mitts if it helps. Some people scratch only when they are sleeping. Let me see your hands. Are your nails long?"

He reached for her hands and this time she didn't pull away. Her hands looked more like a field worker's than a lady's.

"Well, what did you expect?" she asked. He hadn't realized he'd spoken aloud. They had that in common, it seemed. "I've been planting and sowing and everything else."

"You've been working too hard, it seems to me." He tried to keep his voice mild. He'd driven her to this, hadn't he? First he'd taunted her that she was nothing but a fair English lady above common work, and then when she'd done that work, he'd hoped she would tire herself so that she would give it up.

She pulled a hand back, waved it. " 'Tis nothing." Had she learned that stoicism from him? He didn't know whether to curse it or admire it. Certainly Joanna would never have worked so hard among the wounded if it hadn't been for her mother. It had been Joanna's mother who had kept her daughter going through the long days and nights in the hospital camp. He hadn't noticed it then, but after watching Rose work, he certainly knew it now. In fact, when Joanna had gone home, her mother had stayed on. All in all, the mother had been superior to the daughter in every way. Including her integrity.

Peter leaned forward to pull a pillow up behind her head. Her lips were inches from his. "No, it isn't 'nothing,' Rose. Rarely have I seen a woman pursue her dream harder, and for all our differences, I must acknowledge that. And you." He leaned forward just the necessary inch and kissed her lips in a brief salute.

"Now rest, and let someone else take care of you, my lady." Her eyes, which had closed as he came closer to her, remained shut, and he rose before the brief surge of disappointment could induce him to do something stupid . . . like kiss her again . . . and again . . . and again.

Fortunately, he met Eunice on the way up the stair. He told her he was riding to Oak Grove for supplies and instructed her on what to do in the meantime.

Chapter Ten

Thou source of all my bliss,
and all my love.

—Oliver Goldsmith
The Deserted Village, 1770

All the mature reflection and self-control for which he'd congratulated himself the morning they'd struck their deal over the dock had been premature, Peter reflected. It was the week after she'd recovered from her poison ivy rash, and at the moment, all he wanted to do was to shake Rose until her teeth rattled.

She might have given him the agreement to build the dock, but as with the planting, she seemed to want to do it all herself. Now that she was back on her feet, none the worse for her rash and with no scars, she was underfoot every time he turned around.

It was nearly November, and he wanted to get the dock completed before the water got any colder. The days were getting shorter as well, and he couldn't build by candlelight.

Rose wasn't foolish enough to think she knew anything about carpentry, thank goodness, but she wanted to inventory the supplies and make sure he had enough wood and nails. She seemed to think of a hundred other useful details every day that he didn't need help with.

It was late in the afternoon. Peter had dismissed the workers for the day and was just finishing up when Rose came down to the water. She tried to lift the planks to inspect them, saying she wanted to make sure the wood wasn't worm-ridden. Her efforts to lift the large, heavy lengths of wood were ridiculous, of course, and he told her so.

That only put her back up.

And that put him into a blazing temper.

They were standing at water's edge in the descending half-light of dusk. The fall foliage that she'd been capturing in vivid watercolors flamed all around them and across the river.

"Listen to me, you stubborn wench. You can't do the same work I can. I know I was not . . . encouraging of you in the past, but this is no disparagement of you." The stubborn set of her shoulders told him she wasn't listening.

He put his hand on her shoulder, and they both jerked back at the contact. How could he make her see reason when at one slight touch he was fast losing his wits? "There is no dishonor, no contest, no wager on this. You are a man and I am a woman," he began, then realized her shoulders were trembling as she turned away.

"Rose?" he said, feeling oddly troubled that he had hurt her so easily, when really he should be relieved that he didn't have to hammer at her over this as with everything else. "Don't take on. Women of your kind weren't meant to do the work of field hands."

Then her shoulders shook and she turned, and he realized she'd flummoxed him again. She was laughing, the minx. "What?" he demanded, courtesy gone as it always was around her. She seemed to drive it out of him.

"I may not be a carpenter, Peter Walters, but well do I know which of us is man, which woman."

Oh hell, he'd said it backward.

He grabbed her arm and turned her toward him. With the fire in her eyes, her tall form held proudly, and her hair as bright as nature's colors around him, she was irresistible.

"Dammit, stop turning my world upside down," he said, plunging his hands into the richness of her russet hair. The pins scattered beneath his probing hands as he positioned her head to better receive his kiss. Although her body stiffened, it was for a mere instant only, and this time she met him more than halfway.

Her response to his impassioned assault on her mouth was to pull his head closer, her hands going to his hair. She stripped the queue ribbon off as swiftly as he'd dispensed with her pins, and then her mouth was open, receiving, giving, twining, taking in a kiss of such blazing heat that he forgot the night falling around them and the cool fall air.

He didn't notice the coldness of the ground when he bore her down in his arms onto one knee, never surrendering her mouth. He held her with one arm, her torso arched over his other knee, while with his other, he undid the laces at her bodice. Since she was attired in day clothes, there was no stomacher in his way, just laces closing her bodice over her chemise.

Her gown parted and only her thin white chemise covered her breasts. He was too inflamed now to be a soft and teasing lover. He pulled her chemise down, and the setting sun caught the rich, creamy glory of one breast swelling above her stays.

His hand immediately cupped the sweet weight against his palm. As Peter lifted his lips from hers, he trailed his mouth into her hair, then to her ear, where he whispered her beauty in phrases that he wasn't sure had any meaning. If her sweet moans and whimpers were any answer, she didn't care. With light darts of his tongue, he kissed his way down her neck and collarbone, and over her chest.

The nipple of the breast he held peaked as he trailed his fingers across it, and he caressed it to further tautness while his mouth sought its twin from beneath the muslin garment. Her hand in his hair tightened as he kissed and licked his way closer and closer to the peak that remained covered. Nuzzling aside the fabric with his mouth, he found his goal. Surrounding the nipple he could feel had budded, he took the crest whole into his mouth.

Her back arched, she moaned, and her fingers tugged at his hair in the same rhythm he was using to suckle her breast. With her hands in his hair and her back supported against his knee, he brought up his hand from behind her back so he could pull the chemise down farther. He raised his head to admire her fully exposed breasts, which were the most beautiful sight he had ever seen.

He used both hands to cup her breasts, and moved his mouth from one to the other, nuzzling them before claiming the peaks, delighting in the little gasps she made every time he did so.

Moving back to her mouth, he took her lips again, while carefully lowering her onto her back in the grass. He kept her head within the crook of his arm, so it didn't touch the ground. His free hand roamed over her breasts and down.

His tongue was in her mouth, and her hands had dipped inside the open collar of his shirt to move over the planes of muscle on his chest. Peter caressed her waist, slid his hand down, found the outline of her hips, and pressed the fabric of her dress between her legs as he came closer to the juncture of her thighs.

Rose was near to writhing now, wanting a deeper caress but not knowing exactly where or how to ask for it. She had boldly put her tongue in Peter's mouth now and was exploring it, but was finding it hard to concentrate with his hand on her body.

Then his mouth resumed its exploration of her breasts, while his hand delved ever lower amid her skirts. She wished he would lift her hem, but she knew there were countless petticoats to wade through. Still, her body had a mind of its own, and her legs shifted and parted.

Suddenly his hand was there, the place that had throbbed when she'd woken from her dreams, the place that had tingled when he'd kissed her in the driveway of Oak Grove. She made a sound, and he lifted his head to look into her eyes.

Above him she saw vivid red maple and golden oak leaves frame his head. "Do you like that?" he asked, green eyes intent.

She had no words, only nodded. Her legs fell apart a little more as he rubbed there, and the fabric between her legs felt more and more like an obstacle.

"Dear God, you are beautiful," he said, "you look like a pagan goddess, Diana in her glory." And his clever, knowing mouth came down again to heat her breasts, which had grown cool with his mouth's absence, while his hand determined more closely the feminine heart of her, and he came closer to the place she so desperately wanted him to touch.

He knew that too, it seemed, because he lifted his head again and looked down at her. "Will you let me touch you, Rose?"

How could he even ask? He bent over her as she whispered, "Yes."

"Help me," he said. She was puzzled, and then, feeling the cool air around her ankles, she understood what he wanted. She half sat up, his arm supporting her, to reach the bottom of her skirts. She helped him grasp the correct number of layers of skirt and petticoat, and then sank back against him as he lifted them and his arm disappeared.

He kissed her lightly as his hand made its way up her thighs, past her petticoats, to the naked heart of her. His knuckles grazed the curls at the top of her thighs and she cried out.

"Hush, darling, I won't hurt you," Peter whispered. It wasn't fear, she thought, it was wonder

. . . and anticipation . . . and need. But she didn't know how to tell him that. When he cupped her heat in his hand, though, she moaned and arched her neck.

"Ah, you like that, don't you, my fiery Rose," he whispered, and though her cheeks flamed, she nodded. He urged her face up to his and began to kiss her again, as his hand cupped and then began to move against her.

He traced his fingers along the furrow, parting her slowly and carefully with each renewed caress of his hand. When he had reached the moist heat that had gathered there, she didn't know which of them was more surprised.

He sensed her question, because he murmured reassurance. "This is your passion for me, Rose, just as this," and a rigid length bumped against her side, "is the evidence of mine for you." Carefully, she put her hand against him, encouraged by his groans, as his hand sank more deeply into her. When he slid a long finger inside her, she thought she might shatter from the exquisite tension, but with his encouragement, she continued to caress him.

They were both breathing heavily now, and he drew back again to watch her as he moved his fingers inside her. Again, she learned from him, because she caressed him with the same rhythm she felt, and his hips pressed into her side. Finally, when she felt she could bear the exquisite pleasure no longer, she began to plead with him in little broken murmurs.

"Sweetheart, you have no idea how much I want you, how much more there is," he murmured against her breasts. "We can't do more than this, though," he groaned. Whatever else he meant to say was lost, though, as she convulsed suddenly around his intimate invasion of her, her hand clenching on him, and the sharp edge of pleasure caught her and sent her spinning into sensations she had never known.

He cried out too, and surged against her. For long moments, there was nothing but cries of completion as their bodies were claimed by passion, then ragged breathing as they struggled into its aftermath.

"Sweet heaven," Peter managed, as he sagged to the ground, rolling Rose against him and over so that she now looked down on him and he lay fully on the ground. Robbed of all energy, she was too limp to feel awkward sprawled on top of Peter. Her hair fell down between them, brushing his face, and she saw beads of sweat around his temple.

She felt lazy and satisfied and very, very feminine. "So you *do* need me to work hard," she said, propping her chin on her hands to peer up at him.

He laughed, and the sound of it rumbled through his chest. Odd, how that warm sound gave Rose a slight tingling of her senses, especially in her body's secret places. Except now she knew what that sensation meant. It was the awakening of desire, a desire that only Peter could fulfill. There was more than what had just occurred, she knew, despite her sheltered upbringing. She knew men put something in women besides their hands. What was in his breeches, for instance.

Then her own wanton thoughts horrified her, and she tried to sit up. Her mama would have thought her terribly common—a trollop, not to put too fine a point on it. Peter must have sensed the change in her somehow, because he pulled her close to him in the rapidly fading light.

"Ah, Rose, sweet, I know this shouldn't have happened, but I . . ." He didn't seem to know what he wanted to say.

"But I . . . but we . . ." she said, interrupting him, then halting, because she didn't know what to say either.

"Don't turn proper English lady on me now, " he said. "We did nothing that was irrevocable, and you are still a virgin," he said, but the open, easy atmosphere between them was gone. Holding her with his arm braced behind her back, he sat them both up.

Rose pulled her chemise up and sought the edges of her gown. Peter wouldn't let her slide from his lap as she tried to do, but he brushed her hands away and did up her gown with a confidence she didn't want to know anything about.

"No proper English lady would have ever done anything like that." She rose, brushing grass and leaves from her hopelessly crushed skirts. Her body still throbbed in secret places, but she ignored it.

"I wouldn't know about the habits of proper British ladies," Peter snapped. Then his face softened, and he reached for her again. She tried to avoid him but he brought her easily into his embrace.

"Don't be ashamed," he said. "Nor should you feel guilty. I haven't spoiled you for whatever nobleman . . ."

She stiffened and trained on him the steeliest gaze she had ever turned on anyone. If he couldn't see all of it in the descending dark, he certainly sensed it.

". . . for whatever *man* you will marry," he amended.

"I have no intention of marrying," she said, pulling back from him.

"Oh, dear one, don't say that. Even though this was a . . . ah . . . a mistake, a wonderful mistake, mind you, but still an error, as I'm sure you will agree . . ." Peter ran a hand through his hair, sounding genuinely pained. "But you are not ruined."

Was that what he thought she was worried about? She had never felt less like laughing, but she was experiencing a grim sort of amusement.

"This has nothing to do with you, Peter Walters. I came here never intending to marry. You haven't . . . what happened here just now, hasn't changed that." She bent over looking for her hairpins, but it was too dark now to see. Despite her brave words, her knees were shaky and she almost stumbled.

He knelt down, too, either feeling around for his queue ribbon or trying to help her. "Rose, dear Rose, you are a beautiful, vibrant young woman. You should never think otherwise. I, on the other hand, am not for you. Not because of you, 'tis I, my . . . Oh, hell," he said and stopped.

Fine, Rose thought. She really didn't want to hear anymore. Of course it was a mistake. Without a doubt, it had been a colossal mistake. But in another sense it wasn't, for a reason Peter would probably never know. And that was because what had just passed between them might be the only taste of passion she would ever know. Even worse, she knew deep inside her heart, this wasn't all she wanted from Peter Walters.

She straightened, putting a hand into the springy

turf for balance, because suddenly she couldn't see
for the tears that filled her eyes. She would not let
them fall. Thank goodness it was full dark now.
Then she fled back to the house, to the solid,
welcoming stability of Willow Oaks. Her house. Her
home. Peter didn't come after her.

Cold weather closed in around them, but the
planting was finished before the first frosts hit in
late November. Hundreds of bulbs had gone in,
and dozens of trees had been planted, their root
balls carefully covered over with mulch against the
long winter ahead. Peter hadn't had time to build
the greenhouse since he'd been concentrating so
heavily on the dock. Rose hadn't walked down to
the water there since her encounter with Peter.

She was aware of his gaze on her when she went
outside, but he didn't approach her except for
anything but the most necessary conversation. He
was neither as cold nor as wary as he'd been at
their first acquaintance, and occasionally she saw
flashes of some deep emotion in his eyes, but he
didn't touch her, and he didn't give voice to what
he was thinking.

Rose didn't know what she could say to him—
more, please, I liked that?—without him thinking
her desperately wanton. She also had trouble envi-
sioning herself explaining that becoming his mistress would be all right with her because, really,
she didn't intend to marry, so he had nothing to
fear from genuinely compromising her. She wasn't
so ignorant that she didn't know of the risk of
pregnancy, but a man who had experience with
women would surely know something about that.

No, none of the conversational gambits she could think of were suitable, or thinkable, or anything to which a gently reared young woman could give voice. Or even a fallen woman, which she wasn't yet, and she didn't intend to become one.

So they marched on, their relationship neither truly friendly nor loving. She was upset and annoyed until she realized that he was no more comfortable than she. And though she didn't wish for him to be in pain, she felt perversely reassured that she wasn't alone in her misery.

Rose continued to visit Oak Grove throughout the fall. Lily was unfailingly friendly and gracious, and Rose was no longer hesitant or concerned that she was imposing on the hospitality of the Pearsons. She had come to love the entire Pearson family, especially perceptive little Violet, and the serenely radiant, increasingly *enceinte* Lily.

She doubted that Lily was unaware of the uneasy relationship between Rose and her brother, but she didn't say anything. Peter had taken to behaving perfectly—too perfectly, perhaps—when Rose visited Oak Grove. He also made certain that he was never alone with her.

One night, Rose showed Lily the watercolors of what she imagined her knot garden would look like when everything came up in the spring. Peter, seated across from Rose and next to Lily, looked at the paintings briefly before returning to his discussion with Adam about putting in new cherry varieties that the Pearsons had received from an Italian friend of Thomas Jefferson, whose estate was located not far from Monticello.

He complimented her work politely. "You added some new plants?" he asked Rose, but didn't scrutinize her work more closely before returning to his discussion with Adam.

"This is phlox, here, that you've used for the border?" Lily asked.

Rose nodded.

"Is this heather or lavender? Oh, I see, you have lavender in this bed, don't you?" Lily's gaze moved over the paintings carefully. "Then you have lavender in your original beds, but the heather here— this is white heather, rather than the purple kind?"

Lily picked up a pencil sketch. "Now what's this? Is this the same bed from a different direction?"

"Actually, the painting is as it was when I first worked on the bed after coming here." She bit her lip so that she didn't say, "And before Peter and I argued about it."

Rose put her wineglass down, and paused to use the damask napkin in her lap. "And this most recent painting I've done, this one is with the flowers in the bed as I have it planted now," she said. "Initially, I had planted all four quarters the same. Then before the weather turned too cold, I put in different plants in this bed"—she pointed to the opposite quadrant of the circle—"and here."

Lily hmm-ed and nodded and complimented her color harmonies, but said not a word about the flowers' meanings. Rose saw Lily look at Peter once, then at Rose, seeming to ask her silently if Peter had noticed what she'd done. Rose shook her head imperceptibly, and Lily said nothing more, although she laid her hand on Rose's arm once, and squeezed lightly, as if to reassure.

Rose returned her smile weakly. Lily knew the

flower meanings. In two of the quadrants that were Rose's initial beds, she had planted flowers representing her original intentions: carnations for boldness at her initiative in coming to America, the bachelor's buttons that meant she had no desire to marry, columbine for resolution, and flowering white dogwood for durability to symbolize her intention to remain in America. Finally, she had planted lavender for her hope that she would succeed.

Then, as her feelings for Peter had grown, she had allowed herself to express in flower language what she could never say to Peter or discuss with anyone. The yellow mimosa, with its heavy, nodding blossoms, meant secret love, complemented by pink azalea with its meaning of first love. She was sure Lily had noticed that instead of ivy as in the other bed, Rose had bordered these two quarters in phlox, the pretty, early blossoming ground cover that meant "our souls are united." The aromatic herb rosemary, of course, was for remembrance, while the red and yellow tulips she'd planted meant, respectively, a declaration of love, and in a brief moment of despair, the more realistic assessment of "hopeless love."

There was no point trying to hide things from Lily, although Lily, bless her, had the delicacy not to pry. But then there was Peter, who was opposed to the whole idea of her special circular knot garden with the gazebo in the center. He had barely shown any interest in the sketches, and she seriously doubted that he remembered the flower meanings, if he'd ever known them. So she needn't have worried that he would notice what she was doing.

And that was just fine with Rose. She hadn't planted the flowers hoping Peter would notice and suddenly discover her love and that he reciprocated it. She was neither that stupid nor that naive.

Chapter Eleven

I am monarch of all I survey,
My right there is none to dispute.
  —William Cowper, *Verses Supposed to Be
      Written by Alexander Selkirk*, 1782

Peter hadn't been entirely unaware of the conversations between Lily and Rose that took place
at their frequent dinners. He hadn't looked at a
flower vocabulary in ten years, since that long-ago
time when Lily had used her artistry to help the
Patriot cause, and he couldn't have told the difference in meaning between one color of carnation
and another. But he did know that the flowerbeds
were meaningful to Rose, and that he'd been rather

harsh about the subject the one time they had discussed them.

He wasn't totally insensitive. He knew that the beauty of the site, the arrangement of the plants, her romantic desire to have a gazebo—all these were important to her feminine soul.

And perhaps, when there was time, he could do something about it.

In the spring. If she was still here. If.

But that wasn't why he was here this clear, chill January morning, standing on land tucked away in the farthest corner of the plantation. Accompanying him was Will Evans, Adam's longtime employee and factor of Oak Grove plantation. It was early because he wasn't interested in attracting Rose's attention. This project wasn't so much secret, as that he regarded it as a gift to her, and he didn't wish to be thanked. He just wanted it done.

Simple, straight, to the point. Just like a man would do. Adam would approve, he was sure.

But who could tell with women? Therefore, he'd decided that it was in his interest to avoid any feminine input altogether.

Peter would have denied to the ends of the earth that what he was doing was romantic—and there was nothing romantic about it, that was true. But he did have Rose's well-being at heart, and next spring, when she discovered what he'd done, he hoped she would understand that all he'd wanted to do was help her.

Although there were other plantations between Oak Grove and Willow Oaks, Rose's plantation was deeper than the two adjoining it and the land curved back far enough that it actually abutted a bit of Oak Grove at its farthest, deepest point. It was here, hundreds of acres back from the water, that he had asked Will Evans to meet him.

There were many reasons to plant a variety of crops—to work the land in rotation, to be self-sufficient, to have a cash crop—and he was here for the last reason. Although she had not chosen tobacco as a crop, and would have florists' flowers for Lily in the spring, it would take a year or two for those bulbs to divide and yield enough new bulbs to send to their clients abroad.

The ornamental trees would take even longer— four to five years before they would bear fruit. Peter had every confidence that Rose would not be here when that day came—that if she was even still here in the spring, it would only be because winter weather had kept her from taking ship. Yet he would put in tobacco anyway, to give her the cash crop she so desperately needed.

"Will, just have this area planted all across here," Peter said, gesturing to make his intentions clear. "Burn the trees in between to clear the rest of the land." It would look as if they hadn't known where the property of one plantation ended and the other began, if Rose ever discovered this. Not that there was any reason for her to inspect every inch of the plantation. Few owners did; as a woman she was even less likely to do so.

He should know better than that, he chided himself. There was no predicting what Rose would do. He'd never met a woman he'd understood less. Nor had he any need to. He finished giving instructions to Will, and then let him and the field hands get started.

"I would prefer that you not discuss this with

Lady Lansdale, even if she questions you." Will looked uncomfortable and opened his mouth as if to speak.

"Don't worry, Will," Peter said, clapping the younger man on the shoulder. "I am not asking you to lie. Just send Mistress Rose to me should she happen upon the planting before 'tis completed."

As he walked back to his horse, Peter told himself that since this would all belong to him in the end, he was actually acting for selfish motives. That was what he told himself anyway, grimacing a bit because he knew he lied.

He rode back toward Oak Grove along the river path, admiring the view along the James as the sun came up. His restlessness of the past two years had faded, to his surprise. Perhaps now that he'd gotten the dock in, and was able to concentrate on the shipbuilding, he had a sense of coming close to completion on his goals.

But he had less desire to captain them himself, as he'd originally thought he'd do. He had never quite worked out how he was to captain the ships and sell Tidewater Nurseries products when he'd vowed never to set foot on English soil, but he'd postponed that to the time when it would actually occur.

He was beginning to feel more proprietary about the land and the business, that was all. He wanted to supervise Willow Oaks, which he expected to buy. He wanted to see Rose's face when the flowers bloomed and the greenhouse was put up. No, Peter told himself. Lady Rose, Countess of Lansdale, was not a part of his long-term plans. Or a part of his plans at all. No, and no, and no.

* * *

Bertram Fairchild, 11th Earl of Lansdale—until recently he had only been Viscount Muncaster—stepped into the vestibule of the family's London town home one morning in late January. He turned to let Davison take his greatcoat. As if the passage from India hadn't been bad enough, there was the English climate. He wasn't accustomed to it anymore, not after India, with its beastly hot, dry climate that burned a man half the year, then made its inhabitants moldy with the hideously soggy monsoon season the rest. Not that he wasn't glad to have a reason to come home—no longer the second son, he exulted briefly—but he'd forgotten how the cold seeped into one's bones, and bloody quickly too.

"The chit has fled, Bertram," his mother, Fanny, said in her most dramatic tones.

Hello and welcome back to you, too, Mother, he thought.

"Chit, what chit? One of the servants?" His mother, as usual, couldn't be bothered to remember their names. Then he looked closely at her hand draped on her forehead, her smelling salts, and realized this was far more serious. Whatever she was upset about, she actually meant it.

What other chit could matter to his mother? His sister, Rose? Surely not. But why else would she be so upset? "Do you mean Rose has decamped? Gone where?"

Bertram knew he must have missed several developments in his family's life in the six months it had taken for the news to reach him in India and for him to return here, but this coil was beyond any trouble he could have predicted or expected. If he recalled his mother's letters, Rose was to have been married by now.

Rose could be feisty, but she'd never been flagrantly disobedient. Then again, she had loved their father fiercely but had always clashed with their mother. His dear mother had never concealed the fact that she preferred her sons and that she found Rose's height and coloring to be nothing but a difficulty for a girl whose principal worth lay in her eventual performance on the marriage mart.

Bertram, who knew something of what it was to be judged in life based on one's position in it—he'd been nothing but a no-account Viscount until recently—was inclined to be sympathetic to Rose's feelings. But outright disobedience, let alone a scandalous disappearance, was quite another matter entirely.

"Rose should have been married, or nearly so by now, should she not?" he asked, crossing to stand before the fireplace. And his mother should have been well set up with a rich son-in-law, even if the man wasn't much different in age from her own.

At Rose's name, his mother reached for the smelling salts. "Spare me the vapors, Mother, there's no one here to appreciate them. I'd just as soon hear the whole story quickly, then we can decide what to do." And you can take to your bed with the staff hovering over you later, he thought, but didn't say so.

"She's gone to America, Bertram," Fanny Fairchild began in her most dramatic tones. "To America, that hideous backwater."

"America? No, no vapors, Mother. Oh, blast," he swore, tugging at the bellpull.

When Davison returned, he ordered sherry for his mother and port for himself. He remembered that Rose had always loved Willow Oaks.

"Does Chilters know? How long has it been?" He hoped Rose's elderly suitor, the Marquess of Chilters, didn't know. A runaway female was bound to lose her reputation, no matter what she might have done or not done, and his mother's letters had given him to understand in no uncertain terms that they desperately needed this marriage. Women only had one shot at a reputation, and once it was gone, it was gone forever.

"She left shortly after Ralph . . . dear Ralph . . ." This time Fanny did dissolve in a flood of tears. Well, Bertram reflected, Ralph had always been her favorite.

"She's been gone since July? Bloody hell. Does anyone know?"

"No, since the Season was over and it coincided with Ralph's death," Fanny choked out. She bravely sniffled a few times, forcing Bertram to go over and hold her hand. "I retired to the country, and of course we were in mourning, so we attracted no great attention. The Marquess has such a horror of the country, he never bothered to come see her, although he did inquire after us. I wasn't worried about Chilters discovering that she wasn't here, what with the usual requirements of mourning."

"When is the wedding scheduled for now, Mother?" If he could get to America and back, perhaps there was time to save his family and its fortunes after all.

" 'Tis scheduled for May, before the Derby."

Bertram breathed a sigh of relief. He had time to get Rose back, and as long as she wasn't with child, everything might still fall into place. In exchange for marrying Rose and getting the use of her nubile young body—she was his last chance for an heir—the Marquess was prepared to be very generous with his family. Ralph had written him all the details. In fact, Bertram himself was going to be able to buy out his colors and return. Chilters had agreed to quietly endow him as Viscount Muncaster with a bit of property. Now Bertram himself was Earl, and sadly, after Ralph, more in need of that largess than ever.

But Chilters was such a slimy sort. Bertram hadn't needed to buy out his colors, not with his inheritance taking precedence, so he no longer needed Chilters for that. But the Fairchilds needed Chilters's blunt—or that of someone who had equally deep pockets.

"Have you heard from her since she left? Why did you come back to town, in that case?" he asked. "Wouldn't it have been better to wait quietly for my return?"

"Bertram, really. I was positively languishing there. I came up to town for Christmas, because it is so dreary to rusticate in the country this time of year, and because I expected you would be arriving shortly. I wanted to see you immediately, of course. You'll need to take ship very soon."

She might be prostrate with grief still, Bertram reflected, but her mind was working just fine.

"So I'm to fetch her like an errant child? Really, Mother." He took a long swallow of port.

"You are not of such consequence to give yourself airs yet, my boy." Fanny sat up and fixed her only remaining son with a steely glare. She pulled a drawer open in a side table and removed a few letters. "Read these, Bertram. The child thinks she is running a plantation in America. This wasn't a momentary, addle-pated idea. The ungrateful child," she muttered bitterly. "Oh no, Rose had a *plan,*" she said, sarcasm oozing through the last word.

Bertram held out his hand. Fanny rose, slapped the letters into his hand as if she couldn't wait to get rid of them, then reseated herself on the divan. "Your sister is managing Willow Oaks—can you imagine?" she said acidly. "She will make it a thriving success and keep us all happy with its income."

"What does she get out of it?" Bertram couldn't help asking.

"Any number of things, apparently. She shan't have to live in chilly, hated England any longer, marry an old man she doesn't love, or do anything else a well-mannered child should do to help her family." The Countess waved her hands dramatically in the air before falling back against the cushions.

Rose's scheme was utterly chuckle-headed, but Bertram had to give her points for daring. Still, it was hard to conceive a woman undertaking such a bold plan on her own, even his sister.

"She didn't run off with anyone, did she? And this plantation idea isn't some lackwit's plot to get hold of our family's patrimony and wrest it from us?"

"No, dearest. She wants to live on her own, is happy to remain forever loveless and unmarried. She *wishes* this." Bertram, who knew Chilters from his club, winced. He did feel sympathy for Rose.

If their mother perhaps had found someone a bit younger and with a less sour outlook on the world, Rose might not have chosen spinsterhood with such abandon.

He leafed through the letters. Rose had not even had the good sense to replant the tobacco that had been their main crop before. The mention of a name caught his eye.

"Eunice—that was her lady's maid? Traveling with her might have helped protect Rose's reputation, thank God. Not that anyone is to know where she went or what she did, if we can help it." But if it ever did get out, the presence of a chaperone could only help.

He rose and went to his mother, then bent to buss her cheek. "Don't worry, Mother, I shall retrieve our errant Rose. 'Twill all be made right, I promise you. I shall make it so."

Though he would never say it and risk a fresh bout of his mother's hysterics, he reflected that it was a good thing Rose's flight had occurred not long after Ralph's death. With the long mourning period expected of them, she could easily have been missing from society for as long as she had.

No one need know that he had arrived home, either. There was black at the town house door; they were still in mourning. So there would be no appearance and disappearance of the new Earl to explain away. He would sail to America, fetch Rose, and explain to her where her duty lay.

If she could not be made to see reason, well, she would just have to return with him anyway. One had no choice about one's place in life. Just look at him. He'd been resigned to being a second son, to the military, and to life as an inconsequential

Viscount. Now he was an Earl and he had to act accordingly. It was now his *duty* to secure all their futures, and that included his wayward sister Rose.

Thrice-damned bloody hell, Bertram thought as he left the room. He wouldn't even have time for his things to be unpacked. He had a thousand details that must be attended to, and first among all of them, was to book passage—quietly—on a ship to America. More travel, another ship, another savage land. Not to mention the bloody cold weather he'd have to endure. This wasn't exactly what he'd imagined his first duties would be as Earl. Bertram sighed, put down his goblet, and rang for Davison.

Rose was enchanted by the early signs of spring. She had forgotten how mild the Tidewater's climate was compared to the chill, damp winter at home in England, and that spring came so much earlier here. First the delicate white snowdrops bloomed, then yellow, white, and purple crocuses poked up through the softening ground. And like the crocus's meaning of youthful gladness, Rose was enchanted at seeing botanical drawings and descriptions come to life all around her.

As Lily grew larger, small problems developed, and Rose began visiting Oak Grove and staying over to help her out. Adam had quietly thanked her, although Lily kept insisting she was fine. Occasional bleeding, swollen ankles, fatigue—Lily kept saying they were nothing. But she would yield to Rose and put her feet up, and nothing pleased Rose more than watching over the children or learning from Lily about various uses for herbs and fruits, and other domestic secrets that Rose would never have learned otherwise in her ridiculously upper-class, snobbish household. Lily and Peter had had a loving mother until Amanda Walters had died when Lily was nineteen, and Lily had learned much from her mother.

Whereas Adam tended to order Lily to bed for her own good, which put her back up, Rose was careful to ask for information, launch into a spirited discussion, and then profess herself to be the tired one. Or Rose would say she needed to sit down to copy out Lily's recipes for dishes, or for her various lotions and salves.

Once Rose managed to get Lily off her feet, and Adam or Peter took the children to the stables or off to another part of the house, Lily would often nod off by the warm fire. Then the entire household would conspire to keep the environment around her quiet in order not to wake her up.

As if it weren't hard enough to be around a woman blossoming with happiness and growing large with her fourth child, the sheer beauty of the land and its scent rich with promise seemed to conspire against her and Peter. Bouquets of flowering branches were scattered everywhere indoors. Walking out of doors was to find oneself surrounded by symbols of temptation—the apple tree, which had been Eve's downfall—pears, which were a symbol of affection, while peach blossoms proclaimed "I am your captive." The gazebo at Oak Grove, surrounded as it was by azaleas, which meant first love, and dogwood, the symbol of durability—what could be more reassuring to someone in the throes of first love, than the protective dogwood hovering lightly over the azalea, as if to reassure it that love would last—was no escape.

Peter had taken to escaping out of doors whenever possible. But when even the evenings were scented with breezes off the river blowing through the area, there was no place to go to escape. Rose would go home and remain restless in her bed. Or she would paint feverishly, now that she had the real items in front of her.

What Peter did with himself, she didn't know. Just that it was increasingly clear that he was as uncomfortable as she. And while that thought occasionally cheered her, as when his burning glance met hers and she knew enough now to read what that look meant, more often it saddened her, because she could also read the determination in his eyes that he would not be her first love—or lover—intent as he was on protecting her for some mythical future husband.

In the end, the sweet spring air and its abundant blossoms undid the fiercest determination and the strongest will.

Chapter Twelve

If this be not love, it is madness,
And then it is pardonable.

—William Congreve
The Old Bachelor, 1693

Peter hadn't been drunk in a long time and he wasn't sure he was now. But his restlessness had grown with spring's advance, and he had taken to spending the evenings with a flask in his pocket, sometimes riding or walking by the river, more often going anywhere but where the happy people were—his family. He still had no greenhouse, no chance to build his ships, and the spring blooms were nearly upon them. But that was not at the heart of his problem.

He swung a hand at a low-hanging branch. Ha. Heart. *That* was the trouble. He'd begun to realize he still had one—and that was the real problem.

Rose had spent a great deal of the winter closeted at Oak Grove and Peter could hardly stand to be in the same room with her anymore. Since that night in November, he had tried to make the frost that had descended on the land similarly engulf his heart, but damn it, that had proven impossible. Cozy fires, the radiant and pregnant Lily, the children gamboling everywhere—a man would have to be a saint or a misogynist not to be affected by so much fertility and happiness.

Peter also had deep respect for Adam, a respect almost as deep as the love he felt for his sister, and he had to admit, Adam evinced a bone-deep contentment that had grown over his years with Lily. The loner, leader, and commander of the revolutionary years had mellowed into a man whose authority was still unquestioned but whose life was built on a deep, abiding love. Love that Adam gave and received in full measure.

He had spent some time at Willow Oaks as well. Rose had entertained the Pearsons and Peter, but she didn't have the establishment yet to be the kind of hostess Lily was. And when he was at Rose's, Peter took even more care not be alone with her. The memory of that dusk at the riverbank seemed to have seeped into his bones worse than the winter cold. Every time he saw her, he remembered it. The yielding of her lips against his, the heat of her mouth when she allowed him entrance, the ivory and dusky rose of her breasts and nipples, her fair skin and the creamy complexion that so few redheads possessed. He heaved a gusty sigh and tucked his flask back into his waistcoat pocket, aware that his breeches were also uncomfortably tight.

Now he'd added a third sin. In addition to being drunk and loitering, he was randy. He should have gone into town, but after the blissful taste of Rose he'd had last fall, he'd been unable to think of anyone else, touch anyone else. He simply didn't want anyone else.

Peter stopped for a moment at the plants around the open area Rose had planted, hoping some-one—him, of course—would build her a gazebo. Who had time for women and their ridiculous romantic notions?

Suddenly the thought assailed him that if Rose returned to England, there'd be no one to look after this plot, to tend it lovingly as Rose had. He'd be busy with the dock and greenhouse, supervising the tobacco crop, putting plants in the greenhouse to go on the ships. No, he'd have no time for flowers.

And yet, hadn't Adam wooed Lily through the language of flowers?

Peter jammed his hands into his waistcoat pockets with frustration. He didn't want to woo her. No, what he wanted was to feel her under him as he sought her warm heat, the feminine depths that would welcome him, know him. To teach her pleasure . . . ah, God, what joy there would be in that.

Peter adjusted the fit of his breeches again. Hell, in this mood, he was a danger to himself and to Rose. For her sake, if not his own, he'd better get home. He turned away, stopped, turned back.

Hell and the devil. He was tired of skulking

around in the background, wanting something he couldn't have. Rose was a grown woman and, to judge from her response to him, wanted him every bit as much as he wanted her. She'd made her unconventional life and goals known to everyone, and if she hadn't exactly asked him into her bed, he didn't think she was going to chase him out of it either.

He saw light flickering from her office, the room that at Oak Grove was the music room. Rose also favored the dining room for her painting because of its light, but of course she didn't paint at night.

Peter tested the door, not surprised to find it locked. In his parents' day there would have been concern about Indian raids, but then, locked doors wouldn't keep Indians out. Only someone who observed the conventions of polite society would find a locked door a deterrent.

In spite of himself, his mood lightened. He stepped back and knocked. Rose opened the door herself after a brief wait, clad in a wrapper that covered her chemise. The wall sconces near the door were lit.

"Peter," she said with a small frown, seemingly unconcerned about her dishabille. "What is it? Is Lily all right?"

Oh. He hadn't even thought about that, but her concern was quite logical.

"No, she's well. I didn't mean to worry you." He leaned one arm against the door frame, which brought him nearly nose to nose with her. "May I come in?" he said softly.

The question "why" sprang to the tip of her tongue—he saw it struggling to leave her lips—but she swallowed it. He looked at her, a long, burning look, and watched while the expression on her face slowly changed. Peter's desire turned to flame and he hardened in a rush. She knew he had no business being here. Perhaps with some kind of feminine intuition, she guessed, or her body simply understood the call of hers to his.

Suddenly she clutched the sides of her wrapper, pulling it together. The gesture drew his attention to exactly what she sought to cover. Her nipples had peaked. When he looked up, her eyes, dark and glittering in the candlelight, mirrored what he felt.

"Let me in, Rose," he said simply. "I want you."

Still keeping hold of her wrapper, she stepped back. Peter stepped into the hallway and, as he did so, took her into his arms.

"I want you," he said again, in a voice that surprised him with his huskiness. "You know that, don't you?" The answering spark he'd seen in her eyes gave him the confidence to close the distance between them, fitting her lips to his in one fluid, urgent gesture.

The rightness of the action, of the feeling that swept through him as he tasted her, almost weakened his knees. He bent her back across his arm, forcing her to cling to his shoulders to stay upright. As he did so, he teased open her mouth, then took it with the restrained violence that had been building in him since that evening at the riverbank.

Soft sounds came from deep in her throat as she yielded to him. He pursued his advantage, lifting his hands to thread through her hair. Her tresses were still pinned up, a restriction he couldn't tolerate. He wanted her hair wild about her shoulders, between his hands. By swiftly spearing his fingers through her hair, he dislodged the pins, then her hair tumbled down her shoulders and back in a glorious russet spill. The candlelight caught golden and copper glints, and as he deepened the kiss, he massaged her scalp, reveling in the sensuous feel of her hair against his palms.

He lifted his mouth from hers, moving to graze her neck where a sudden pulse leaped. Her head was tilted back, her neck arching in the same graceful arc as her back.

"Divan," he gasped.

"Yes," she answered.

"Where?"

"What?" She sounded puzzled.

"What?" He was confused.

"Where's what?"

"A sofa."

Rose pulled back slightly. He looked at her. "I thought you said 'divine,'" she said. "I agreed."

He smiled, resting his head against her forehead briefly. But the insistent desire that pulled at him was whetted, not eased, by the light moment. She was so honest, so unlike . . . No, he would not let his thoughts go there. Not tonight.

"Well, my lady," he said, lifting the hair at her nape and placing a kiss there. "Where then?"

Rose felt her heart hammer against her chest, so loud that she was convinced Peter would hear it. Silently she led him up the stairs to her room, hoping he wouldn't condemn her boldness. She would have loved to be swept up in Peter's arms and carried but knew she was too tall, and therefore weighed too much, for a gesture so foolishly romantic.

Doubt surged in her all at once, just with that small thought. She turned, as if to go back downstairs, and Peter took her in his arms to keep her from running into him. He leaned in to kiss her. She moved her head back a tiny fraction. Her retreat was imperceptible, she thought, but apparently not to him.

"What is it, Rose?"

"This is madness. You can't want me."

"What on earth do you mean?" Peter smoothed her hair against her back, following the curve of her spine, but the chill that had lodged there was not so easily dismissed.

"I'm too tall, I'm red-haired. I'm too old . . . I— I—" She hadn't stuttered since she was a child beneath her mama's critical scrutiny.

"Rose, sweet, stop." He lifted a finger to her lips, stroking them gently when she closed her mouth. Another old, bad habit had her biting her lip, but again Peter's gentle finger smoothed the impulse away.

He gathered her to him as she began to tremble slightly. "I've been attracted to you since the moment I first saw you," he whispered against her hair. "You are the liveliest, most intelligent, and yes, most beautiful woman that I have ever had the good fortune to meet."

Rose's hands twisted briefly in his hair, then dropped to his shoulders. She continued as if she hadn't heard him. "I've had three Seasons. None of the m-m-men really interested me, and I wanted nothing to do with those who were. Papa encouraged me to choose whom I liked, although Mama was quite out of t-t-temper at that. Then Papa died, and after mourning, I had to go back onto the m-m-marriage mart.

"By that time, my older brother Ralph had dined and gamed his way through London, so our debts were mounting, and I had gained a reputation as too outspoken and too choosy. Only old men or social climbers desperate to marry a peer's daughter wanted me. After Ralph d-d-died and his debts landed at our door, Mama felt she had to act quickly, because Bertram was too far away in India to come home anytime soon."

Rose was barely aware of Peter's soothing hands on her back. "So Mama chose a horrible old man, the Marquess of Chilters. He tried to g-g-grope me at the party Mama gave to make our betrothal announcement . . ."

"Hush, that's enough, Rose. You don't need to tell me this. None of it matters to me."

But she couldn't stop now, compulsively clutching the fabric at his shoulders. "He said it didn't matter what c-c-color the hair was there, because we were all—we are all alike in the d-d-dark." Filled with shame, she lowered her head.

Peter understood. She could tell from the tension that tautened every muscle in his powerful body, although his hands never stopped stroking her. Rage for the man who had been so coarse to her filled him until he shook with it, but apart from a few savage curses under his breath, he never stopped his gentle reassurance.

He lifted her head so she would look him in the eyes. "A fool and his foolish words are easily parted," he said, "and those words mean nothing. They are less than nothing," he said, holding her chin with one hand to emphasize his words. "Nothing he said was true, Rose. You are a beauty and a wonder, a gift without price. I want you until I lie awake at night, wondering how you have invaded my being, my very soul. And it is only you I want, not someone else, not a woman, any woman. Just you."

He took a step backward, keeping hold only of her hands. "I would be honored and humbled if you wanted me too, Rose, although I will not, cannot, make you any promises." His eyes were a clear green, honest and direct in the lamplight that shone from her bedroom.

Rose was excited and sad all at once. He wasn't making her a vow of love, she understood that. She straightened her shoulders and, pulling her hands free, stepped toward Peter and clasped them about his waist.

Wasn't what he was offering exactly what she wanted herself? If she went to her death a spinster, at least she would have had the knowledge of what could take place between a man and woman, untainted by lust for her title or the desperate attempt of an old man to prove his virility. With Peter she would at least have honesty and truth. Given the world she had come from, how much more could she ask of a man?

"I do . . . want you, Peter. And I understand that there are no terms and no conditions. What you offer is good enough for me."

Peter's arms encircled her, blocking out the hurtful memories, and his breath on her cheek was pleasantly warm. Now all the surging excitement had come back. Just before he closed the distance between them with a kiss, she felt his erection brush her thin chemise and wrapper, and her insides melted to a hot, deep liquid flame that burned only at his touch.

He lifted his mouth a fraction from hers, just enough to whisper, "No questions, Rose? No regrets?"

His confidence in her, his confessed longing for her, had restored her spirits. She pulled back until her gaze met his. "Oh, I have many questions, Peter Walters, but no, no regrets."

With those words, she had the courage to take his hand again and lead him the rest of the way to her bedroom, forgetting that he had seen her sick and miserable-looking here before. All that counted now was this moment, this candlelit moment suspended in time where they were only a man and a woman testing the gossamer-and-steel link that bound them.

Once Rose had opened the door to her room, closed to keep the heat from the fire Eunice had built inside, Peter took her hand from the doorknob and turned her. She thought he would kiss her again, but instead, he lifted her—lifted *her*, Rose Fairchild—easily and carried her to the bed. He kissed her as he walked, and kept kissing her as he laid her on the bed, following her down. There was nothing but Peter, Peter around her, Peter above her, Peter next to her heart.

He eased her wrapper open and began to kiss her neck and the soft skin below her throat. She arched her head back, and her hands went to his hair. She threaded her fingers through it, loving its thick feel and richness beneath her hands.

But even richer were the sensations of him touching and cupping, stroking and caressing. He was more at ease, more leisurely than when he had first caressed her on the riverbank, but she knew that the fire was only banked. He murmured unintelligible things against her skin, slowly pushing back her chemise, exploring more skin, and giving her more kisses with every inch uncovered.

Rose slid her hands down from his hair, smoothing her hands along the strong muscles of his neck and shoulders. He had shrugged off his coat at some point, and as she reached the limits of his shirt opening, she reached down to tug his shirt up from his waist.

He obliged, sitting up and pulling off his shirt in one smooth motion. He reached for her, pulling the laces of her chemise apart and peeling it down her arms along with her wrapper. He lifted her up to pull the fabric from beneath her hips, and then she was unclothed and Peter's warm strength covered her from head to toe, his murmurs more and more ardent as he stroked from her legs to her shoulders.

Rose felt as if she were simultaneously floating somewhere above her body and yet more fully alive inside it than she had ever been. Peter's mouth had moved from her lips to her breasts, where his hands shaped and molded them until the nipples peaked and were astonishingly sensitive, and the deepening ache between her legs became almost too much to bear.

"Peter, touch me, please," she whispered to the top of his head as the thick bright hair she had longed to caress again brushed across her breasts. She held his head and he looked up at her, his eyes gleaming in the candlelight from her bedside table.

"Where, fair Rose? There is no inch of your skin that I would not kiss." For answer, she took one of his hands and moved it down her body. With her other, she reached for his breeches, amazed at her own daring.

"Let me help you," he said, moving onto his knees. He swiftly divested himself of his remaining clothes. This time, when he stretched his length along her again, she knew the amazing feel of the different textures of his body and his warm strength.

He settled himself between her legs and instead of the fear she'd thought she would feel, there was only a rising sense of anticipation and building need. His manhood stirred, hard and hot against her, and it was the most natural action in the world to part her legs.

"That's it, sweet." He encouraged her in a low voice made urgent by his passion. "Open for me, there, like that. Feel me against you here." He took her hand and moved it to him. She closed her hand around him, wondering at the softness of the warm, supple skin that encased his hard arousal.

"This will . . . ah, fit?" she asked, a bit dubious. He was not only hard but also big.

Peter nudged against her center and she felt a melting that allowed him to push a little way inside her. He withdrew and she felt open and aching. She gave a tiny, involuntary moan. "I will fit, sweetheart, 'twill be like a hand and glove." He reached down to fit himself more closely to her, parting her and stroking his fingertip along that most sensitive place that she had never even known she had until he'd touched her there the last time they had been together like this.

Rose gasped and he slid a little deeper. "This may hurt, sweet love," he said, "but stay with me." He thrust and she moaned.

She pushed her hands against his chest. "Stop, Peter, that hurt."

Peter rested his temple against her forehead. "I know, I know. Don't move," he whispered. "I will remain still and you will feel better in a moment, I promise."

But she wriggled with the pain, wanting to get out from under him. He sucked in a breath. "Don't, Rose, this won't help."

"I can't help it. You're hurting me."

"Rose, I am so aroused that I can't stay still if you don't also. Every movement of yours is sweet agony to me." His hips had surged as he spoke and he pushed farther into her. "Just . . . try to stay . . . still. Please." He sounded as if he spoke with clenched teeth. Was she hurting him somehow?

She tossed her head restlessly, her body shifting. With a groan, Peter lowered his head and took her lips again. But this time the kiss was not so tender; it was a kiss of passionate plunder. He seduced her mouth, seducing her into forgetting the little sting of pain she felt at the introduction of his manhood deeper into her. Responding with abandon, Rose became wholly involved with the sensation of his tongue in her mouth, with the pull of his clever, roughened fingertips at her nipples, finding that the pain retreated, just as he'd said.

Her moans turned to murmurs, her pain to purring. Her body's tension eased and her limbs melted to honey under his caresses. Peter must have felt her yielding, because his thighs pushed hers a little wider and he deepened his presence inside her. Suddenly Rose found she wanted him there, and she trailed her hands from his shoulders down his back to urge him more fully against her.

By the time Peter broke her maidenhead, the pain had disappeared. The floating feeling had returned, and she felt she could both see Peter above her and feel him within her. The soaring feeling rose with each thrust; her legs rose to clasp him closer.

The world had narrowed so that it now consisted only of the two of them, striving toward one goal with one accord. She felt the moment when pleasure seized her and held her fast. As she had that other time, she convulsed around him.

The rapture seized Peter just as fiercely, so that he cried out her name, then summoned his last vestige of will to pull away from her. The wave of pleasure was too far gone to turn back, so it broke over them both, surging, pulsing, then receding slowly until only the two of them were left on the far shore, their lives, themselves, never again to be quite the same.

Chapter Thirteen

Remorse, the fatal egg by pleasure laid.
——William Cowper
The Progress of Error, 1782

Peter woke before Rose, not surprised to find himself hard again. After he had gently cleansed her and then himself, she was nearly asleep. She had turned on one side, and as naturally as breathing, he had fit himself against her in the night, his arms cradling her back against his chest. But now his hardness pressed against her, insistently demanding his attention and definitely seeking hers.

Smoothing his hand down her back where her tumbled hair flowed, he marveled at its texture, its vitality so much a part of her personality that it flowed through her, even here, even now, in her sleep. Slowly, he spread the strands around her, her neck, her back, and her satiny arms. Gradually, his arms moved around her, until he found himself gently arraying the strands in curves that modeled the rounded curves of her breasts.

Stroking up from the undersides, he cupped the weights in his hands, his thumbs sliding across the silky texture of her nipples, feeling them pebble under his touch. He'd love to see her in the light, his Diana with the russet hair. Her body was long and lithe and, he couldn't help the thought . . . made for his touch.

Rose stirred, her voice a sleepy murmur, "Peter?"

He nuzzled her neck. "Aye, love?"

"Do you want to love me again?"

"You're a brazen one, aren't you?" he chuckled against her warm skin, opening his mouth a bit more widely to dapple her shoulder with kisses.

"And you're not?" she replied, wriggling her hips against him.

"You learn quickly."

"I have a good teacher," she said, and then laughed when he rolled her onto her back and rose above her. She didn't laugh long.

"You didn't need any teaching," he said, his mouth descending on hers. This time it was all heat and light and fast, sharp pleasure. Neither of them spoke for a while because this time their bodies were so attuned that she met him when he moved. She didn't question him when he pulled out before climaxing again this time. Sleepily, he wondered how much she knew about pregnancy prevention, then fell heavily into sleep.

Sometime toward dawn, when the earliest birds began to chirp, and the sky beyond the shutters to lighten, Rose felt the loss of warmth at her back and turned to find herself alone in bed.

She drifted off to sleep again, not terribly concerned. The evening's glow still clung to her; her dream state seemed not that different from the middle-of-the-night interlude they'd shared. She was sore, but pleasantly so, and she looked forward to a full bath a bit later. Peter had ever so gently bathed all the sticky and secret places. She was aroused again by the time he'd lifted the damp warm cloth from her, and she found that he was too, but he had gently, laughingly pushed her away.

"You're sore now, or if you aren't, you will be," he had said, smoothing back the tumbled hair from her forehead. "It wouldn't be right or fair of me." Too sleepy to protest and insist—she knew he was probably right—he'd cradled her against his chest, his arm beneath her head, until she'd fallen asleep again.

When she finally stirred, the sun was fully up. Peter entered the room a few moments later, bearing a breakfast tray in his strong capable hands. Rose smiled sleepily and sat up, drawing the sheet up with her. She looked around for her chemise and wrapper, but they were hard to distinguish from the crumpled linen that seemed to be everywhere in the room.

Peter's shirt had somehow miraculously ended up over a chair back, and looked positively crisp. Peter saw her wry look at his clothing and hers, then handed her his shirt. She pulled it on quickly while he arranged the tray.

"Mmm, you cook, too?" she said teasingly. "I'll marry you."

"Fortunately for us both, you already have a good cook," Peter said. Rose knew Cook didn't get up this early, and never made her biscuits and ham in the morning, but she didn't quibble. Peter had done this, but if he wanted to pretend Cook had, she would let him.

But after her few short teasing words, she became aware that the easy, sometimes teasing intimacy of the night before had vanished.

It didn't matter whether she'd meant what she'd just said about marriage. Nor did it matter that she had said there were no expectations between them. How worried about giving away his own heart must he be to react as if her words had somehow seized him by the throat?

"Rose, marriage is not in the cards. Not for me, at any rate."

"I was jesting."

"You wanted honesty between us," he pointed out, the look he turned on her searing and intense.

"I am not interested in marriage either," she protested. "But suppose we were, both of us. Why not, Peter? Just what would be so wrong about a union between us?"

"You don't belong here," he said bluntly.

"What do I need to do to prove to you that what you say simply isn't true? And why should I bother proving it anyway? I was born here, Peter. I can be an American. I *am* an American."

"But you are not," he retorted. "You've spent the last ten years in England. What assurance do

I have that you wouldn't just leave and return there?"

"Why would you need such assurances?" She stared at him in complete confusion. "If we love each other, what assurances could possibly be needed?"

"That you wouldn't leave . . ." She thought he'd been about to say "me" but he stopped and let the sentence trail off.

"How would I know that you wouldn't leave here and go back to England?" he asked again.

"But Peter, I came here from England. I came back to Virginia, to Willow Oaks. I did that all on my own. I would have lived here even if I hadn't met you."

"You wouldn't have stayed." He picked at the crumbs of a biscuit on his plate, not meeting her eyes.

"What makes you so sure of that? You've said this from the start, and yet I can't remember a single time, a single day, when I ever thought, 'Oh, this is too hard, I want to go back to England.'"

"Yes, but what keeps you from going back?"

"I love Virginia. I love Willow Oaks. And I love you." Oh, her foolish tongue. She put a hand to her mouth, instantly mortified. "I wasn't supposed to say that, was I?"

"No, you shouldn't have. Still, I'm glad at least that you listed me third. No matter what you say, a woman's love may not . . . may not . . ." He hesitated.

She was starting to get seriously annoyed with Peter now. "Prove true? You think I would do all that I have done, and just give it all up . . . you,

Willow Oaks, our flowers . . . to go back to England?"

He frowned. She assumed it was at her use of the word "our." Rose pushed the tray aside, got up, and began to pick up her clothes, aware that Peter was trying not to look at her legs extending from beneath his shirt. He began to pick up his own.

She turned back to face him. "What is it, Peter? What is all this truly about? Did someone hurt you?"

He turned his face away from her, leaving only a broad male chest with its mat of curling golden hair that, despite the argument they were having, made her mouth go dry. She still had on his shirt, but he didn't seem to notice he had on nothing above his breeches.

She wasn't going to let clothes, or their lack, distract her. At last, she thought she had grasped the essential truth here, and she wasn't going to let it go.

"That's it, isn't it?" So Lily *had* been right. "It was the woman that you loved, the one in New York that you were engaged to. She hurt you, and then she left you? Was that it?"

"I don't wish to discuss this." The look he trained on her was turbulent, his eyes full of hidden depths, green and gray and stormy.

"I think you should. Don't we owe each other honesty?"

"I don't know that we owe each other anything," he said, folding his arms.

Rose almost reacted to his dismissal of their night together, of her virginity, and then realized two things at once. One, she had given him her innocence, freely, in full knowledge of what they were doing. She had not been deceived or fed lies or pretty promises he didn't intend to keep. He had promised her nothing.

Two, she must remember that she had asked nothing in return. He had asked her if she was sure, and she had said yes.

But then, she hadn't thought she wanted anything in return, at least not then. What she had done with Peter was meant to be her final emancipation. Having broken all of society's conventions, she was supposed to have been free. Free of conventions, free of expectations. She had the plantation now; it would yield its bounty sooner or later.

And so, to solidify her freedom, she had decided to take a lover. That had taken all her daring; she hadn't thought ahead to the morning after. Perhaps she should have. She seemed to be a creature of convention after all.

But could she have known she would lose her heart along with her innocence? And would it have made a difference? Wouldn't she have done this anyway? It didn't take much for Rose to lose her head when Peter was around. All her senses—her body's senses, at the very least—had yearned toward him.

Peter had turned back to regard her as the silence lengthened. "We owe each other nothing, 'tis true," she finally said. "But you are not an insensitive man, I have learned, despite your care to hide your better nature. The one who hurt you— she was English. Is that why you reacted so strongly to me when we first met? I thought 'twas just the war that had made you dislike the British."

" 'Twas just the war. I don't like the English."

That was too easy. "Your brother-in-law is English, is he not? And a lord?"

"That's different."

"Why?"

"I knew him before the war and before . . ."

There, he'd almost said it. Before *her*.

"You never have talked of this, have you? Not even to Lily?"

He shifted again to look out the window, presenting her his profile. At least it wasn't his back this time.

"Peter, there is some demon riding you. Don't you think 'twould be better to let some of it out? To exorcise its power?"

"Nay," he said.

"We have just shared the most intimate things possible between a man and woman, and you still can't tell me of this woman you used to love? Surely you do not love her still?"

"Love her still? Hardly," he said with an edge to his voice she had never heard. He turned and his storm-green eyes were almost gray, as bleak as she had ever seen them.

"All right, Rose, I shall tell you. But what I am about to relate to you is something that I have not told to a single living soul. Not to Lily, not to Adam. To no one."

For a moment, Rose wanted nothing more than to reassure him. Yet even knowing it would hurt him, it was better that he talk about this. So she restrained her impulse to take him in her arms, to offer comfort, even if physical intimacy was the only kind he would accept. He had decided to tell her, at last; and now, she must listen.

"I shall keep your confidence, Peter." She strove to keep her tone light, knowing that his statements of distrust ultimately had little to do with her, and more to do with his past. "You should know me well enough by now to know that I am no simpering fool."

"Of course you are not," he said instantly. "I would never think such a thing. Your reaction is all the more reason not to tell you. You see now how surly and ill-tempered this subject makes me."

"You shan't get out of this so easily, Peter." She smiled; he did not.

"Very well." Rose returned to the bed to sit. Peter had moved the breakfast tray to a side table, and sat again on the other side of the bed, where he had sat since first entering the room a lifetime ago. He'd carried breakfast in his hands and winter in his heart.

"As Lily has probably told you, I was an officer in the American Navy. My friend from Williamsburg, Ethan Holt, and I stayed in Philadelphia after the Continental Congress appointed General Washington commander in chief. Ethan had come from a seafaring family, and he persuaded me to stay. We enlisted on the spot."

"We served together, fought together. We were even wounded together, in a sea battle off the coast of what was then New York Colony. The ships had closed with each other; we were fighting hand-to-hand and man-to-man as they tried to board us. Ethan nearly lost an arm; he took a terrible injury. I had a gash in the leg from the falling mast, but thank God, I was in no danger of losing it.

"My leg was useless for a time, but it did not fester and did not need amputating. The woman I met, Joanna, was a volunteer nurse at the hospital, along with her mother, Anne. Joanna's father was a banker, and as many of the richer men did, he favored the Loyalist cause. But Anne was more in sympathy with the cause of independence, so she thought she had persuaded her husband to remain neutral.''

"And your nurse?" Rose prompted gently when he fell silent, and looked as if he did not want to continue speaking.

Peter rubbed at his neck, looking decidedly uncomfortable. "I ... ah ... Well, like many a patient, I suppose, I began to fall in love with my nurse."

"What was she like?" Rose asked quietly.

"Does that matter?"

"It does to me."

"She was lively, vivacious, quite the chatterbox. The men loved to have her around because she brought the presence of a world seemingly untouched by war into the hospital with her. She loved many of the things that are difficult to come by in war: fine clothes, evening entertainments, dancing, and the like. Though such things are of little interest to me, I found it understandable. She was young and frightened by war; I was young and trusted ... and loved, too easily, I suppose."

Eunice poked her head around the doorway just then, probably looking to see if Rose was up and wanted breakfast. She looked shocked, and her little mouth parted in a silent "O" of surprise, but Rose waved her away quickly with a small gesture, hoping Eunice would understand it and leave.

Peter had his back to the door, and Rose did not want anything to interrupt his telling of this story. Who knew if he would ever choose to speak of it again?

Eunice took the hint, fortunately, and vanished silently. Rose breathed a sigh of relief.

Peter had resumed speaking. "Then word came that the British were close to retaking the town where we were. Those of us who were mobile were discharged, the rest packed up and taken to a secret location not far away. I stayed, since I didn't want to leave Ethan, and did what I could, despite my leg, to help move the patients and the hospital supplies. Anne worked far into the night with many of the women, but Joanna did not come. I was too busy to wonder about it at the time. I supposed I might have thought Anne wanted her daughter away from any danger, because she was fearless for herself, but always concerned about Joanna's welfare, like a good mother.

"Things settled down once we had moved; the danger seemed to have been averted. The redcoats were still nearby, but we did not think they had discovered where we had been moved. I had received permission to keep our ship's company together, and try to get back to the ship as a group.

"Despite the uncertainty of where we would go next, and when, Joanna and I became affianced with her mother's warm approval. But by this time, something about Joanna had changed. I thought 'twas just that she didn't like the nursing. Certainly, she didn't have the same compassionate empathy as her mother. Anne would stay late at the hospital; often, she would not be home in time for dinner.

"I began to see more of Anne than her daughter.

Joanna, when she did come in, would talk about the interesting company at her father's table, and although she tried to avoid saying who they were, I worked out from her conversation that they were mostly Tories, rich bankers and merchants who did not want trade with England affected by war.

"Even Anne was worried about the change in Joanna. She knew her husband was contemplating leaving America for England. She didn't want to go, but knew she would have to as the duty she owed her husband." Rose winced at the word "duty," but Peter was so engrossed in his tale that he didn't notice.

"One night, Anne told me that if I truly loved Joanna, I should elope with her. Perhaps for love, her daughter would stay in America." Rose couldn't help her involuntary movement of surprise.

Peter noticed, and smiled briefly. "I know, I know, a mother suggesting elopement. 'Twas most unusual. A brave woman, Anne Lewisham."

"With her mother's blessing, I was emboldened to press my suit with Joanna. I talked to her about marrying now, said we could always have a bigger affair after the hostilities were over."

His hand went to his neck, but the habitual kerchief was not there. "Joanna was reluctant; there is no other word for it. She said she couldn't abandon her parents. But her mother suggested it, I argued. So eventually she went along. I supposed I should have sensed then that her heart wasn't in it. But Joanna was beautiful and could be so charming, and she hid her reservations well. Or had she already planned this? I never knew."

Rose broke in. "So she turned down your suit." The tightness in Peter's voice and the bleak ending to this recital made her want to spare him any more of this too-painful confession.

Peter looked at her, and for the first time, she saw a deep-seated anger and bitterness she had never suspected. His laughter was short and ugly. "Jilted me? That wasn't the half of it. She did much more than that. Let me finish, Rose. This isn't easy and I do not mean to tell this tale ever again."

She nodded, chastened.

"I pressed her, knowing all the while that her mother thought this was the best future for her, away from the marriage mart in England where her family's wealth would be the determinant of her worth and ultimately her destiny. Finally, she accepted."

Rose certainly sympathized with Anne Lewisham's aversion to the marriage market. Would that her own mother had thought the same way.

"So we agreed to meet late one night outside the hospital. We were to go to a local minister— I had already talked to him and had the banns waived—and we were to be married that night. But when we met near the hospital, along with Joanna, out of the shadows stepped redcoats waiting for me."

"They thought she was a rebel?" Rose gasped. "What happened?"

Peter's gaze was so hot with anger that she thought the room would catch on fire. Yet she knew that he looked past her, that he barely saw her, if at all. He was reliving that terrible scene. "She gave us up to the redcoats—me, Ethan, the hospital's location, and all the men in it."

Again, Rose gasped, completely shocked; she hadn't seen this coming. "Joanna had been seeing someone those evenings when her mother worked at the hospital; of course, her father had approved. There was a smirking young lieutenant with her, leading a company of soldiers. This was his opportunity to score a major coup and impress his commanding officer. We were all 'captured' and marched off to a prison camp. We were sent off in a field cart, which bumped and rocked, causing indescribable pain to the more seriously wounded. Our destination was more than two hours out of town."

"Oh," Rose breathed. This denouement was even worse than she had thought. All this time, she had been imagining just a "normal" jilting that had broken his heart, but not so much that it wouldn't mend. This was so much more terrible.

"None of us were spies, thank God. The British weren't going to hang us. But no prison camp is pleasant, and men died, men who would otherwise have lived, men who shouldn't have been moved from the hospital, not so roughly, at least. Men like . . . men like . . ."

He passed a hand in front of his eyes.

"No, oh, Peter," Rose said. "Your friend Ethan?"

He nodded. "Ethan's wound festered in camp. By the time a British field surgeon had been summoned, his arm had to be amputated, but 'twas already too late. The gangrene had set in. It worsened. Ethan . . ."

He didn't need to finish. Rose reached out a hand, but Peter didn't even see it.

His voice hardened. "Those of us who survived remained prisoners until the war was over, and the peace treaty signed."

"How long was that?"

"About two years." Dear God, no wonder he was bitter.

"What happened then?" Rose asked.

"I learned that the Lewishams had returned to England. I knew that Anne had to have been opposed, but also that she would not—or could not—go against her husband's wishes. And Joanna had not only helped set those wishes in her mother's absence. No, she had become something more. A traitor. Or at least from an American perspective."

With the subtle emphasis on the word "American," Rose knew that he had never forgiven nor forgotten his betrayal. At the hands of an English woman. Well, that certainly explained Peter's disdain.

"That's why you didn't like me from the start."

"I told you 'twas not your fault."

"No, but 'tis still unfair. I had nothing to do with any of this. But you blame me for my birth, as if I could help it."

"You wanted an explanation, Rose."

"I didn't say it had to make sense, now did I?" she smiled, hoping he didn't see how much his words had hurt her.

"What is there that doesn't make sense?" he said sharply.

"What doesn't make sense to me is how this has anything to do with us," she returned with asperity.

"In one sense it doesn't. In another, it hangs over everything I do. I can't trust a woman now."

"You can't trust a woman," Rose repeated slowly. "Any woman?" she asked, incredulous. "What about your sister?"

"Lily is an exception, of course. As you know, she is my sole family."

"Fine," Rose said stiffly. "But how could I betray you, assuming I would ever even want to, or would be in a position to be able to do so? The situation does not even begin to obtain any longer. I am not Joanna, and there is no war. How could I betray you, even if I wanted to, which you must know I do not. I never could. Never," she finished emphatically.

"Ah, Rose," he said, unfolding his arms at last. "There is more than one kind of betrayal." A last somber look from those green eyes and he was walking past her. Past her and out of her life, because they could not go backward after this.

Joanna had done more than betray him to the enemy and hurt his pride. She had done more than break his heart. She had shattered his trust. And if that most basic requirement for human interaction had not been restored, as she very much feared that it hadn't, how could she possibly be the person to do it?

In the end, Rose did not bother trying to go after Peter. Staring silently out the window beyond which the sparkling James River flowed, she didn't move until Eunice came to her to help her dress.

She had asked for an explanation, after all. And now she had it.

Chapter Fourteen

The gentle mind by gentle deed is known.
For a man by nothing is so well betrayed,
As by his manners.

—Edmund Spenser,
The Faerie Queene, 1590

Bertram alighted from the ship at Yorktown, looking around him with distaste. True, the London docks could be brutal and were inhabited by scum but behind them rose the magnificent cupola of St. Paul's and the spires of a dozen churches. That was London, in all its magnificence and with its spectacular history. Here there was naught but dust and dirt and crude dwellings.

Ah well, he didn't plan to be here long. Just long

enough to get Rose and get back on this ship. He'd
already made arrangements with the captain, who
planned to sail in the next few days.

Did a town . . . a dwelling place, for this was no
true town, even have hackneys? He had to get to
Williamsburg—surely there would be a coach—
then take a boat upriver.

Rose no longer knew what to think. She had
thought the night with Peter was the beginning of
a glorious new stage of her life. She was a woman
now and had a lover. She hadn't expected it to
lead to marriage. She didn't want to be married.

But Peter had just assumed . . . and Rose had
really been in no hurry to explain. That was her
fault, but despite her personal declaration of independence, she still wasn't so brazen as to enter
into a cold-blooded discussion of their affair.

That was the real trouble with passion, she
reflected. Easy enough at the moment—and here
she blushed—but later when it came time to think
and review and plan, well, those things just weren't
compatible with passion. Not that she was an
expert, by any means.

But off Peter had gone and she hadn't seen him
since. She knew he was working because the workers told her he was in the farthest fields but he
never came near her or the house. She had no
idea where he had spent the last two nights. Lily
had sent a messenger over to inquire after him,
and she'd had to say he wasn't here.

If Lily weren't so heavily with child, Rose knew
she would have come over herself. She knew she
ought to go over to Oak Grove herself, but how

could she hide from Lily what had passed between her and Peter . . . and its awful aftermath?

Eunice came bustling in with her morning tea. "I've had word about Master Peter, I have, miss," she said self-importantly.

"Good morning to you too, Eunice," Rose said, attempting to keep her face and voice neutral.

"Oh, miss, you needn't pretend with me." Rose raised an eyebrow but didn't comment. Eunice had certainly blossomed in America. She was as small and plain as ever, but she'd told Rose how much better servants were treated here and how mistress Lily treated hers almost as her friends. Rose also thought Eunice had her eye on the strapping new lad in the stables, judging from the number of trips Eunice made when Rose was in the vicinity, always bits of information or questions that could wait until Rose returned to the main house. But Rose begrudged her not a moment of her flirtation or any happiness that might come of it.

"Pretend with you about what, Eunice?" Rose sipped her tea and waited.

"That you're not that tore up about Master Peter."

"Tore up? Wherever do you learn these expressions?" Rose asked, wrinkling her nose at Eunice's colorful language.

"You can't distract me, mistress," her cheeky maid replied. "Don't you want to know what I heard?"

Rose sighed. She did, quite intensely, but some amounts of British reserve couldn't be overcome.

"All right," she said, aware that she probably sounded peevish.

"Master Peter's been sleeping in the fields with

a bottle of whiskey for company," Eunice said with the air of someone delivering news she knows is certain to both titillate and repel the listener.

But Rose was almost relieved. She hadn't been aware quite how much she feared that Peter had sailed off on a trip to the West Indies or gone to a harlot in town until Eunice spoke.

"Isn't that scandalous? You must have had quite the row for him to go haring off to douse himself in liquor," Eunice declared as Rose seated herself at her boudoir table. With the ease of long experience, Eunice picked up the silver brush and began to brush her hair. An involuntary shiver ran through Rose at the memory of Peter's hands in her hair, his fascination with its color, its texture, the way he'd wrapped it around her . . . Rose knew she was blushing and kept her eyes focused on her teacup.

"Anything that passed between Master Walters and myself is not your concern," she reminded Eunice.

"Course it's not, mistress," Eunice agreed cheerfully. "But Master Peter, though he be moody, I never seen him go off like this. Have you?"

Rose thought privately that neither of them had been here long enough to know what Peter did when troubled, but she'd never seen any inclination to drink. And her heart told her he wasn't that type of man. But then, after what had passed between them, she hardly knew her own heart anymore. She certainly didn't know his.

"Between you and his sister, he's probably afraid to go home," Eunice continued blithely. "But sleeping in the fields like a field hand, oh my."

"Oh no, what about Lily? Won't she be worried?"

How selfish of her, to think only of her own problems. Lily was probably worried sick.

"Don't worry, I sent that Malcolm over to Colonel Pearson right smart like, soon as I heard." So Eunice had had at least one genuine reason to visit the stables. Perhaps that new fellow Malcolm had been the source of her information. It didn't matter.

"You acted well," Rose said, meeting Eunice's gaze in the mirror.

"Should I go over to Oak Grove?" she asked Eunice.

"I don't think so, mistress. Colonel Pearson will know what to do. This is a man's business, drinking and whatnot."

A man's business. A man could turn to a bottle, Rose thought. What was a woman to do? Having chosen to be brazen and independent, she supposed she would go on acting independent. The trick was not to regret being brazen.

Hot color flooded her face and neck. Being brazen wasn't all she'd thought it was. She'd like nothing more than Peter's arms around her and reassurance in his lips against her mouth. Did he regret what they'd done? Would he ever come to her again?

She met Eunice's eyes in the glass as the little maid laid down her brush and pulled back Rose's hair to dress it. "They be trying, men, aren't they?" she said with sympathy. Rose nodded. If only Eunice knew.

Rose was tending her special garden, resolutely ignoring the empty circle at its center that reminded her of her own empty heart, when a man-sized shadow fell across her. She looked up, shading her eyes against the warming March sun, stifling the glad cry that came to her lips. Peter had come back.

"Rose, get off your knees," a cool, cultured voice said. Rose scrambled to her feet, her heart pounding, glad she hadn't cried out Peter's name. She recognized that voice.

"Bertram," she managed, tucking her hands behind her back so her brother wouldn't see how dirty gardening had made them. Damn it, already he'd made her feel childish and guilty. She wouldn't allow herself to be bullied. She was the mistress here.

He stepped forward, kissed her cheek briefly. Subtly planting her feet, she tossed her head back and met his gaze squarely. "Welcome to America, Bertram. Do you recognize our old home?"

"Of course I do. I was fifteen, remember?" She kept her gaze steady and inviting. Finally he looked around impatiently. "It's been well kept up, I see."

"No, I did all this, Bertram. The fields had gone to seed."

"You did all this alone?" He sounded skeptical.

Rose felt herself bristle. "I had help, of course, but 'twas I supervised getting this plantation back in working order."

"With my money," he replied, but without heat. "In any event, it matters little. This foolishness has come to an end."

"What do you mean?" she asked, although she knew very well.

"This is not your life, Rose. You may have enjoyed playing at it, and God knows, having the talent to run a household is necessary for any woman of your station, but you are not a tobacco planter. Nor are you a horticulturalist, or whatever 'tis you think you are doing grubbing about there in the dirt.''

Rose had never had the legendary temper of the redhead, but thought she might be about to develop it. How she longed to tell Bertram he was an ignorant boor. Sadly, he was not only her brother, but also the head of her family and her last remaining male relative.

"I will explain everything, Bertram, would you but give me the opportunity." She drew on reserves of politeness she didn't know she possessed. Bertram was not the bully Ralph had been; perhaps she could win him over.

He was gazing at her speculatively, then seemed to make up his mind, nodding once. "All right. I shan't act as our late brother did. I mean to do well by the title and by the family, Rose. Make no mistake, I am the head of this family now."

As if she could forget! As the Earl of Lansdale, Bertram now had complete rights to this property, all monies, and everything else that pertained to and was part of the title.

And that more or less included her, for although she was of age, Papa had not provided specifically for her in his will. Without an income, she could hardly continue being independent.

Bertram offered her his arm in a gallant gesture she hadn't expected, but the anxiety he displayed as her dirt-stained hand rose toward his arm—at least he'd had the sense to wear a fine broadcloth rather than silk to come here—almost made her laugh.

She put her trowel and shears into the split wood basket that contained the flowers she'd just culled—she had hoped to take them to Oak Grove for a flower-arranging lesson from Lily—and used both hands on the handle to keep from sullying Bertram's pristine sleeve.

She hid a smile as he emitted a nearly audible sigh of relief.

That was her last smile for some time.

"I won't, Bertram, I won't," Rose said for perhaps the twentieth time in three hours. They had breakfasted in the dining room, surrounded by the easels on which her watercolors stood, but any semblance of gentility between them had disappeared. The flowers she'd been gathering that morning sat forlornly at one end of the table. Eunice had served them breakfast, then disappeared. Her face had turned so white upon seeing Bertram that Rose thought her teeth might chatter with fright.

"I'm tired of discussing this." He dabbed at his lips with a napkin. "I don't even know why I am bothering. You will come home with me. 'Tis your duty."

Rose twisted her hands together more tightly at the word "duty." "I thought you might understand, Bertram. You, having been a second son. You knew you wouldn't get the title. Wasn't that why you bought your colors, went to India? To make a life for yourself, to get away from England? Can't you understand I might have felt the same, wanted to make a life for myself, too?"

"Rose, you're a woman. 'Tis different for you."

"Why?" She was so tired of arguing. She had to try, but she knew by now that nothing she said would make a difference. Women of her station weren't independent, unless they were extremely wealthy or widows.

"You must do your duty by your family. We all must." Easy for him to say, she thought rebelliously, since his "duty" meant acquiring a title, lands, and property he'd never thought to have. Instead of the modest title of a Viscount with a small parcel of land in the country and an apartment in town, he now had a large estate in Gloucester and a house in a fashionable district in London. All he'd done was benefit from their brother's death.

She had to marry. "That is what you say my duty is, Bertram, to marry some rich old man? So you and mother can live well?"

Bertram's gaze lit on one of her paintings, but he didn't comment on it. "We each provide for the family in our own way."

"But that's what I did. 'Tis why I came. If I can make a profit here, get the plantation working again . . ."

"That is my concern, not yours. I've no interest in Colonial backwaters, not after India," he shuddered. "Do you know there are so many diseases there that some of them have never even been given a name?"

"America is no longer a colony," Rose started to say hotly, but Bertram raised a hand for silence. He rested his hand on the cherrywood table, tracing a small scar on its surface with a well-manicured nail. If he recalled the dinners spent at this table when they were small, he didn't show it. He smiled, but there was no warmth in it. "Rose the radical, hmm?'' he said. Abruptly, he stood up. "That's enough. I don't intend to engage in any further discussion on this. You'll return with me, you'll marry, and I will either auction this plantation or offer it as a dowry.''

"I won't marry that horrible old man,'' she retorted. "Bertram, do you know what Chilters tried to do at the ball when Mama announced my engagement? Took his hand and tried to put it up my skirt.''

"I don't know if Chilters would have you now anyway, if he ever learns you've not been in mourning for Ralph all this time.''

"Then I'll tell him I went to America and became a harlot.''

He had been about to walk into the salon, but he turned now, fury on his face, his complexion as pale and English as if he'd never been in India. He gripped her wrist. "You'll do nothing of the sort. You're a clever girl, Rose, so don't make this harder for yourself. You could do worse than Chilters.''

Rose tried to pull her arm out of his grasp. "Have you become a bully like Ralph? That was always the biggest difference between you two. When it was just the two of us, you were never cruel.''

He dropped her arm, his eyes narrowing. "I'm not a bully and I shan't become one. But you answer to me now as the head of this family. And so you shall.''

"You can't make me go, Ralph. I won't leave.'' Had he always been this tall? Rose had never thought of Bertram as very prepossessing—and he wasn't, compared to Peter—but his years in the Army clearly had done him good in that area. He could overwhelm her physically, if they fought. Oh, where was Peter when she needed him?

Rose almost laughed hysterically at the thought. What an idiot she was. Who was to say Peter wouldn't help Bertram escort her out the door, and the two of them sign a contract on the way to the dock? No, Peter wouldn't be any help.

And that left her with no choices. "I'll come back with you on one condition, Bertram."

"You're hardly in a position to bargain." Still, he looked as if he was listening. He lounged against the archway between the dining room and the salon, one booted foot crossed over the other. Rose stood at an easel, and began to sketch in flowers with a hasty hand. She thought desperately.

"I'll only go back with you if I don't have to marry Chilters."

"Fine."

"What?" She was flabbergasted. She'd hardly expected him to agree, much less agree so easily.

"Rose, I'm not an ogre. I never liked Chilters and his reputation is unsavory. I wouldn't have agreed to such a union or forced you into it, had I been there."

" 'Twasn't Ralph, 'twas mother who was behind the match."

Bertram crossed to her, laid a comforting hand on her shoulder. "I know. But I'm Earl now and Mama has to listen to me, too. We both know Ralph was Mama's favorite." His rueful, almost conspiratorial look lightened her heart somewhat, reminding her of when they had both been the younger siblings, before Bertram had realized that the only way to get along with Ralph was to do what he wanted. Rose could never bring herself to do that, and she and Ralph had never gotten on well together.

She wasn't going to blindly follow Bertram either, no matter that he seemed at least somewhat sympathetic to her plight. Who knew if that conciliatory mood would last, or if, in the end, he would really face down their mother on her behalf? It wasn't something she could afford to rely on. "I'm glad you agree about Chilters. Then you will also agree that I must choose whom I shall marry."

"Choose? That's asking a bit much."

She'd let that go for now. It wasn't as if she ever intended to choose anyone, but Bertram needn't know that. Rose tried another tack. "And what about the future of Willow Oaks?"

"I must sell it."

"What about the income from it?" The cry came from her heart. Surely he couldn't just cold-bloodedly sell it all.

" 'Tis not enough. Ralph ran up huge debts. I don't want to worry about this place in addition to everything else."

"Then let me worry about it!"

"No, Rose."

"But over the long term, you would derive so much more income from holding on to it than just selling it now as it is without established crops or a history of recent profits."

Bertram paused, a considering look on his face. "Actually, you have a point there. Perhaps I'll only need to hire someone to oversee the place."

"I can do that. 'Tis what I want to do. 'Tis why I came."

"I'm sorry, Rose," he said as he came toward her. If she hadn't had those tears she was trying so hard not to shed in her eyes, she might have seen his intent. This was Captain Fairchild now, not her brother Bertram. And Captain Fairchild had learned how to fight in India, where British notions of honor and civility were quaint hindrances in a system that respected only blood and conquest.

Bertram's arm shot up from his side. He clipped Rose on the jaw before she realized his intent. He caught her as she sagged, then dragged her back toward the dining room.

"I wish you hadn't forced me to do this, Rose," he muttered. She was too stunned to take in what he was saying. "But you have always been a stubborn wench." Holding her around the waist with one arm, he pulled a packet out of his coat pocket and emptied it into the liquid remaining in the teapot.

He pushed her into a chair, stirred the mixture with a spoon, and then lifted it to her lips. Dazed, Rose struggled, but she was too weak. Bertram poured the bitter liquid into her mouth and kept her jaws open.

"It's a sleeping draught. You'll be all right, I promise." Bertram held her in the chair firmly, until her already weakened senses succumbed to the draught and she slumped over.

Bertram picked her up from the chair and carried her into the salon. Then he went to look for Eunice to tell her to pack her mistress's bags. He was certain the chit wanted to keep her position. She no longer had one here in America, and only his good word to mother would ensure she kept it. And the recommendation to keep her on would depend on her assistance in getting her mistress, suddenly taken ill, packed up and on board that ship with the minimum amount of fuss and attention.

Chapter Fifteen

We must take the current when it serves,
Or lose our ventures.
—William Shakespeare
Julius Caesar, Act IV, 1599

The March sun shone warm this morning, but to Peter it meant nothing but pain. The wind blowing off the river ruffled his hair, making every separate strand hurt. The sun, warming the land, heavy with the rich promise of spring, hurt his eyes. When he'd chucked the bottle upon waking at dawn— if you could call emerging from his stupor "waking"—sick of what it had done to his brain and body, he hadn't been able to rid himself of its effects so easily.

He had walked out on Rose after telling her about Joanna without a backward glance or further explanation. At the time, the pain of reliving the betrayal had been too much. Her sympathy had been too much. He had given Rose his body without thought for his heart—or hers. He had not thought about marrying her, but neither did he want her to think he had cared for her for only one night.

If she was willing to continue as they had begun—an arrangement even more unorthodox than her attempt to run Willow Oaks—perhaps they could go on. At least that had seemed to make sense when he was drunk. Somewhere deep inside, however, he had known that it didn't make enough sense for him to leave the fields and his bottle and approach her.

But now that he had recovered from his own temporary insanity, he knew that he owed Rose more than the curt explanation he had given her. And so he had gone to Willow Oaks this morning without even stopping to shave and clean up. He had been gone three days, three days too long. As he had come to her in the night, urgently and without warning, so he owed her the same urgency now that physical desire had been satisfied—at least temporarily. He didn't think he'd ever get enough of Rose, because no matter what haymow he'd gone to sleep in, he'd dreamt of her.

He couldn't call it love, not yet, but he also had to assure Rose that he didn't fear betrayal from her. That had been his past hurt talking.

And when he got there, what he had found was . . . nothing. No Rose. No Eunice. Nor any evidence that she was out for more than a walk. But no one had seen her or Eunice since the day before yesterday. Finally he had hunted up Malcolm in the stables, who'd said Eunice and Miss Rose were off for a trip to Philadelphia with Lady Rose's brother.

That had not seemed right, given Rose's desire to get away from her family. And so he had come to Oak Grove as quickly as he could. It was late morning now, and Adam looked up in surprise as Peter walked in and waited, impatiently, until Adam's tenants and workers had cleared the room.

"She's gone, Adam." Peter leaned over the desk in Adam's plantation office, a small room where he met with workers, factors, and others on Oak Grove business. Adam had deliberately built it as a separate outbuilding because he had found that the workers and indentured servants were often too intimidated to come up to the big house. And with the children into everything, he had a bit of privacy for the few times when he needed it. They had that privacy now.

"What do you mean, she's gone? Gone where? And what the devil is the matter with you? You look like you've been on a three-day bender."

Peter scratched his head, where a piece of straw or two remained. He had been, so what was the point of defending himself? Adam had been a spy. There wasn't anything Adam didn't know. His tracking abilities were outstanding, so who better to help him find out where Rose had gone, and if she had gone willingly.

It wasn't as if he hoped something untoward had happened to Rose. After, he'd fully expected her to decamp. He just hadn't known when, he told himself. He *had* expected this. After all, hadn't he secretly hoped that the physical encounter between them would end his attraction for her and make her realize that there was nothing to be obtained from him except bodily pleasure?

Except that his "strategy"—if one could dignify what he'd done as that—hadn't worked. He wanted her more, not less. He had wanted more of her then, and he wanted more of her now. Leaving hadn't been of any use. Peter groaned, running his hand across the stubble of his beard. Adam didn't look up from the papers before him on the table, but Peter suspected he'd heard.

He'd gotten himself drunk to avoid the inescapable conclusion of that night, which was that all the surprises had been his. Having her hadn't sated anything in him, far from it. It had only whetted his appetite for her, and his need. It had made him realize that in fact he had needs: not for her body, not for the comfort of a female body, but for her, for Rose, anything and everything that made her who she was. That was what he wanted. Needed. Had to have.

Was it love? He still shied away from thoughts such as those. If he could get her back here, he could figure it all out. Eventually. Getting her back was all that counted. Especially if she hadn't left of her own volition.

Adam had watched patiently, but now he broke in on Peter's thoughts. "I've been where you are now, Peter, so I won't bother wasting time with words. Were Lily here, she'd have a few, I know, but I will spare you." He looked up, eyes crinkling with his smile. "At least until she catches up with you."

"Can you come with me to look for Rose?" Peter asked bluntly.

"I would, but Lily's expecting the child at any time. I can't be away for as long as this might take."

"A day or two." Peter was surprised. Adam was protective but Lily was no fragile flower, and she'd borne three healthy children with no previous problems.

"A day or two? You haven't talked with Lily then. Did you come directly here?"

"Yes." Peter shook his head, gesturing at himself and his state of general disarray. "I haven't been around. Nor, as you no doubt surmise, have I been fit company."

"Sit down, then. This is more serious than you know. Lily thinks she's been kidnapped, not run away because of your lover's quarrel."

"How the hell would you know that?" Adam didn't answer. Had Lily guessed through women's intuition or had it been gossip? Maybe Rose had talked to Lily. More likely, Eunice had talked to one of the servants here. But that didn't matter now either.

"Trust me, Peter, we've known for some time that there's been something between you and Rose. Even when you didn't know it yourself."

Peter, who hadn't bothered to sit when told, smacked his hand on the desktop. Stupid gesture, he thought. It bloody hurt. "Why does Lily think Rose has been kidnapped?"

Adam pulled something from beneath a stack of papers on his desk. "Here. Do you recognize this?"

" 'Tis one of Rose's drawings . . . ah, paintings. Watercolors. Whatever." Peter pulled at his kerchief but realized he'd lost it somewhere in the fields. "So what?"

" 'Tis fortunate Lily isn't here, or she'd have your hide and I would let her. Don't you remember the flower vocabulary?"

"Yes, but that was years ago."

"Where does your mind go when you are at table with us, Peter?" Adam asked, but his tone carried more exasperation than anger.

Peter ran a hand through his disordered hair, dislodging a few more bits of straw. "I don't have one. I'm usually concentrating on avoiding Rose."

Adam waited, the sounds of plantation life around them muted in the distance. Morning sun streamed in through a window. His eyebrow rose.

"Avoid Rose? Or avoiding your feelings for her?"

"Damn it, Adam, if you must know, I'm trying to avoid having an erection every time I'm in the same room as she is. It doesn't leave a lot of room for additional thought. And don't laugh, damn your eyes."

Adam's rueful smile was full of male understanding. "I wouldn't dream of it."

"So why is the vocabulary important now?" Peter asked, still unsettled by the admission he'd made, though he was sure Adam had known it already.

"First, tell me what happened," Adam said. "Sit."

Peter allowed his aching body to finally settle into the chair in front of Adam's desk. "We quarreled and I went out to drink it off. That's about it. When I came back, I thought she'd finally given up on . . . on making Willow Oaks what she wanted, and had decided to go home."

"What you really mean is you hoped you had

browbeaten her into believing that you didn't want her in your life, and that she had finally taken your less-than-subtle hints and departed. And when you found that out that she had gone after your drinking binge, you felt—or feel—immeasurably guilty?''

Peter nodded. Damnation, Adam had always been keen. Peter suspected he knew about the lovemaking, too, but if Adam knew about that from his own experiences with Lily, Peter didn't need to know that much about his sister's early experiences with Adam. He also didn't intend to discuss with his brother-in-law his intimate evening with Rose.

"Don't flagellate yourself too much over what happened, Peter. I tried to keep Lily out of my life, too, thinking it better for her, and I failed miserably at it. I thank God for that nearly every day," he added fervently.

"So what about the flowers?" Peter asked.

"Lily went to Willow Oaks looking for you. It must have been the day Rose disappeared because the flowers she had apparently picked, probably that morning, were not yet dead. Lily found the beginning of a sketch, not filled in, and the real flowers on the dining room table near the easel.''

"Rose always paints in the dining room. What of it?"

"That's the odd thing, you see. Lily saw at once that the flowers in the sketch did not match the flowers on the table. And when she realized what flowers were in the drawing, she became convinced that Rose was trying to send a message."

"Even you must remember that iris indicates a message." Peter nodded, not wasting energy on Adam's dig. He deserved it. He deserved a thrashing, more like. "Lily was pretty certain the shape of the foliage indicate they are laurel leaves. One of its meanings is perfidy. Yew means sorrow, and zinnia—which isn't even blooming right now—stands for thoughts of absent friends. And periwinkle is for memory or, ah, 'sweet remembrances,' Lily said."

Peter understood. "The perfidy is in taking her away against her will, the yew for sadness at leaving. We are the friends from whom she is absent. Hell, hell and damn. It must have been her brother or some creature of his who instigated this. Or her fiancé."

"Rose was betrothed?"

"Her mother was trying to marry her off for money. The randy old goat tried to grope her at their betrothal ball. She despised him. That is when Rose decided to leave."

"What about the brother?" Adam asked.

"She never said much about him. He was in India, but perhaps he returned upon learning of his inheritance."

Brother and brother-in-law looked at each other with understanding dawning in their eyes.

"Oh, hell." Peter spoke first. "He's come to fetch her home, hasn't he? Either to make good on the marriage that had been previously contracted for her, or to marry her off to someone else, the highest bidder probably."

Peter pounded his fist hard, and didn't even feel it this time. "God in heaven, why didn't I think of that sooner?"

"You were drunk," Adam said dryly. Peter was nearly over the desk when Adam knocked him back with palms flat against his chest.

"Hit me if you must, Peter, but don't lay blame elsewhere."

"What the hell . . . ?"

"Peter, I love you, you know that. And Lily and I haven't wanted to interfere. But you've made a bloody mess of the last few months, and if you lose Rose—or if harm comes to her—there will be even harsher words between us. Lily cares for her."

"As do I."

Damn it, Adam was right, Peter conceded to himself. Adam hadn't spoken to him as if he were a boy in many years. It hurt to think that he deserved it now. Of course, it also hurt to think. Which was Adam's point in the first place. He hadn't been thinking. He hadn't been paying attention. And he had been so sunk in his own imagined hurts that he had lost the one woman he had come to care for at any time in the last few years.

Adam's thoughts seemed to run parallel to his own. "Perhaps you realize that you care for her now when we think she is in danger, but what you were thinking to make love to her, and then quarrel and part the way you did?"

"How did you . . . ? Oh, never mind. Did that happen to you and Lily?"

"I had to leave Lily for her own safety," Adam said a bit stiffly.

"She didn't know how you felt, though, did she?" Peter countered. "And I do know that you tried to keep her out of Sons of Liberty matters. She was quite upset about that."

"I remember." Adam's face was tight, but he nodded. "Again, I did it for her safety."

"Rose is às headstrong as ever Lily was. But I had no idea she could ever be in danger."

"Yes, but what did you say to her that made you think she had returned to England? If you had suspected earlier . . . if you hadn't disappeared . . ." Adam stopped. "There is no point in blaming you. The simple fact is that her brother has three days' lead on us and they could be anywhere."

"No, I know where they are. He's taking her back to London."

"From what port?"

"Does it matter? I can't stop a ship that's sailed. I'll just have to go to England." Peter grimaced. "That's my punishment, I suppose."

"I can't go with you because Lily is too close to her confinement and she has been having some difficulties."

"What difficulties? You haven't told me of any."

"No one's told you much of anything, Peter, because even when you've been here in the flesh, you have been too wrapped up in your own misery to listen. Lily hasn't been afflicted with anything serious, but she's experienced some bleeding. I just don't want to leave her now."

Peter didn't bother wasting his energy on anger. Adam was right. He had been selfishly immune to others' problems.

Adam blotted the last bit he'd been writing, and then set his pen aside. "If you want that lovely girl back, you'd best exorcise your demons." Peter rubbed his neck again. Hadn't Rose said something to that effect, about him exorcising his demons? He should have taken her advice. If it wasn't too late, perhaps he could still take Adam's.

Adam closed the ledger that still lay open on his desk. "Come, we have to make plans. You can't catch up with them by ship, so we might as well plan this properly. I'll send you to my barrister in London. He can make the arrangements to get you into the proper circles."

Peter's thought processes had been slow all morning. There was no difference now. "What, into society? What the devil do you mean? I'm just going to fetch Rose."

"Do pay attention, Peter, or I will let Lily box your ears, so help me. If Rose's brother has indeed taken her, even against her will, you cannot just 'fetch' her. She is properly in her brother's care, as he is now the Earl. He will have to set her up in society, telling a plausible story for her absence these last months. Then he will marry her off, from what you've told me, either to the randy old goat you mentioned, or to the highest bidder. If you want to stop that, and try to woo Rose yourself, you'll not only have to go to England, you'll have to get close to her and her family. And that will mean dealing with society."

Peter had known from the moment Adam mentioned kidnapping that he would have to go after Rose. To England—the place he'd sworn he would never go. "But if Rose doesn't want to be with her family, can't I just . . . just . . ."

"Just what? Take her away? If she was taken against her will as the flower message indicates, then it won't be so simple. You can't just show up and she will walk out of a ballroom and onto a ship with you. You will have to get access to her, court her, and get permission to marry her."

Peter began to sputter about English atrocities such as courtship and marriage customs, the strictures of society, and the barbaric nature of the marriage mart. Adam held up a hand. "Wait, let

me finish. You will have to approach her in a manner above reproach to at least ascertain if she still
wants you. Then you may plot a way to get her
away from her family. But the only way to get in
is through the front door, even if you end up running out the back. There'll be neither shame nor
dishonor in that way out, if her own family took
her against her will, no matter what bloody English
law may say. Bear in mind that leaving the back
way assumes that you both intend to return here
to live because she could never live in England
again."

Adam and Peter exchanged a look of grim understanding, and a purely masculine smile that contained no humor or good feeling, but left them in
perfect accord. He didn't have to like going to
England, but in his brisk nod to Adam, he acknowledged that he had botched his relationship with
Rose quite thoroughly. Peter knew what he had to
do.

Damn. Why couldn't men and women communi-
cate as effectively as men did between themselves?

Chapter Sixteen

I hardly yet have learn'd
To insinuate, flatter, bow
and bend my limbs:
                    —William Shakespeare,
                        Richard II, 1597

Rose was furious. Not only had she been spirited away from Willow Oaks by her brother, but also there was nothing she could do about it. She couldn't very well jump off a ship in the middle of the ocean.

"Must you prattle on, Rose? Talking won't achieve a single thing you want," Bertram said from the chair that was bolted next to the cabin's table, also similarly bolted down. "I vow, I shall have to do something if you do not stop railing at me."

"What, you would resort to more force, my dear brother? If my talking makes you miserable, I'll happily settle for that," Rose retorted. "You kidnapped me, Bertram."

"I did not. I am merely taking you back home to the bosom of your loving family." But Bertram had the grace to look uncomfortable.

Eunice threw her apron over her head and went back to sniffling. She had apologized to Rose a thousand times, and Rose had forgiven her. But the little maid still felt guilty for her part in helping get Rose to the ship, lying to the rest of the servants that Master Bertram was taking her and her mistress to Philadelphia for a visit, and that they would be back in a month or so.

Rose had forgiven her, but Eunice might not ever forgive herself.

At night, however, alone in her narrow ship's bed, Rose acknowledged the hopelessness of her plight. After their last encounter, Peter would think she had at last returned to England. As for leaving matters at Willow Oaks without instructions or arrangements, well, that would just prove his point that she had never been equipped for this undertaking, that she was a dilettante, that she didn't know what she was doing, et cetera.

With her sudden departure, she knew that all his worst ideas about her—the ones she had thought to teach him by example were untrue— would be confirmed. She hadn't betrayed him to anyone, of course, but she had left without a word of explanation. That made her capricious, willful, unreliable . . . all the things he hated about women, thanks to Joanna. And for having put her in that position, for taking her beyond the reach of communication or explanation, she had Bertram to thank.

"I have to do what?" Thunderstruck would be the closest match to Peter's emotions at that moment. Adam had warned him not to go directly to the barrister's from the docks, so Peter had repaired to an inn to wash, shave, and change into what Adam called "town clothes," and then he had taken a hackney to the law offices that clustered near the Temple.

With Adam's letter in his hand, Cranwell, the Earl of Dalby's barrister, knew a brief moment of sympathy, but he wasn't certain whether it was for himself or the man before him.

"You will be participating in the annual social season, with the Dowager Countess of Dalby as your sponsor." The Earl of Dalby's letter, while short on background, had made it plain that his brother-in-law Peter Walters would not be an easy client. Nor was Cranwell certain that putting the American with the Earl's mother was the best arrangement. But Cranwell was a barrister, not a nursemaid, by God, and the Countess had demanded that she be the one to host her son's brother-in-law.

The Earl had softened slightly toward his mother over the years. Cranwell was sure the American woman that the Earl had married had been the one to exert that softening influence. He'd seen no signs since the Earl had been a young man that he would ever forgive his mother, even though Lord Dalby had never altered the provisions of his father's will, despite her perfidious behavior. After the unfortunate circumstances of long ago, the Dalby fortune and a circumspect life had restored the Countess to society's good graces.

The Earl had even permitted the Dowager Countess to visit America to see her grandchildren. She'd come home in high dudgeon that the Earl still wouldn't return to England, however, especially now that he had heirs. She had sworn she would never visit again.

Still, the Earl's wife did write to her, and the Countess continued to keep abreast of her son's affairs. That is, as much as the Earl permitted his mother to know. The Earl had given his title to a relative when he'd decided to become an American, but with the late hostilities past and the relative in an early grave, the title had again reverted to him. And that was how Cranwell preferred matters.

"London is in the midst of the annual season," Cranwell repeated, "and Lady Rose, sister of the Earl of Lansdale, is on the marriage mart."

"The marriage mart? How barbaric," the American said with feeling.

"Yes, well," Cranwell smiled thinly, wondering if the American knew how ironic his words were, coming as they did from a citizen whose nation of rebels had thrown off the rule of their rightful King. Barbaric indeed.

"Regardless, the only way you will be allowed to see Lady Rose is by gaining admittance to society events to which you and she have been invited. She has the entrée by virtue of being a member of the *ton*. You, as an American, are at rather a disadvantage, I am afraid." He respected the Earl of Dalby and enjoyed the prestige of managing his lordship's legal affairs even more, so he supposed he could not actually sneer.

Still, he did allow his upper lip to curl just the slightest bit, certain the American wouldn't notice. Walters was too busy being outraged at the thought of having to wear silver shoe buckles and learning to bow. His lordship's mother would have quite a time with this American. Pity he couldn't watch his "education," but Lady Dalby had a sharp side to her tongue, too, and he'd no wish to be the target of it.

Cranwell signaled for a clerk and asked him to collect the papers that Walters would need. He would send Peter Walters to Lady Dalby and wait for reports from his contacts in the household and society. The season should be entertaining for this, if for no other reason. And perhaps a scandal would ensue. The prospects were rich indeed.

"What are you gaping at, young man?" the Countess of Dalby snapped.

"I'm not that young, and if you think I shall bow and scrape to you, my lady, I had best take my leave." Peter reached for his beaver top hat, ignoring the walking stick she had placed beside it. He didn't even spare a glance for the gloves.

"Not if you want the gel," she said in her haughtiest tones, observing with satisfaction that he stopped moving at once.

With a muttered curse that she would have pleasure teaching him to restrain, he swung back to her, anger and frustration evident in every line of his powerful frame. He was tall, about the same height as Adam, she thought. She suspected he was built far more like a worker than a gentleman, but she knew he would stand out like an eagle among pigeons, and that was all to the good. Whether Rose Fairchild was on the marriage mart by choice or compulsion mattered little. For Peter Walters to win her, he had to get to her first, and that meant entering society.

Failing that, perhaps he could kidnap her back to America, but that would be a dicey business and she'd play no part in something of that ilk. Not that she wouldn't mind seeing Fanny Fairchild humiliated.

Adam's mother, who had always despised the Countess of Lansdale, smiled to herself. Now there was a set-down for which she would most happily claim credit. Furthermore, if she could witness it, then she could die a happy woman.

But for now she had to turn this handsome sow's ear into a silken purse, something she knew he would hate. And oh, she would enjoy every minute of it.

"Pick up the gloves and walking stick," she instructed imperiously, aware that his back had stiffened at her tone. "One never disagrees with a lady," she said, smiling sweetly. "Follow me into the drawing room. I have much to teach you and very little time. You must attend the Assembly at Almack's in three days' time."

Peter looked around him in disgust. This was his second week at Almack's, and he thought he'd never seen such a collection of well-dressed, insipid-looking women. For the most part, their hair was blond or heavily powdered—unless they wore wigs, even worse—their faces were pale with powder, and they looked as if they'd never spent a day outside in their lives. These English misses also had a lamentable tendency to giggle, and their eyes apparently glowed in direct proportion to their mama's estimate of a man's wealth.

He hadn't wanted to come again, but Lady Dalby had said Rose was sure to appear tonight, since she had missed last week. One couldn't afford not to be at Almack's if one was on the marriage mart, she'd said in her distinctively haughty voice. It amazed him at times that this woman was Adam's mother.

His hand rose to tug at his kerchief, and a voice below his ear said quietly but sharply, "You're wearing a cravat, my boy, not some homely workman's scarf."

Peter might have smiled at her dismissive language—he had become used to the acerbic Dowager Countess, "likable" never being a word one would think of in connection with Adam's mother—but he was too damned uncomfortable. He hated these overdone clothes, and he had ordered his as simple as Lady Dalby would allow the tailor to create.

"There are at least twenty-two ways to tie one of those. As far as I know, you know only how to fold it over once, or so Timons tells me." She waved one jeweled hand in the air. So I warn you, one tug and you'll ruin those folds," she hissed in her best, dramatically hushed tones.

"So what?" he muttered back ungraciously, without turning his head away from his slow contemplation of the room to look at her.

"Timons is not here to repair the destruction,

my boy, and I assure you that you cannot repair it on your own."

Thwarted from tugging on something, Peter's hand next went to his hair, but he stopped. He'd absolutely refused to wear a wig or to have his hair powdered, but it was combed and tied back more elaborately than would be the case at home and he knew he couldn't disturb that either. Timons was really an agreeable man; it was his employer that one couldn't offend.

Lady Dalby wasn't finished with him. "Now remember, you are not to act as if you know Lady Rose when you see her. I'll thank you to remember this is not savage Virginia, where people have no manners and one may introduce oneself to anyone one likes. You have a voucher to Almack's on sufferance, so you are not yet accepted. If the hostesses accept you—and wearing those dreadful boots, I have my doubts—then we shall see what we shall see. Now, try to look interested in some of the young ladies here."

"Why?" Peter thought it a reasonable question. He wasn't interested in anyone else, nor did he seek to make Rose jealous. Why should he lead any of these silly young girls on and make them think he was interested in them, when the reality couldn't be farther from the truth?

"You cannot be too obvious. 'Twill make her family suspicious. You don't want them to think you have an intimate connection to Rose from America, or they may send her off to the country or betroth her to the first likely man they find. Any hint of scandal will ruin Rose."

"What makes you think she hasn't told them?"

"Because if I know Fanny Fairchild, and I do,

she will not only have forbidden Rose to speak of her American adventure, she will have refused to listen to it. And while that younger son of hers may have grown enough spine to fetch Rose in America, it was at his mother's command, and he isn't going to cross her now. Therefore, neither of them is likely to know about your true place in Rose's life when she was in Virginia."

Lady Dalby had turned to face him now, holding the cup of orgeat that she had forced him to fetch for her from the drinks table as part of his "training." She'd already confided that it was abominable, and he had asked her why she'd bothered—other than to torment him, of course. She said she was protecting the shrubbery.

When he'd raised an amazed eyebrow at that, she said that she suspected the stuff had killed a certain bush outside the Assembly Rooms in St. James, because she couldn't imagine anyone actually drinking the remnants after the assembly ended for the night.

After that, Lady Dalby had gone on lecturing him while his attention wandered. With effort, he focused his eyes on her, aware only that he had yet to see any redheads come through the door. Then she said something that forced him to listen to her. "Don't even begin to think that Lady Rose's social ruination is an acceptable outcome until you have her permission."

Peter looked at her, startled. Had Adam written to her that his brother-in-law was potentially a hothead, or was this something Lady Dalby had figured out on her own? She wagged a finger at him, her gloves tucked in her reticule now that she had a glass to hold.

"I'm on to you, my boy. The worst possible thing you could do for that young woman would be to ruin her, and only then find out that she doesn't want you, or she doesn't want to go back to America. This flower message business of my daughter-in-law's is a surmise only. If you act too hastily, *you* will have ruined her life, rather than her family, and left her with no choices."

Even with his frantic sense of urgency to regain Rose before she slipped away from him forever, Peter had to admit that the old dragon was right. He could not act precipitously until he knew what Rose wanted.

He didn't particularly want to give the old "gel" the satisfaction of knowing that, however, so he heeded her urging and began to request space on dance cards, though his jaw grew more tense with each vapid response from the young ladies.

He was in the midst of some tedious dance— Almack's was old-fashioned enough that the dances he knew from America, now hopelessly out of fashion elsewhere in London, were still danced here— when he saw the top of a russet head, piled high with curls, enter the ballroom. Trust Rose not to allow herself to be powdered or bewigged either.

Here they were at last, in the same room. Peter was ready to part the Red Sea to reach her side, but Lady Dalby miraculously appeared at the end of the line of dancers and hissed, "Stay," at him.

He glared, but complied. His partner, thinking he meant the frown for her, hurried away from his side as soon as the set ended, which was fine with him. Then he started for Rose's side of the room.

Chapter Seventeen

Give me a storm, if it be love.
— Thomas Carew, "Mediocrity
in Love Rejected," *Poems*, 1640

Rose had gone even paler than she had been lately. She had just entered the Assembly Rooms and had seen Peter dancing with a highly eligible young miss. In the last week, she had heard about "the American." She had hardly dared to hope that it was Peter, but she had guessed it was he, once she'd heard about his connection to the Countess of Dalby.

This was the first event they had mutually attended. Actually, she had forced herself not to speculate on what he was doing here. She knew he didn't love her; therefore, he wouldn't have come after her, not all the way to London, to hated England.

Rumor had it that he had come to hang out for a rich wife, but the very thought would have made her laugh, had she been in the mood for it. Whatever it was—and she was very much afraid it was the pursuit of Willow Oaks—it couldn't have anything to do with her personally. Yet for all that, anticipation glittered through her veins as if she'd drunk champagne, which Almack's refused to serve.

A woman who had to be the Dowager Countess of Dalby appeared at Peter's elbow and he accompanied her. She couldn't tell if he had cast a glance her way because at that moment one of the patronesses of Almack's came up to Bertram, blocking her view. Although Bertram still had a hand at her elbow, Rose heard them as if they were a long way off.

"Do you wish for Lady Rose to meet the American?" she asked.

"Not particularly," Bertram said.

Lady Whoever-it-was frowned. "Why, is there something untoward about him?" she inquired. "Is he not from Virginia where your family once lived? We thought you might know something of his people."

"Indeed, we do," Rose said, for the woman's words had pierced her absorption. Ignoring Bertram's pinch on her forearm, she began to explain. "Master Walters is from a family that has done a great deal to foster trade between England and America since the late hostilities. The most discrim-

inating noblemen eagerly seek after their botanical
specialties. And his family's plantation is near to
William Byrd's of Westover, one of the largest plantations on the James River and one of the most
prominent of Virginia families.''

Rose smiled triumphantly, knowing Bertram
would not protest now. Their mother might have
offered further argument, saying that money was
not lineage or some such, but she had declined to
appear tonight. She hated Almack's, thought it
too tame, and appeared only when she felt it was
required, such as two weeks ago, when Rose had
first returned to the marriage mart.

But Rose quickly learned that she hadn't given
Bertram enough credit for cunning. "Oh, no, you
misunderstand. We would love to meet him," Bertram said with apparent sincerity. Then, by all
appearances placing an affectionate arm around
Rose's waist, he jabbed his arm deeply into her
side in one swift gesture that was blocked from the
patroness's view.

Rose gasped with pain and crumpled against Bertram. He held her against him, again seemingly
tender and solicitous. "As you can see, my sister
is suddenly indisposed," he said imperturbably.
"I believe the cause must be the tea service this
afternoon at Lady Darnton's. Her cakes were too
rich for so late in the afternoon," he confided in
a low tone to the patroness, who hung on his every
word as if titillated by the gossip.

Rose was still panting for breath; Bertram's arm
was now actually necessary for her to remain
upright. "We'll be taking our leave now," he said,
as smooth as butter. "Please extend my regards to

Lady Dalby and her pet American. I'm certain we shall meet them soon."

"I shall convey your greetings, my lord. Good night, Lord Lansdale. I do hope your sister feels better soon."

And so Rose was ushered out the door and into their carriage before anything more could be said or done. She fell back against the cushions as soon as Bertram had solicitously escorted her to her seat.

"Bertram, are you trying to kill me? You can't do that, not if you hope to make a match for me," she said bitterly. "Nor does it help your cause to make a scene at Almack's." Then she slumped against the squabs, winded from the few brief words she'd just uttered.

Bertram tapped on the roof to give the driver instructions to go home. *"Au contraire,* I prevented you from making a scene, my dear sister." He straightened and the pose of the indolent lord fell away. He was all military strength and bearing now.

"Now listen to me and listen well. You will stay away from that American. I know who he is; I've talked to Eunice. I don't know the extent of what was between you, and I don't care to know, but 'twas clear from the look on your face just now that you've fancied yourself in love with him."

He settled the tails of his cutaway coat and took off his top hat. "You aren't with child, are you?" he asked with no preamble.

"You would have known that by now after all those weeks on the ship, wouldn't you, Bertram?" Rose asked, no longer shocked that her brother would ask such a question. It surprised her only that it had taken him so long. "Or didn't you get all the details on *that* from Eunice?"

"I should have turned the chit off as Mother wished, but she's loyal to you, Rose, and that counts for something."

At her look of surprise, he smiled grimly. "I'm not an ogre, Rose, I've told you that before. When you showed no signs of pregnancy, I decided 'twas not my business what had transpired between you and the American, as long as you were not spoiled for marriage."

"What about my vaunted virginity?" Rose asked, although every breath hurt. She was going to have a bruise from what Bertram had done to her side, but there was no point in screaming about it. No one would believe that her own brother had punched her in the ribs, and she had no business being surprised at his action, not after he had drugged her to get her out of America. The law was on his side as Earl, and despite being of age, she was still little more than chattel.

"By the time you are married, it isn't going to matter," he answered. "No man is going to admit he's been cuckolded before he ever got to his marriage bed, especially with a doctor's certificate that you were a virgin. And I would resort to that only if any questions should arise, which I doubt is likely."

Rose stared. Here was her older brother calmly explaining how one bought proof of virginity. Had he no scruples? Would he stop at nothing?

"Furthermore, an active woman such as you have always been can always plead vigorous horseback rides in the country," he continued. "More than one woman was ruined when her maidenhead broke quite naturally, but it only takes a logical explanation and the willingness to listen. I can produce a certificate to that effect and I will, if necessary."

Rose was sickened that he had thought this all out so far in advance, but no longer astonished that he knew so much about such intimacies. All men, it seemed, knew more than women when it came to such matters. "You're prepared for any eventuality, I see."

"I told you 'twas my duty to look after the family and I take that seriously. I won't let Mother badger you, which means I assured her that there would be no questions about you, no hint of scandal. In exchange, she is to keep her own counsel as well, and that specifically includes leaving you alone."

How odd that Bertram could be relatively thoughtful in this one respect, while displaying such ruthlessness in others. She'd wondered why her mother had been so circumspect since her return. Expecting daily interrogation, Rose had been surprised to be left mostly to her own devices—as long as she stayed at home. When she went out, Bertram was always with her.

"There are several servants and professional men, such as clergymen and apothecaries, who are prepared to testify that you and Mother were prostrate with grief for months after Ralph's death, which tragically followed so soon after Father's."

Money, perhaps, or some other threat or inducement, had allowed Bertram to effectively box her in. Now she would have to attend parties she hated if only to see Peter. And as much as Bertram might want to keep her away from Peter, he also had to have her out for display on the marriage mart.

She hardly knew how she felt about Peter, particularly since she'd had no opportunity to speak with him. But he had made his position plain after their one night together. Hadn't he? And if he had, then why was he here?

Well, with Bertram determined to defend her honor for his own purposes, she had nothing to lose by meeting Peter. If she could arrange it. If he even wanted to see her. With ribs aching at every sway of the carriage, Rose tried to forget the tangled coil she was in. She would gladly run away with Peter. The question was, would he want her to?

Given what had happened to him in the past, would he ever trust any woman again enough to ask?

After two days passed during which Rose impatiently scanned invitations and wondered—then pointedly tried not to wonder—which Peter might attend, Rose heard that he would attend the annual ball given by the Duchess of Rotherford, one of the season's biggest events. Eunice, perpetually worried about her position since she had been forced to help Bertram spirit Rose away from Williamsburg, had been trolling the gossip nets attentively as a way of showing her mistress loyalty.

Rose thought she hoped to hear some news of whether her beau Malcolm had accompanied Peter. Privately, however, she thought it unlikely that Peter would have had any need for a stable hand on a trip to England.

Eunice had even managed to keep what she had learned known to only herself and Rose, so when Bertram did not see Peter anywhere, he had gone on to the gaming room, satisfied that "the American" was not in attendance. Since the event was an important one, given the Duchess's social standing, her mother had come. Thus Rose was, unfortunately, not alone. It seemed she was never alone these days, and yet so alone in others.

At the moment, however, she was not being besieged by suitors, so she was able to scan the ballroom surreptitiously. Bertram had at least kept his word when he said she would not have to marry the Marquess of Chilters if she didn't want to.

In her absence, the old man had had a stroke and was now even more decrepit. His current tendency to drool made him less than desirable among the fashionable set, her mother had said with perfect seriousness. Without Bertram, Rose thought, her mother might still have married her off to the old man. She shuddered.

Rose not only didn't want to marry him, she didn't want to marry anyone. But no matter how reasonable Bertram professed to be, he wasn't really. God knew her mother wasn't. Even if Bertram showed any inclination to yield, their mother never would.

So Rose danced when her mother glared at her, which was at nearly every set. Dividing her attention evenly among the men, she hoped to avoid encouraging any of them. In the end Bertram and her mother would choose whom she would marry, unless by some unlikely chance she found someone agreeable both to her and to her family. But the odds of that happening were about as good as her returning to run Willow Oaks on her own.

And yet, some sort of miracle had just occurred, because when she looked across the ballroom after the set she had just completed, Rose instantly recognized the tall form and richly gold unpowdered hair. Her heart thumped painfully. Not only had Peter Walters set foot on English soil, he had entered this ballroom.

From the top of the staircase, Peter descended to the ballroom level with the Dowager Countess of Dalby. Rose watched as Peter bowed to their hostess, halfway across the ballroom from her. Even if her eyes had not been utterly parched for the sight of him, she would have been impressed. He bent over the older woman's hand with the correct degree of formality; he made a proper leg.

Peter looked even more elegant than he had the other night. He wore a coat with cutaway tails that she had never seen him wear in Virginia. That modern fashion had not even arrived in Virginia; Peter must have been to the tailor's at Lady Dalby's insistence. Since she could not imagine Peter having gone to a tailor otherwise, she hid a smile; there must have been an interesting contest of wills if the old lady was half as stubborn as Peter.

Clearly, the Dowager Countess had prevailed. There was no other word to describe him but elegant. Even at Oak Grove's Christmas ball last year, she had never seen him dressed with such formality. A silver-gray embroidered waistcoat complemented the rich golden sheen of his hair, while his charcoal gray coat and breeches conveyed an image of muted elegance. Eyes regarded him from every corner of the Duchess of Rotherford's capacious ballroom.

"Look at that man," her mother's voice near her said. "No wig. And boots, in a ballroom?" Rose smiled reluctantly; trust her mother to find the irregularities. The Countess of Dalby must also have objected to the lack of traditional pumps and silk stockings, but Rose was certain that Peter would never observe anyone else's formalities if he did not wish to.

He wasn't wearing clocked silk stockings or shoes with silver or diamond buckles, and boots were for day wear, not evening, but they were new and glossed to a high sheen. Peter looked vital, alive, more than a match for any man in the room, and more a man than most.

"Is that the American?" her mother asked. "The one that old witch, the Countess of Dalby, is sponsoring?"

Rose nodded. " 'Tis." A vast yearning filled her, but she did not move. Even without Bertram's and her mother's eagle eyes, convention did not allow unmarried females to approach men. Remembering Virginia's much less stratified ways, she sighed. She would wait. But not forever. After all, did she really care about her reputation?

Remembering that Bertram did not have to make a good match for her, only one advantageous to him, she realized that it was in her own best interest not to damage her reputation. Resigned to her fate, she schooled herself to as much patience as she could muster.

Peter's thoughts were in turmoil. He had pinpointed Rose's position as soon as he'd surveyed the ballroom from the staircase's top step. He'd wanted to rush over to her and ask if she was all right, although he could see for himself that she was, at least on the surface. She was beautiful. Tall, and with that glorious red hair, she outshone the milk-and-water misses so decisively that Peter could not have described a single one of them later.

Yet Adam's mother demanded that he dance with the most eligible of the silly misses. She insisted that it wasn't to make Rose jealous, but to enhance Peter's standing and prestige to ensure he was invited to the best social engagements, and so that Rose's family would not be suspicious of any approaches to her.

"Fanny Fairchild would probably die rather than let her daughter marry an American, but you are the social season's novelty, and she is too much the creature of the moment to pass you up, even on grounds of social standing. In addition, I imagine it must be positively slaying her to attempt to figure out what my connection to all this is. As far as anyone knows, you are merely my son's brother-in-law, but as they all imagine America to be one great wilderness, I doubt anyone has connected Oak Grove with Willow Oaks. Or else she could be suspicious."

"And if they do become suspicious?" Peter had gratefully stopped dancing to get the old lady a glass of punch, while he had something stronger. Rose had been dancing but he'd lost sight of her when he'd had to dance attendance on Lady Dalby. "What of her brother Bertram?"

"Ah yes, you are itching to display your manly pugilistic skills, are you not? But your Rose is quite unharmed, as you have seen."

"She is now, but . . ."

"Unclench your fists, Peter. And remember, all in good time, my boy. You shall have your revenge, but 'tis not only Rose's family you must worry about. I imagine the lady's heart is bruised or she would

not have agreed to return to dear England's
shores.''

Peter hadn't told her the details—indeed he
didn't really know them for certain, but he didn't
for a minute think that Rose had returned of her
own accord—and so he remained silent. The
Countess looked at him shrewdly, but he had
learned by now to school his expression. Returning
her look blandly, he cradled the snifter in his palm.

''Therefore, winning her heart is your particular
task, and haste will win you no points,'' Lady Dalby
concluded.

''I thought her brother wanted to marry her off.''

''Yes, he does, but haste is suspicious, and most
marriages take place after the season. Now is the
time for negotiations, displaying the wares, dick-
ering over the dowries . . .''

Peter nearly spit out his brandy. He managed to
set the glass on the table before exploding in as
low a tone as he could manage. ''Women are not
prime horseflesh.'' He glared at her, even though
he realized that she was enjoying this exchange.

''Perhaps where you come from, dear boy. Here,
women still know their place.''

Peter and Rose both ''lost'' their escorts eventually. The Dowager Countesses had finally come face
to face and were intent on outmaneuvering each
other verbally, socially, and in any other way they
could gain advantage. Nearly every widow and
many an older matron had gathered discreetly
around the two society dragons to hear the badi-
nage.

Peter and Rose, from opposite sides of the huge

room, made their way toward a quieter corner shadowed by large potted trees, drawn toward each other as if bound by invisible, yet irresistible threads.

At last they found each other in the same corner of the ballroom, as alone as they could be in a roomful of crowded people. Bowing over her hand, Peter kissed the air above the glove covering her hand. Though there was nothing lingering or improper about his kiss, Rose felt the heat from his fingers gripping her palm all the way to her soul.

"Rose," he said softly as he straightened, his eyes clear and green and intent enough to make her feel giddy.

"Peter," she said, trying to keep any softening out of her correct and proper voice.

He smiled. "After all the required titles and correct forms of address here, it sounds so . . . natural to hear your name. Does your mother know we are on a first-name basis?" he asked.

"My mother doesn't know anything at all."

"You haven't told her?"

"She doesn't want to know. And besides, what is there to say? I don't even know why you are here."

"I came for you."

A shiver ran up her spine, ending at the nape of her neck where, with her upswept hair, she could almost feel the soft, downy hairs rise. The soft, emphatic statement made a wild flare of hope burn through her senses, which had been dulled by so many days of quiet despair. Still, she couldn't succumb to his charm so easily; why would he come all this distance to woo her? He had never acted this way when they were neighbors in Virginia.

"Do you expect me to believe that?" she challenged him.

He never dropped his gaze. "Why else would I be here?"

Rose had a number of possible retorts to that, but she didn't have the chance. Her dance card had been filled since long before Peter's arrival. Although she'd have liked nothing better than to forget that, her next partner spotted her through the palms and had come to claim her.

Since the Duke had found her, that meant others could as well—what a shame she and Peter were so tall—but Rose knew she dared not make a scene and risk an appearance by her mother or Bertram. As the Duke of Devonbury led her away, she watched Peter silently fume. His fists clenched at his sides, and he took a step forward as if he meant to pull her hand from its polite resting place atop the Duke's coat sleeve.

She frowned and shook her head in a "no" gesture. As the Duke led her away, Rose turned slightly, formed the word "later" with her lips, and hoped Peter understood.

When the dance ended, she escaped from the Duke and made her way to the same corner before her next partner could claim her. Peter stood there, his frame and face tense with purpose. He wasted no time on words, but took her elbow and propelled her from the ballroom's edge through the first door he saw.

Fortunately, Rose recognized the hallway as one that led to the retiring rooms for women, and to the powder rooms where both men and women went to see to their toilette. The gaming rooms that were the exclusive purview of the men were located off a hallway at the opposite side of the ballroom, so there was little chance that Bertram would stumble on them here.

Still, she could not risk her mother seeing them, so she pulled the door to a powder room open, then shut it quickly behind them. She locked it and turned to face Peter.

Chapter Eighteen

Ye Gods! annihilate but space and time,
And make two lovers happy.

—Alexander Pope
On the Art of Sinking in Poetry, 1728

Peter moved so quickly, she had no chance to speak or even move. In one fluid gesture, he clasped her waist, maneuvered her against the wall, and lowered his lips to hers as if he were a man dying of thirst.

He drank of her deeply, one warm, familiar hand smoothing up the silk of her gown from her back to her neck, where he gently cradled her head against his palm and tilted her head back to a deeper angle for his kiss.

Rose was lost the instant his lips touched hers, as wild sensations streaked through her. Streamers of fire fanned out from every place he touched her, and even when his lips left hers so they could both breathe, she couldn't. She would rather breathe in Peter. Even though she knew he was as immaculate and polished as any gentleman for the ball, her senses recalled his normal masculine scent of soap and horses, green things and the good earth. That was Peter's scent. His mouth was warm and intimate and she wanted desperately to feel it again on hers.

She was sure they should talk, but not certain she could, and anyway, with these sensations ravaging her, she couldn't think. Nothing was more important at this moment than the remembered touch of Peter Walters, his lips, his hands, his hard body pressed against hers, his warm breath fanning her cheek. The scent, the touch, the taste of him— all things that she had thought she would never experience again.

Peter appeared to be similarly intoxicated. His low comments were seductive, but murmured against her skin so that she hardly understood them. It didn't matter—the tone of voice, his touch—told her what she wanted to know.

His touch grew bolder, his caresses more ardent. Feeling air whisper against her breasts, she realized that Peter had freed them from her bodice, and was about to take a hardening crest into his mouth. His other hand cupped and kneaded her bottom through the dress, edging it up so she felt a draft there too.

"You can't ... we can't," she gasped. "Not here."

"What?" he challenged, a trace of bitterness in his voice, but not stilling the movement of his hands, as if he knew her body wanted what her conscious mind might seek to deny or delay. He pressed a knee between her legs, causing her to moan with pleasure. "Am I too much the country bumpkin for you now?"

"Oh, Peter how can you think that's true?" Couldn't he tell what his touch was doing to her?

"You didn't seem to be objecting too much just now, to that, whoever he was, to being in his arms." So he had watched her dancing.

"You're jealous," she exclaimed. Who would have thought it?

"I came to rescue you from that disgusting old man, and instead you go off to dance in the arms of a . . . a . . ."

"Of someone who is neither old nor doddering?" What devil prompted her to say that, she didn't know. She knew the Duke was considered a catch, but he didn't appeal to her at all.

Peter still had her pressed against the wall, his knee between hers. She knew even through all her skirts that he was aroused. It wasn't that she had to feel his erection. She could see it in the tautness of his pose, his nostrils flared like a stallion about to mount a mare. Her senses caught fire at that extremely wanton thought.

All thoughts of propriety fled. Leaning toward him, she pressed against his leg. Even if she couldn't feel his erection, he would feel her body's movements.

"That's it, isn't it Peter?" Her tone was low and very seductive. "I am yours. You want to stake your claim on me, mark me. Go ahead. I'm yours, Peter.

I don't care what you've seen or heard. Nothing has transpired between me and any man since you were . . . since . . ."

"Since I made you mine," he said in a low voice that immediately made her lower flesh tingle as if he were touching her already.

She leaned back against the powdering room wall. "Make me yours again, Peter. You know I already am."

His mouth captured hers in a kiss that did not even wait a decent interval to reestablish matters between them. He took her mouth as a pirate takes plunder, as if he had every right, as if they hadn't been parted for weeks.

As if . . . as if he had her beneath him in bed. Rose moaned and found her hand had strayed to his breeches. Peter could not reach for her in the same way, not through all her skirts.

"I can tell you're still an innocent, Rose," he said in a low, frustrated voice. "You've no idea of the logistics of doing this in a room such as this."

"Because there are no divans?"

"Because I want you in a bed, stretched out beneath me, nothing covering that glorious body of yours. Because I want you to part your legs for me. Because I want to watch you watching me enter you." With every "because," his hand waded through another layer of petticoats.

At last he groaned in frustration and dropped to his knees. "But there is no way to do that easily, so . . ." He pulled her skirts up and away and said, "Take your skirts in your hands, Rose, and lift them for me. High, as high as you can."

She complied, feeling the draft on her bare legs as she inched her skirts higher. Peter clasped his hands around her knees, but instead of using his hands, as she had expected, he began to kiss her knees.

It tickled and she almost giggled, but he muttered "Higher, Rose," in such a strained voice that she kept lifting and then, to her surprise, she felt his lips on her thighs. As her skirts came higher, so did Peter's mouth, until she stood, trembling, her skirts nearly at her waist, and felt Peter's mouth graze the soft nest at the juncture of her thighs.

"Lean back and brace your feet, Rose," he ordered, still in that thrillingly rough voice. She did, and he moved his hands from her knees to hold her hips, and then his clever tongue was suddenly against her there, and she would have fallen if he hadn't been holding her up. He pushed her trembling legs apart, and she thought she would melt against the wall.

Peter's tongue evoked such wild sensations that Rose did not know how her heart stayed in her chest. She had the absurd desire to touch her own breasts, just to feel hands on them, because how could this paradise of feeling exist alone without Peter's kisses on her lips and his hands on her body?

But transfixed by pleasure, she continued to hold up her skirts, while Peter slowly brought one hand in from her hips to trace down the passage he had opened. Then while his tongue stayed at the topmost point of pleasure, he insinuated one finger, then two, into her.

Small cries began to bubble up from her throat without any conscious volition. "Hush, Rose," Peter's voice came thickly. "Stand still, and be still." So the pleasure went on and on while she fought the trembling that consumed her. Peter wouldn't even let her scream when she climaxed, just kept pulsating into her while his voice warned her, low and rough, to stay quiet and of the dangers that discovery would bring. He put his thumb against that most sensitive flesh while he laid his flushed cheeks along her thighs and blew his hot breath against her, and she came again almost immediately.

When he at last stood up, she all but collapsed into his arms. Somewhere in her pleasure-mazed brain, she realized he was shaking too, and then she found the two of them in their slick silks sliding down the wall, until they sat on the floor in each other's arms, gasping for breath.

Peter was unsatisfied, though, she saw at once, because the tight fit of his breeches left no doubt of his state. And she was suddenly aware of how much pleasure he had given her without taking his own. Without even thinking about it, she bent over him, releasing his buttons and reaching into his smallclothes.

Peter had his eyes closed and his head tilted back against the silk-clad wall, attempting to strangle his unslaked desire so they could get up and go on with life, as if they hadn't just blown all semblance of it to kingdom come, when he felt her busy hands.

"Rose, what are you doing?" he asked, but made no attempt to push her hands away.

"I have done nothing but take, Peter. I want to give pleasure to you now," she murmured.

"You could start with taking off your gloves," he said, and they both laughed weakly at the spectacle of what they had been doing in the powder room while she still had on her proper lady's gloves.

She touched him, smoothing up his hard length with her gloved hands, and he had to acknowledge that there was a certain guilty pleasure in that sensation, the contrast between the elegance of her attire and the rawness of his need, but the feel of her own warm, capable hands was what he really wanted, and she quickly complied.

It took every ounce of self-control he possessed not to destroy her coiffure when her head bent over his lap and she took him into her mouth. He wanted to bury his hands in her hair and wrap those russet strands around them both, but they'd never explain their way out of the mess that would make of her hair, so he kept his hands clenched at his sides while encouraging her to wreak the greatest havoc with his self-control that he had ever allowed a woman.

And when it broke, he didn't even have the discipline to pull her away from him. All he could do was softly call her name while she took care of his needs in a fashion he would never have imagined any woman would. Ah, his wild, unconventional Rose. How had he thought he could live without her? Her generosity astonished him.

Afterward, he pulled her up to rest her head against his shoulder, while their breathing returned to normal, and they helped each other rearrange their clothing. Fortunately, the walls still held them up, because he would wager that she felt no steadier than he.

Everything seemed to have returned to normalcy, until he helped her to stand, his arms supporting her waist. And the touch and scent of her filled him again as if what had just transpired had never been. He pulled her tight against him and took her mouth. She opened for him and he plundered her mouth again, as if they had not begun this interlude in exactly the same way.

"Despite all that has just happened, I still want you beneath me, Rose, and me inside you."

"As do I," she admitted in a low, sultry voice.

Then, blessedly, the patent absurdity of carrying out what they both still wanted, here and now, came to the fore, as it apparently did for Rose, too, because they quietly laughed themselves breathless. Otherwise, they could only have seethed with frustration. They had nowhere to go, nowhere to be together, and they had to get out of the powder room before they were spotted and their presence missed. Rose explained how little time it took to ruin a reputation.

"Do you want yours ruined, Rose?" he asked, remembering what Lady Dalby had said, his fingertip running over her sweetly swollen lips.

Her body swayed irresistibly toward his for a moment before she pulled away from him. Disappointment marked every line of her body. "Is that all you want, Peter?" His senses were still awash with their passion. He didn't know what to say, wasn't prepared to go on, not yet, not so suddenly.

She straightened, picked up her reticule from the floor, and without a backward look, she slipped away from him, out a door against the far wall he hadn't known was there. After looking in the mirror to ascertain that his hair and cravat were still in reasonable order—just enough to get him out the main door and back into the hall—although his mind screamed that he had to breathe fresh night air *now*—he left the powder room, and the house, and strode away into the London night. Let Lady Dalby fend for herself and make excuses to their hostess.

As he had done in Virginia, he had made love to Rose without a thought for the consequences. The emotional consequences, that is—he hardly felt like congratulating himself for remembering, *in extremis*, about the physical ones. He almost wished there *had* been the possibility of her becoming pregnant. Then he would have his choices made for him.

Peter shook his head, appreciating the sting of the cool May night that was so much chillier than at home, against his cheeks. These English homes were like hothouses with too many flowers, too many candles, too many unwashed bodies covered in too much scent. No, getting Rose pregnant would have been the coward's way out.

Oh, he would have married Rose without blinking if he'd thought, even for a moment, that she might be carrying his child. But that would not have answered the question of whether he loved her, or just couldn't live without her. Sadly, they were not necessarily the same thing.

" 'Tis time to arrange the auction," Bertram said at breakfast the next morning.

"You're going to sell me? I'm not a slave, Bertram. I don't care what barbarities you learned to like in India."

"Hush, Rose, I don't mean you." He looked at her with exaggerated speculation as if hoping she would smile at the absurdity, but after all that had happened to her recently, Rose didn't find anything amusing about it. She now believed Bertram was capable of just about anything.

"No. I mean Willow Oaks, of course."

"That's not part of my dowry?"

"No. I'm trying to get by with as little dowry as possible."

"Of course."

"Now, don't take umbrage, Rose. As a peer's daughter and one reasonably attractive, even if not fashionably so, you have been much sought after this season. But the quickest way to raise the blunt to pay off Ralph's creditors—who are now mine, as you well know—is to sell the plantation."

"What about hiring someone to look after it, especially if they could make it more profitable?"

Bertram tried not to look interested. "Go on."

"Haven't you wondered why Peter Walters came here?"

"Not for you, I take it, since he hasn't called here." That hurt, but she couldn't let Bertram see that it had.

"I think he wants Willow Oaks," she said, managing to find her voice. If this was the only way to save her beloved plantation, so be it. She'd vowed not to give Peter what he wanted, but when faced with the choice of seeing it disappear from her own control, she'd still rather it went to someone who would look after it properly like Peter. An absentee landlord from England or someone like Bertram, who thought only of profit, would tear out all her flowers to plant tobacco instead.

"Does he? I'd wondered why he was hanging about. Since he hasn't called on us, I'd assumed it was some business of his family's."

"And if he wants to buy it?" Rose held her breath but tried to seem casual by buttering her toast.

"If he has the ready, then he's as welcome to bid as any other gentleman present."

"Why not just sell me to him along with the plantation?"

"I have no problem with that. If he has enough blunt, he can have you too." He smiled as if bestowing a favor on her. Rose seethed.

"Oh no," their mother put in, "she needs to wed a Marquess or at least an Earl. I won't have our position in society jeopardized."

Bertram grimaced. "That's right, Mother, you want it all, don't you? Money and position."

"Well, of all the ungrateful children. I hadn't expected it to be you, Bertram. I didn't think you were like your shameless sister. Don't tell me you don't want the same things as I do. You aren't fooling anyone." Fanny then swept out of the room, offended, in a dramatic whoosh of muslin.

Bertram leaned over and tried to pat Rose's hand. "Rose, just ignore Mama. Our position in society is secure. At least I intend to keep it that way. So far, news of our debts has not traveled outside a small circle of banks and creditors. If I get enough cash from the sale of Willow Oaks to pay off Ralph's debts, you can marry whomever you like. But if the American is here to bid for the land, I hardly think he wants you too."

Rose hated to admit it, but she feared he might be right. Peter had said he was here for her, but she was too afraid to believe him. When she had challenged him, he hadn't replied—he'd kissed her. Soon, she and Peter weren't talking at all. Impulsively, she had welcomed his touch, let him

renew their liaison, and nothing had been resolved
between them.

Later, she found that she had no desire to go
out that evening. She did not think she could even
look Peter in the face after last night, although the
aftermath of that encounter had left her feeling
strangely sated . . . and yet unsatisfied. Remembering the hot excitement of the night brought a flush
to her body—that was the satiety. But she also
wanted his possession, and even a part of her that
was not wholly physical felt the ache, the ache of
her desire for Peter to have claimed her wholly as
his.

Yet Bertram's words remained with her all day
and into the night. That night she dreamed she
was on the block for sale, along with the Willow
Oaks house, its lands, livestock, and property. She
stood, while on other pedestals around her, were
miniature models of the house, the orchards—
grown tall and lush in her dream, the dock Peter
had built, even the fields of flowers. Peter was
among the bidders who crowded the foot of the
dais where she stood on display. But he repeatedly
ignored her, bidding instead for the dock, the
house, the orchards, even the horses and stables.
She might as well not have existed for all the attention he paid her.

Rose awoke in the night, shaking. If she could
not have Willow Oaks, if Peter did not want her,
what was left of her and her desire for independence? To be a spinster in her mother's house or
in Bertram's, should his wife even allow a maiden
sister to live with them—oh, the humiliation. Living alone in those circumstances was not at all

comparable to her dream of an independent life
in Virginia.

If her fate was reduced to her mother's house
or Bertram's, then she had better make the best
match she could. When morning came, Rose
picked up the invitations that lay on the silver salver
in the entrance hall, and began to really look at
them. This time she did not ask Eunice to find out
if Peter would be at any of them. She did not want
to know.

Chapter Nineteen

She's beautiful and therefore to be woo'd;
She is woman, therefore to be loved.
—William Shakespeare, *King Henry VI*,
Part I, 1589–90

"Why has Rose suddenly taken an interest in the social whirl?" Fanny asked Bertram in the ballroom at the next soiree they attended. "Surely she doesn't agree with me? I've given up hoping she would ever be understanding or obedient."

Bertram, who had noticed a certain disheveled look about Rose the night of the Rotherford ball when she'd taken the carriage home early, had his own suspicions, but chose to keep them to himself.

"I do believe you're right, Mother. Perhaps

someone has caught her eye. Whatever the reason," he sighed, trying to sound bored, "she's easier to deal with when she's participating."

Fanny nodded, then left in a rustle of silks and
feathers to play her usual game of superiority with
the other ladies of her class. Bertram suspected
there had been an encounter between Rose and
her erstwhile swain the other night, and that it had
not gone well. Perhaps that was all to the good.
Rose seemed to have taken his words about the
American's presence here to heart. She looked a
bit despondent, though he'd not been trying to be
cruel when he'd said what he did.

And sure enough, the American had responded
to the discreet invitations he had sent out about
the auction of Willow Oaks. He'd sent a note over
to Lady Dalby's and received a written card from
the American in reply. He hadn't had the heart to
tell Rose that his suspicions had been correct. If
she had now decided to play the marital game, and
had begun to concern herself with finding a match
for her own reasons, then all the better. As he'd
told her, he did want her to have some happiness,
if possible.

He himself had managed to escape the toxic
presence of their mother, and realized finally, that
underneath his suavity, his brother Ralph had been
nearly as poisonous. Luckily, Bertram had found
a life of his own and developed the confidence
that went with it. Rose had tried to do the same
in America. A pity it was that she hadn't been born
male; he could have left her alone in that case.

Now that Rose seemed to have become more
compliant, he could concentrate on his own marital prospects. He might wait until next year, when

his financial situation looked better, but if some lovely piqued his interest tonight, he could always pursue it. Bertram strolled off to the billiards table, reflecting with satisfaction that life was good. And also, he was certain, it was going to get better.

Rose had rarely been so miserable in her life. The Duke of Devonbury was attentive, charming, and a good conversationalist. He was nearly forty and his wife had died in childbirth with their second child, but the Marquess of Chilters had been sixty and had drooled even before his stroke.

He appeared to be willing to slay dragons for her, though, because he became protective when she stiffened upon seeing Peter heading their way.

"Is this American someone you do not wish to speak to, Lady Rose?" he asked.

"You are most kind, Your Grace," Rose answered, "but no, he has not bothered me. I knew him in . . . ah, when I was . . ." She stopped suddenly, remembering Bertram's warnings against revealing where she had been.

"Ah, that is, I met him recently. The Countess of Dalby, you know, she is his sponsor . . . she, ah . . ." Rose searched her imagination frantically. What could she say that wouldn't sound suspicious?

"The plantation where we used to live in Virginia Colony, before the war. Well, you see, Lady Dalby's son is married to Master Walters's sister."

"Ah yes," he smiled, "the American Earl. Most unusual."

He turned to shake hands just as Peter arrived at her side. Devonbury's friendliness seemed to soothe any incipient violence in Peter, although

Rose knew from the storm-cloud green of his eyes that he might welcome an excuse to fight. If the Duke had shown her the least signs of overt affection, she'd no doubt that Peter might have started a brawl in this very ballroom.

Rose looked around while the men exchanged strained pleasantries, wondering why Peter's keeper, Lady Dalby, wasn't around to put a stop to any uncivil behavior on Peter's part. She assumed that Adam must have sent Peter to his mother to make sure he passed muster long enough in society for him to bid for Willow Oaks.

Why he didn't just conduct business with Bertram, she had no idea. Why bother showing up for these society events that he had to hate?

"I say, my dear, did you hear the question?" Devonbury was asking her.

"No, I'm sorry. What is it?"

Peter's voice interrupted. "I asked you to dance, Lady Rose."

She stared at him, disbelieving. "Really?" was all she could manage to say. She felt the blush starting at the neckline of her low-cut gown, felt it travel to her face. Fortunately, Peter had the grace to look abashed, too, although he'd planted his feet in such a way that Rose thought he would finish this on sheer bravado.

Mutely, she held out the dance card that was affixed to her wrist with ribbon. There were no spaces on it. Peter opened his mouth, looked like he wanted to say something, then bit off whatever it was under the careful scrutiny of Devonbury's gaze.

"My dear, 'tis time for dinner," Devonbury said jovially from beside her. "I believe you agreed to let me escort you. Shall we go?" He smiled at Peter, who had not yet looked away from Rose.

"Lady Dalby is just there, Master Walters," he said helpfully, gesturing in the direction of Adam's mother.

Then Devonbury tucked Rose's hand through the crook of his arm and took them away from Peter.

Peter endured a lecture from Lady Dalby that night about approaching a lady before she had left the dance floor and was still with her current partner. He hardly heard her. His hands itched to do something, especially since Devonbury had not afforded him with an opportunity to break his straight aristocratic nose. Peter was not a violent man by nature—war had taken care of that—but his frustration at the situation with Rose had left him feeling so out of sorts that a punch or two might have relieved his feelings.

He smiled with no great humor. Wouldn't the old lady have had a fit if there had been violence at such a high-flown society gathering? Given the virulence of her dislike for Lady Lansdale, she might even have welcomed a brouhaha that reflected poorly upon her rival, but punching Devonbury would only have embarrassed Rose and had himself barred from any future ballrooms. Then he really would have received the rough side of the old virago's tongue.

Until he'd ascertained how and why Rose had returned to England, he didn't even have the satisfying task of rearranging her brother Bertram's face. There had been so little talk of where Rose had been—absolutely none, in fact—that Lady Dalby believed Rose had been forbidden to discuss it.

Peter knew how matters stood, how little action he could take, all right; he just didn't have to like it. He hated the enforced idleness, and Lansdale's auction was still several days off. He could do nothing until then, and after the rebuff tonight, he knew he'd get nowhere with Rose until he could get her alone so they could talk. Talk, he reminded himself. Something he should have done the other night.

As he'd confessed to Adam, that was a difficult task around Rose. He wanted her so badly when he was with her that it clouded his judgment. Of course, Rose hadn't really asked him any questions either, other than to doubt that he had come here for her. With Willow Oaks up for sale now, was she right? If he couldn't have her, would he buy the plantation and sail back to Virginia without her?

How could he show her how much he cared? Remembering how Adam won Lily over after their argument, he wondered where in London he could get Virginia flowers.

"Go to bed, Peter, or find something else to do with yourself," Lady Dalby's sharp voice interrupted his speculations. "You have a bad case of the fidgets and watching you will not improve my digestion, I assure you."

Find something to do with yourself. Wooing Rose. Suddenly he had an idea. Timons could help him.

Rising, he bowed to Lady Dalby. He suspected she had these late-evening chats with him just so she could have an excuse to drink a little brandy, since it wasn't a usual beverage for a woman. Not that there was anything usual about Adam's mother. Surprising her, he bent over her where she sat stiffly in her corset and bussed her cheek.

He didn't even hear her spluttering as he left the sitting room of her town house, suddenly more cheered than he had been in weeks. He whistled for Timons as he bounded up the stairs. Adam had wooed Lily his way. He would woo Rose in his own fashion.

The first gift arrived the next day. Rose had received gifts from her suitors before. Occasionally she had received several bouquets of flowers on one day. But none of them were as beautiful as the flowers she had begun to grow in Virginia. Many of them would be in full bloom by now, and she had only her imagination to picture them now. But even the best of the flowers she had planted last year could not begin to compare, in her estimation, to the flowers Lily had so carefully bred, cross-bred, and nurtured at Oak Grove for so long.

Her mother fussed over the bouquets that arrived at the house, and indeed took many of them off to her own rooms. Rose cared little. Each glance only reminded her of the flowers she no longer had and the life she no longer led.

But when the first package was delivered, her interest perked up. Instead of flowers or bonbons, the package held a small piece of wood about three inches in diameter and about half an inch thick. It was oddly shaped at the edges, and appeared to have been rounded off, rather than cut. On one side there was a carving. The wood was closely grained and held a high sheen as if it had been carefully polished.

No card or note accompanied the gift. Questioning the maid who had answered the door yielded nothing, except that a boy who looked rather too much like a street urchin for the neighborhood's tastes had dropped off the unmarked package. He had said only that it was for a "Lady Rose."

Rose was not entirely sure what the carving contained, except it looked like a flower or plant. Then she turned it over to look at its other surface, where it appeared that the word "myrtle" had been carved.

What did it mean? She had no idea. Who was it from? She didn't know that either. She didn't know anyone who carved. Carvers in London generally concentrated on stone and marble. She wasn't even sure what this was supposed to be.

Still, she kept it, and enjoyed its smooth feel and texture.

Then, the next day, another one arrived. The plant that covered one side had heavy, nodding clusters of flowers. She thought she recognized the flower as mimosa, but the word "acacia" was engraved on the back. She was going to have to consult a horticultural book of some kind, because she didn't know the Latin names for plants.

At home, although it wrenched her heart, she continued to help Bertram draw up a complete picture of Oak Grove. She sketched the big house, the dependencies out back, and the flowing James River as it looked from her room upstairs. As she filled in the sketch with watercolors, she painted the flowers in her knot garden around the gazebo she had always hoped to have built in its center. It stood white and gleaming like the one at Oak Grove, dogwoods waving their delicate white tracery above it, while colorful flowers bloomed in profusion around its painted wooden slats.

Every so often she wiped away a tear. Bertram might only see crops and profits, but she saw beauty and sunlight and flowing water. Her heart would always belong at Willow Oaks, no matter who owned it.

A week later, Rose sat in her sitting room, a small pile of heavy books around her. Several more pieces of carved and polished wood had arrived wrapped in pieces of colored tissue and cloth. She had identified some of them, but not all. The third piece to arrive, however, had been easy to identify without the books she had borrowed from a peer in the Royal Horticultural Society.

She had recognized the ranunculus with its round head of tightly circled petals, because it was one of the most popular flowers in England, and extremely fashionable. And "ranunculus" was what was carved on the back. Was one of her admirers trying to find a different way to send her flowers?

The Duke of Devonbury had paid her the most attention—or at any rate, the least obnoxious attention—since this whole season business had begun. But she didn't know him that well, and she hardly saw this simple, probably handmade, little gift as his type of offering. He had sent large bouquets of florists' flowers after balls at which they had danced together. But he'd never said anything about these wooden tiles or whatever they were.

Bertram pronounced himself pleased with her watercolors, and said he would use them at the meeting with the prospective buyers. Rose held on to her pieces of wood and pondered their meaning.

The Duke of Devonbury was preparing to make an offer for her, Bertram said, but he had no interest in Willow Oaks. Rose could detect nothing in Devonbury's demeanor that indicated he had sent her the unusual gifts. When she thanked him for his flowers, he seemed pleased, and that was all.

Although she enjoyed dancing with him, she had no interest in him as a man. She told herself that nevertheless he was her best chance for any semblance of a life she could tolerate in England. Lord Robert, Duke of Devonbury, was not horrible, wicked, cruel, or even doddering. He was interested in the New World, treated her as an individual who had a brain, and after coming to know and love Lily and Adam's children, she was not put off by the prospect of being a stepmother to two children.

The problem was that she did not love him and she did not want to marry him. The only man who had ever fired her senses and claimed her heart was Peter Walters. That had not changed. She could not imagine it changing. Was it Peter's fault that he didn't want her heart?

On the seventh day since the little wooden pieces began arriving, a seventh piece and an empty round frame made of the same wood arrived together. The frame had a beveled edge cut into the center, into which the pieces fit.

Rose had given up trying to find the boy who delivered them. As if to avoid detection, they now came at different times of the day, sometimes even at night, when no one was around.

She had finally figured out that the pieces fit together as if they were a kind of puzzle. The pieces did not interlock, but when placed side by side in the correct way, with certain curves against certain indentations, it became apparent that the carvings fit together and that the overall ensemble was meant to represent a bouquet. That must be why the flowers were hard to distinguish one from another, if they all made up part of the same bouquet. They were obviously carved with skill.

Using the frame, she had laid the pieces together to form part of a bouquet, then with the help of the books, had identified the flowers that were represented. She was puzzled after that, because the flowers included an herb—rosemary—and several of them did not bloom at the same time. So they could not be meant to represent a real bouquet.

What was the point? Rose pondered their mystery when she had time, which was not often. Most of her time was divided between helping Bertram collect and collate as much information as possible on Willow Oaks and worrying about the outcome of the auction. Any remaining time was spent deciding whether Lord Devonbury was the best match she could make, and whether she could bring herself to actually marry anyone, even one so apparently kind as Robert. Bertram had appeared kind at times, too, especially when they were in public— and look what he'd proved to be capable of doing.

Magnolia, evergreen, yew, and rosemary. These were hardly traditional constituent parts of a bouquet. Yew meant sorrow, she recalled. She'd planted it in her own knot garden, the one that expressed her secret feelings about Peter.

Then realization dawned. Of course, she had it. Why had it taken her so long to understand? This wasn't a traditional bouquet; it was symbolic.

For a moment, Rose had a wild, brief flare of hope that someone had come to rescue her. Could Lily be here? Then she reminded herself that Lily had been nearly eight months pregnant in May. Since it was nearly July, perhaps she had already even had the baby. Sadness overwhelmed Rose that she wouldn't be there for the birth. It was impossible for Lily to have come.

Could Peter have sent these "flowers"? If he had, then what on earth did they mean? He had never tried to pay a call on her, but she realized that even Bertram, who professed not to care about her past relationship with Peter, was careful that they saw each other only in public. Her mother would probably never let Peter in the door had he tried to call on her.

As for the times she did see him out in public, she was increasingly with Robert, Lord Devonbury. Peter didn't look happy, but Lady Dalby must have told him that if he caused a scene, he'd be thrown out and unable to return to any society affairs. Rose didn't know what she wanted, but she didn't want any time alone with Peter, as much as her body yearned for it, until she knew what she was going to do about her heart. Robert probably represented her best chance within society for a decent marriage.

Still, Peter must be trying to tell her something, if he were the author of these little gifts. And then, just a day before the auction, a piece came that fit in the center, not against the sides of the frame. It was a perfect oval, a round piece that all the

others she received to date touched in part. The
bold iris, which meant message, was that smooth
center piece.

And with that confirmation that she was on the
right track, she applied herself to the horticultural
texts and illustrations even more closely. She
wished she remembered more of Lily's vocabulary,
but of course she didn't have it with her. The flowers in the bouquet obviously held specific meanings. She had eleven pieces now, twelve if you
counted the center roundel. She had rosemary and
ranunculus and a single rose. There were several
evergreen types: yew, magnolia, evergreen foliage,
and spindle, whose berries were deciduous but
whose foliage was everlasting. There was orange
blossom and safflower and myrtle. Yet even when
she had placed everything inside the frame's rim,
the pieces still did not complete the picture. Two
pieces, the last remaining pieces of the puzzle, were
missing.

Chapter Twenty

Thus to persist
In doing wrong extenuates not wrong,
But makes it much more heavy.
> —William Shakespeare
> *Troilus and Cressida*, Act II, 1602

The day of the auction dawned clear and bright, one of those rare beautiful and perfect days of an English summer, when skies were cloudless and temperatures were beautifully warm, neither humid nor sultry. All it did was remind Rose of Virginia. This July weather in London was what Virginia experienced in May. She remembered from her arrival last August how humid Virginia could be, but breezes off the river usually kept the sweating heat away from those within its radius.

Bertram did not want her to attend; her mother certainly did not plan to, but Rose had insisted. "Who else knows Willow Oaks as well as I do, Bertram?" she had asked. "Do you know what price a crop of tobacco usually fetches? And I am certain you have no idea what the flowers are worth."

He had glowered, but she pressed on. "Their worth varies depending on the popularity of the flower. Ranunculus, for instance, command extremely high prices. And the price of tulips is based almost exclusively on the color, its striping, and whether the bulb is capable of reproducing that striping."

Finally, Bertram had grunted, then assented. Rose didn't know whether to be elated or despondent. She was going to attend the event that would put an end to every dream she had ever had.

Rose had dressed carefully in a morning gown of green sateen with the new slightly higher waist and less fullness in the petticoats. She let Eunice dress her hair, trying to ignore the butterflies in her stomach and Eunice's incessant chattering.

"Miss Rose, do you think Master Peter will be able to buy Willow Oaks? Will we be going back if he does? Oh, what do you think will happen?"

Finally, Eunice's questions pierced Rose's veil of self-absorption, but she felt so weary, she could not even reprimand Eunice for her chatter. "What I think will happen, Eunice, and what I wish would happen, are two totally different things. I fear that some British lordling who wants to seek a fortune in America will buy the place and ruin it by planting all the fields with nothing but tobacco. And that is probably a good outcome.''

Rose's hand rose to cup the base of her neck, where a tension headache was building, but Eunice squealed suddenly.

"What?" Rose cried, startled, dropping her hand.

"Sorry, Miss Rose, I just didn't want you to risk touching this 'ere hot hair iron.''

Eunice slid the hot iron tube out of Rose's hair carefully, letting the ringlets tumble before pulling them up to the back of Rose's head. "What would be a bad out . . . out . . . whatever you said?" she asked.

"A bad outcome, or ending, from my point of view, would be an absentee landlord who buys the place and lets it fall apart, exploiting the land for whatever it will yield in the short term and not caring if it doesn't last. Or it could be someone who hires a harsh overseer, who brings in slaves and works them too hard.''

"I—I see, Miss Rose," Eunice said hastily. Eunice probably wanted to hear no more of the depressing recitation than she did herself. "Will you be wearing the bonnet with this today?"

"No, the auction will be indoors and 'tis too lovely a day to hide one's face under a bonnet.'' Her skin now had all the fashionable pallor of any young English miss. Rose wondered if Peter had noticed. She also marveled that his skin seemed to retain its healthy golden color even here. He probably rode in Hyde Park, perhaps even out of town, while she had been hiding indoors for so long, a combination of restraint and constraint, that sometimes she felt as if she would fade away altogether.

Well, her future would be decided today, one way or the other. Willow Oaks would be sold, and she would have to choose a husband. The season would be ending soon. Parliament would adjourn, and those remaining in town until the very end of its session would then repair to the fresher, cooler air of their country houses and family seats.

Rose would have to accept an offer for her hand, the one everyone expected from Devonbury. At least this season would end differently from her others. The part of her that still carried a tiny seed of long-suppressed feminine vanity was secretly pleased, but the part of her that loved Peter— which was all the rest of her—grieved that she would end up making the choice so many women of her class did.

Oh, it would be considered a good marriage. Even her mother would be pleased. So she would have a loveless marriage, but one that nevertheless fit all the usual requirements of her station. She supposed she should be grateful that she liked Devonbury and he seemed to like her. But once she belonged to him, what then?

"Stop fussing, Eunice," Rose said at length, aware that Eunice was attempting to draw side curls down to her cheeks and was pulling wisps of hair to curl around the nape of her neck.

"I'm not going to a ball. It looks lovely," she added hastily, so Eunice's feelings weren't hurt, "but really, 'tis enough."

Rose declined the carriage, so Bertram had to accompany her. She thought she'd have a short stroll in peace, but Bertram feared to leave her alone even that long, it seemed.

"You don't need to accompany me. Surely you don't think someone will abduct me, Bertram?" she asked, with eyes wide with pretended innocence.

"Oh, stop being shrewish, Rose," Bertram grumbled. "I did not feel like walking today."

"Too much to drink at your club? Were you betting on Willow Oaks's future sale?" She knew men entered all sorts of wagers into the books at places like White's and Boodles.

"Don't try my patience. I didn't have to allow you to attend, you know."

"Oh, I know," she said. His remark served as one more irritating reminder of how little influence she had over her own life. Since baiting Bertram was only depressing her, she remained quiet for the rest of the walk.

Bertram had wanted to use a room at White's but Rose would have not have been permitted entrance there, so he had asked the land agent managing the sale to let a private dining room in a respectable inn. Since the auction was by invitation only, he wasn't worried about rough types showing up, but he had hired the Bow Street Runners as lookouts anyway.

When Rose entered the room on Bertram's arm, she saw her watercolors placed around the room. The familiar sight of Willow Oaks almost made her cry, but she handed her pelisse to a servant and steeled herself against the urge. If this was difficult, she chided herself, just how was she going to feel when she saw Peter? She hadn't seen him in more than a week—since the night she'd shown him her dance card—but truth be told, she had also tried hard not to look for him.

She had passively let Devonbury squire her around most evenings, so that fewer and fewer men approached. She'd had a feeling that, once rebuffed, Peter wouldn't try again. Whether she'd been right, or whether he had simply stopped coming as the true object of his trip grew near, she didn't know, and didn't care to work out. But he would be here, that much she knew, and she had to be prepared to face him.

There were at least half a dozen men present, she saw. Bertram had left her at the back of the room, within sight and reach of the Bow Street Runner who guarded the door to the salon. She sat quietly in back, trying to identify the men and looking for Peter, though she had not yet spotted him. She was sure she would have no trouble recognizing him, for who else had such broad shoulders, such commanding height, or such richly colored hair, even if he were wearing a hat?

She did not spot her own suitor, and she hardly knew whether to be relieved at that or not. She had never raised Willow Oaks with Devonbury, although he had to know of the sale, because Bertram mentioned it frequently. Rose had even considered whether to tell Robert of her interest, but that would raise so many questions that the Duke would inevitably refer to their conversation while with Bertram, and then the fat would be in the fire. She had no hope that a Duke would emigrate to America anyway.

* * *

Peter was the last man to enter the room, and
even then he'd had to show the invitation sent to
Lady Dalby's house in order to get in. He'd heard
something of the Bow Street Runners, and while
they were principally investigators, they also had a
reputation for efficiency. The one stationed in
front of the inn and the one at the salon door
inside were certainly no fools. The one at the door
had held on to his card, taken it up to Bertram,
and waited for a nod from Rose's brother before
returning to admit him.

He'd also evidently received some other order,
because Peter saw Rose the minute he stepped
through the door. The Bow Street Runner, however, practically hustled him up the aisle of chairs
to a seat well away from hers. One word—
"Don't"—was whispered into his ear by the burly
watchdog, and a hand firmly pressed him into his
seat.

Peter was about to disregard the order when he
and Bertram locked gazes with each other. "Don't
look back," Bertram mouthed, his brown gaze narrowed to Peter exclusively. There was no mistaking
who was being addressed. The last thing Peter
wanted was to do anything to jeopardize Rose's
position or have her sent from the room, so he
gave a barely perceptible nod and restrained the
urge to turn his head.

His thoughts flew fast and furious in his head,
however. Had Rose received what he'd sent her?
Did she understand? At some point during the
opening pleasantries he became convinced that
she knew he was there, because the back of his
neck tingled and the fine hairs there stood on end.
She had to have recognized him. He was sure she

was looking at him. Damn all this British subterfuge and subtlety. He'd had about as much of society as he could stand. He'd hated the balls, but the only thing worse than attending them was not attending them. So he had continued to come, but had seen her every time on Devonbury's arm. He'd seethed, but Lady Dalby's cutting remarks stopped him from making a fool of himself.

Not that he would have minded a good brawl, not at all. But the old dragon reminded him that Rose would be the one embarrassed, Rose would be the one gossiped about, and while he could let the world hang and not give a damn if he was the subject of gossip, he would not, could not, harm Rose's reputation.

For all his selfishness, the self-pity and self-centeredness he'd been immersed in, he knew that if Rose had chosen this life, he had no right to ruin it for her. Certainly not when he had told her she belonged here, not after he had told her so many times to go home. If she had come back here on her own, or if she had at some point changed her mind, even if her brother had coerced her to return at first, he could not spoil the life she had remade.

He didn't think she had chosen this, but he did not know for certain. She did not seem to be in love with Lord Devonbury and yet the gossips had them betrothed in a matter of days, according to Lady Dalby. Somehow Rose had learned the society art of concealing her emotions, and that he found perhaps the saddest thing of all. He was so accustomed to Rose's honesty, her candor, to seeing what she felt so plain upon her face.

Once she had loved him. Now, he no longer

knew. He had only to remember the way she'd
looked at him when they had made love at Willow
Oaks. Then he compared that look, indelible in
his memory, with the way she looked at him now,
and the glances he had seen her give Devonbury.
Polite, careful. Her glances were decorum itself,
but her heart was cached somewhere deep beneath.

Even the night of their encounter in the powder
room at Lady Rotherford's, he had seen her passion stamped upon her face, and known that he
had been the first—and by God, he swore he'd be
the last—man ever to see it. Sweet God, what a
fool he'd been. There was nothing between her
and Devonbury, just as she'd said. Devonbury
might wish it, and was performing the proper courtship rituals, but even if his heart was in it, Rose's
was not. Although that was hardly a triumph, since
she was not really speaking to him, it told him
something valuable, something that he should have
known long ago.

Rose loved him. And even if she'd been on this
fellow's arm, she had never let him love her. He
blessed her loyalty. That was something Joanna had
never had.

If it was the last thing he did in England—and
it might very well be, because her answer would
send him home one way or the other—he would
see her emotions engaged and worn upon her
sweet, expressive face once more.

Another man sat down beside him. He knew
without looking who it was. He turned to Adam's
barrister, who was seated by his side. "Why don't
we stop this farce now?" Peter asked in a low voice.

Cranwell put a restraining hand on his arm.

"Patience, Master Walters. We have to be certain that the document you have is the latest one extant. It may not be, even though it was written not long before the Earl of Lansdale's death. Do not forget that the first son, Ralph, inherited. He was the 10th Earl for five months before his dissolute ways ended his sorry life."

Cranwell sniffed in disdain, but glanced around surreptitiously before continuing in a low voice. "We have no way of knowing what the 10th Earl might have done with his father's papers or how many instructions he might have superseded or overturned."

"Could he have canceled . . . ?" Peter began in a harsh whisper.

"Of course he could have. He was the Earl. He did not have to respect his father's wishes if the transaction had not been concluded. He could have withdrawn the contract before it was signed by both parties. But since we can argue intent, and because Lady Rose will support you, our case is—"

"Half a moment, Cranwell. I do not know that Lady Rose will support me."

"I thought you and she were to be betrothed," he said, surprise lifting his sparse eyebrows almost to the line of his bagwig. Peter hadn't told Cranwell any further details of what had transpired between him and Rose, although he was sure Lady Dalby knew, or had guessed, everything. But she also didn't know about the contract. Peter simply couldn't trust her not to spill her news when her rival Fanny Fairchild was around, and Cranwell had concurred.

The Dowager Countess of Dalby had mellowed somewhat late in life, but there were many aspects of Adam's legal affairs she did not know about. Adam's man had confided this to Peter, and that Adam had willed it so. She did not know, for instance, that Cranwell had prevailed on colleagues in the Temple to research the matter of the papers Cranwell now had safely tucked in the pocket of his old-fashioned frock coat.

"I hope that we will be betrothed," Peter continued, "but the lady is not in my pocket."

"Then you had best be glad that these papers are in mine," Cranwell returned in his usual acerbic tone. "Even then you will need Lady Rose's assistance. I can't guarantee the legal outcome, should the present Earl challenge this, and we are unable to produce the actual contract. But the very fact that he is holding this auction suggests that he knows nothing of what his father did."

"He was in India during his father's final illness and death, and all throughout the period that his brother was heir. He probably knows very little of what went on."

"Then his barrister is not competent. Odd, since Coverdell is a man of some repute within the Temple."

"Rose told me that her brother fired the family's long-standing legal representation. The new Earl, Ralph, turned to a solicitor who abetted his wastrel life by joining him in his pastimes. When Ralph was killed in a duel over a married woman's honor, and 'twas known that the solicitor had stood as second, thus countenancing an illegal duel, he was ruined and forced to leave London. Didn't you know that?"

"No, I didn't," Cranwell said thoughtfully. "Lady Lansdale is cleverer—or richer—than I gave her credit for. Society knew that there had been a duel, although the lady's name was kept out of matters. The fact that she was married and that the family's legal counsel had been directly involved was marvelously hushed up, I must say, either through generous expenditure or the calling in of chits and the exertion of influence. She's not one to underestimate.''

They turned their attention to Bertram then, who began describing the property, its site along the James River, the dependencies, how many hectares of land it had, and so forth. Peter ignored most of it and concentrated on Rose's watercolors, for he had recognized her work immediately. He hoped Adam had finished the task he'd asked him to undertake in his absence, that Lily and her new child, who must have been born by now, were well, along with his nephews and niece. Most of all, he hoped that he would be returning with Rose and able to show her what he'd asked Adam to do for him in his absence.

Cranwell poked him in the side and Peter knew his attention had been wandering.

"What?" he asked.

"He's asking for sealed bids," the lawyer said.

"I thought 'twas an auction."

"There is such a thing as a silent auction, but there wasn't much need for everyone to come. Men of affairs could have been sent with the bids, in that case.''

Others spoke up, so Peter did not need to register an objection. Bertram consulted with his barrister, then raised a hand for silence.

"Very well. We will proceed as originally planned. I had thought to afford the gentlemen some privacy, but if everyone is comfortable with this procedure . . ."

"Acquit us, Lansdale," one man called out, a beefy man Peter recalled seeing at a few balls, but not one whose name he knew. "Ain't you ever bid on horseflesh at Tattersall's? This is no different, especially if your sister comes with the property."

"She doesn't. What are you implying?"

"Then what is she doing here?" the burly man asked and at least two other men seconded. Several craned their heads to look at Rose. So much for the breeding of these vaunted English aristocrats.

Rage filled Peter. He wanted to leap from his chair and pound them all into dust. Cranwell gripped his forearm and hissed, "Stay in your seat." He subsided reluctantly.

Bertram relaxed his posture with an effort and Peter saw him reaching for the lie. "My sister has a sentimental attachment to the place," he said airily. "She was born there, and was at a tender age when we returned to England before the late hostilities began. I indulged her wish to be present. And you may have noticed these lovely watercolors. My sister executed them."

"How up to date are they?" a man in a yellow striped coat called out.

"I have received reports from a land factor in the area, which Lady Rose has, ah, integrated with her memories. From the reports I have read, these are quite accurate."

"Where are the tobacco fields?" another man asked, his man of affairs whispering busily in his ear.

"Since my sister did not spend much time in the fields, she is most familiar with the land closest to the house. And since most of you have seen engravings of Virginia's fertile soil and its broad tobacco leaves stacked to the ceiling of warehouses, I doubt her delicate watercolors would add much to the business side of matters. Now, my man will give you a few more details, and then . . ."

At that moment, the rear door to the salon was pushed open and a youth entered. The Bow Street Runner burst in behind him, shouting, "You got no call to be here," whereupon all the men turned.

Cranwell gave a start. "That's my clerk," he said, his clipped accent making the word sound like "clark," but Peter knew what he meant.

"Unhand the lad," Cranwell said, rising. "He obviously has important news, or he would not have been sent here to seek me."

"Come here, Colin," he said. "What is it? Do you want to go out in the hall?"

"I am told, sir, that it affects this auction, so, no, sir, I must tell you here and now."

Chapter Twenty-one

Suspense in news is torture.
　　—John Milton, *Paradise Regained*, 1671

Every man in the room had now risen and was looking at them. Bertram appeared to be apoplectic and ready to throw them all out. "What is it, then?" Cranwell said.

"Sir, there has been a storm at Willow Oaks. I have a letter from Lord Dalby for you."

Bertram started toward them. "A storm, you say? What the devil kind of trick is this?"

"No trick, sir," the young man retorted.

Cranwell took the boy by one shoulder. "Remember that you work for me, Colin, and have no need to defend your appearance or your need to speak to anyone but me. Now, deliver your message, if you please."

"There is another message for him, sir, if he is the Earl's brother-in-law," Colin said, indicating Peter, who alone of them all had remained seated.

Peter jumped to his feet. "Does it concern my sister?" he asked, feeling the blood drain from his face. Just then, he became aware that Rose had risen from her seat at the back of the chamber and had come to the edge of those ringing the youth. Without thinking, Peter put out his hand to draw Rose to his side. She came at once, squeezing his hand tightly.

The young man's face cleared. "Oh, no problem there, sir. The Earl of Dalby says she came through splendidly, and you have another nephew." Peter put an arm around Rose's shoulders to hug her. They looked at each other with huge smiles on their faces, then recollected where they were. Peter would have held on, but Rose stepped back and he let her go.

"What about this storm?" Bertram broke in, impatient and ill-tempered.

"To me, Colin," Cranwell reminded the lad softly.

The boy turned his hazel gaze upon his employer and continued. "There has been a severe storm, perhaps a hurricane. The Earl of Dalby's property is in fair condition, but the water rose and drowned much of the new growth in the fields at Willow Oaks. Both the big houses are intact, as is the new dock, but the foundation for the greenhouse was swept away."

"Was anyone hurt?" Rose and Peter spoke simultaneously. They looked at each other and Peter knew her face mirrored his own concern. He felt the same shock of recognition between them that he had the first time he'd touched her. He also knew they were thinking the same thing: property damage could be repaired, but oh, so much more precious were the lives of those who lived there.

"Some livestock was lost, but no one was injured, the letter said."

"Thank you, Colin," Cranwell said. He accompanied the young man to the door, since Bertram looked like he wanted to threaten murder.

Three men were at the door already. "Your sale's off, Lansdale," they advised. Taking up their hats and walking sticks, they took their leave.

Several other men were not so categorical, however. Their muttered comments indicated they thought they had a chance at a real bargain now. No one had addressed Bertram.

Peter observed that Bertram was so incensed, his face had turned a dull beet red. His man of affairs whispered to him from one side, the barrister from the other. Bertram kept directing furious glances at Peter, but did not approach him. The remaining men clearly expected Lord Lansdale to say something in response to this extraordinary news.

"There can be no decisions made today," Bertram said at last. "Come back at the same time tomorrow afternoon and we will sort this out. The property is worth far more than this most recent news would have you believe. The loss of one season's crops detracts little from the plantation's overall worth."

Bertram's solicitor beckoned to Cranwell, who had come back into the room. As Bertram and his group, including Rose, left by the salon's side door, Peter and the other men filed out the back.

Expectations among the men were that the price would have to come down substantially, and one or two men facetiously congratulated Peter on his timing. He was asked how the news had happened to come to him, out of all those present, and he explained that his brother-in-law was the Earl of Dalby, owner of the neighboring property.

"Ah, you're just here to see what kind of neighbor you get, then," one man said. Peter did not answer, merely tipped his hat, and then strode off with Cranwell in the opposite direction from the others. There was nothing to be gained from revealing his intentions.

"What was all that about at the end?" Peter asked Cranwell.

"Lord Lansdale's man told me we were no longer welcome at the auction. His lordship wanted to accuse us of planting the news deliberately, but a runner arrived for him not long after my Colin with the same news."

The day's surprises were not over, however, because Colin, who stood down the street a little ways waiting for them to emerge, said they both needed to go back to the office with him.

"What do you need me for?" Peter asked.

"Sir, there is a packet that came for you with the news from the ship. It is in Lord Dalby's handwriting, and says it may be opened only by you."

Cranwell sighed. "Then you had best come with us, Master Walters."

"Fine," Peter said. He would only have gone out to ride in Hyde Park or found another of those lonely roads out of town. He hated this confining city life. He wrote letters to Lily nearly every day. He doubted Lily would see anything before he returned, because he expected to be home before anything sent on a ship could reach her.

After Peter emerged from Cranwell's office an hour later, he knew he had to see Rose this very night, no matter what the risk to her reputation. After the additional news he had just learned, he had to solidify his position with her and ascertain her true feelings. Because once tomorrow's events unfolded, he might never have another chance to know them.

Had she received his gift? Had she understood it? Even though they had been united in their concern for Oak Grove and its inhabitants, and all those at Willow Oaks, he had seen no spark of recognition in her eyes, no secret shared understanding of the messages he had sent her.

He hoped that neither Bertram nor her mother had been intercepting his gifts. He didn't think they would have come to her family's attention; he thought his offerings were quite innocuous. But now he had to know if they were getting through, because they were his last chance to woo Rose. The day's news had made that task all the more urgent. He hoped she had not accepted Lord Devonbury's suit.

If he'd thought smashing the man to a pulp would have helped, he would have gladly indulged himself there, but he saw no purpose in it. Devonbury wasn't a bad sort and perhaps he was what Rose wanted. After all, he knew how rare it was for a woman to marry for love.

He knew now beyond any shadow of a doubt that he was in love. Seeing her in Devonbury's arms had been enough to make him realize that he could never let another man have her, that he wanted to be the man whose arm escorted her, the man who would lay down his life for her. But what had made him really realize how much he loved her, that she was his soul, his heart, and the best part of himself, was her instant and shared concern at the fate of those on the plantations. She did regard Virginia as her home, Willow Oaks's people as her own, Oak Grove's family as her family. She was loyal, loyal to those she loved. He need never doubt that again.

He had been blind, and deaf, and dumb, and he had almost lost her.

If she didn't know what he had sent her, he would go tonight and make sure that she knew. He would tell her that he loved her beyond any ability to doubt.

Rose let Eunice brush her hair the hundred and fifty strokes she was usually too impatient to sit still for at night. She wasn't sure what to make of the news that had interrupted the auction today. If the price went down, did that make it easier for Peter to buy Willow Oaks? Or did it mean Bertram would wash his hands of the place, take the best price he could get, and not care what became of any of it?

Of course, she suspected that's what Bertram had intended anyway. He didn't really care to whom the plantation went, as long as he got the best price he thought he could possibly squeeze out of it. He'd looked such daggers at Peter, however, that she wondered if the intervention from the barrister's clerk had ruined any chances of Peter's being able to buy Willow Oaks.

"There, Miss Rose, it fair gleams now," Eunice said with pride.

"Thank you," Rose said tiredly. She was in the awkward state of being exhausted but also in no mood to go to bed. She hadn't been sleeping well lately; she doubted tonight would be any different. Worse, probably, because the anticipation that had eaten at her nerves last night was redoubled now with worry for the people suffering from the damage done by the storm. And Bertram still intended to dispense with the auction and the plantation tomorrow.

So she didn't feel much like going to bed, but she let Eunice turn down the counterpane and lay out her nightrail.

"Do you want some warm milk, Miss Rose?" Eunice asked, a little frown creasing her brow when she saw how listless her mistress looked.

"No, thank you. I'm not really hungry. Or thirsty," she amended.

"Well, you didn't eat none of your dinner either," Eunice muttered.

Rose realized she had not told Eunice the news. "I'm sorry I didn't tell you sooner," she concluded after telling her of the dramatic arrival of the news about the storm. She knew Eunice wanted to ask about her friend, but she had no specific news. "I can't tell you anything about Malcolm, Eunice, but the clerk did say that no one was injured, so I think your friend must be all right."

Eunice blushed, and then curtsied. Finally, she threw her bony arms around Rose's shoulders and hugged her tightly. "Thank you, Miss Rose, thank you. I hope we get a chance to go back to Virginia, oh, I hope we do. I know you liked it ever so much better there. And . . . and I did, too."

Rose simply nodded, so Eunice closed the door quietly. After she left, Rose took off her chemise and put on her nightrail. Then she reached for her wooden puzzle, the candle Eunice had left at her bedside giving her plenty of light to see by. Peter hadn't said or done anything today that made her think he was the person sending her the gifts, yet who else could it be? She gathered her papers together where she had scribbled notes, along with such flower meanings as she remembered.

The horticulture books were wonderful for descriptions, but they did not have the kind of information Lily had gathered over the years. How Rose longed for the vocabulary now. She had copied out many of Lily's lists, but when Bertram had grabbed her so rudely, of course they had been left behind, like everything else of value to her.

And yet the only thing that really mattered was here in London with her.

As if her thoughts had conjured him, the curtains covering the French doors that stood ajar onto her private terrace stirred and a dark-cloaked man stepped through.

But he had not covered his hair, and Rose knew at once that it was Peter. She stifled the greeting that rose involuntarily to her lips, forcing herself to remain in bed with the sheet drawn up to her lap. She tried to hide the pieces of paper she'd written on, but there were too many.

Peter halted as if surprised by her lack of greeting. He saw the movement of her hands, however, and smiled. "What do you have there, Rose?" he asked.

"Is that what you ask when you burst into a lady's bedchamber?" she asked, trying to sound angry at the intrusion.

Peter smiled. "As I've never burst into a lady's bedchamber before, I'm not sure what I am supposed to say."

There was no point in debating propriety, so Rose cut to the heart of her question. "Did you send these?" she asked, indicating the frame and wooden pieces that she had arranged.

"Yes," he said simply.

"Where did you get them?"

"I carved them."

"You?" she blurted out, surprised. "I never saw you carve anything before."

He smiled again, and the easiness of that untroubled smile that she had seen so rarely lulled her. She did not even notice when he came closer and sat on the edge of the bed. He picked up one of the carvings between his strong fingers. A little shiver ran though Rose at the memory of those hands on her.

"At home, I didn't have much time," he said quietly, "between the work at your plantation and at ours."

"True," she said, and nodded. "But where did you learn to do carvings such as these?"

"On board ship. Most sailors learn to carve figures or work knots to pass the long hours at sea. I had more time to learn the craft in prison camp." He looked up at her, his gaze moving from the pieces she held in her palm to land caressingly on her face.

"I thank you," she began, when Peter leaned forward and took her hand in his.

"Don't thank me, Rose," he said. "Tell me that you understood what I was trying to say."

"Ah well, no, actually, I didn't. Not very well. I don't have Lily's vocabulary, you see, and while I could remember some of the meanings—such as rosemary, 'that's for remembrance,' I didn't know some of them."

His gaze was on her mouth, and she returned the look with interest. They leaned toward each other irresistibly, then for the second time that day, spoke simultaneously.

"We need to talk."

They both sat back, Rose against the pillows, Peter still at the edge of the bed. He reached for the frame and took it from her hand with a gentle caress against her fingertips.

What had changed in Peter? she wondered. He seemed more at ease with himself than she had ever seen him. Was it the news from home?

She was about to ask him when he began to speak. "Myrtle, here," his fingertip outlined the branch he'd carved, "means home. Mimosa," the tile with the nodding flower clusters, "that means secret love."

Peter's voice wobbled for a moment, but he did not look up. He reached for another tile. "This is—"

"Ranunculus," she put in. "That one I recognized right away. They're quite fashionable here in London. But I don't remember what it means."

This time he looked up and held her gaze. "It means 'your charms are radiant.' " He leaned forward and kissed her, a gentle brushing of the lips that nearly overwhelmed her with its tenderness. She couldn't look away. He learned forward and brushed her lips again, but when she would have leaned into him and deepened the kiss, he pulled back.

She couldn't help the little disappointed sound that came from her. He gave her that luminous smile again but said nothing about that, just went back to cataloguing the carvings' meanings.

"You identified the rosemary, you said, and the next here, this foliage, is from a yew tree."

" 'Sorrow,' " she said, remembering her secret garden. "What is it for?"

"My sorrow at losing you."

Rose drew in a breath, moved, but Peter went on in the same even voice. "Did you recognize the magnolia? It's native to my region."

Magnolia grandiflora," Rose said. "I love that name. It's called that for its big glossy leaves and huge white blossoms. Yes, I remember."

"Magnolia represents love of nature, something I think we share. And it stands for sweetness."

In the brief pause, he held her gaze intently. Shivers raced up her spine. She had never thought Peter would ever talk to her this way.

"The evergreen was not too hard to puzzle out," Rose said. "It's 'everlasting' or 'forever,' isn't it?"

"Very good. What about this?" He had worked his way around one side of the frame to the other. "Where is the center piece?" he asked.

"Oh, 'tis here," Rose said. She reached out to the mahogany table at her bedside. "It's so lovely and smooth. The iris is what made me realize there was a message in the flowers."

"I should have remembered you didn't know all the meanings. I'm sorry," he said.

"I copied out a lot of Lily's meanings, but—"

"Never mind," he said. "Let's finish this. You know what this is, of course."

"Mmm," Rose said, "a rose."

"And you know what that means," he said softly.

"Well, what color is this meant to be?" she said in a teasing voice, almost unable to bear the weight of the intimacy between them.

"What color would you like it to be?" Peter returned, his voice light, but she could still sense the emotion behind his words. "That's the problem with carvings. They're so monochromatic. Your watercolors are more expressive, with the way you use color." As he spoke, his fingers wandered from the carving to her hand, tracing patterns on her palm that only he could see.

He leaned toward her again, and she toward him, and their lips met so effortlessly, so naturally, that the kiss made her feel as if she were floating. Peter's hands reached for hers, and he intertwined his fingers with hers as he continued to kiss her with surpassing gentleness.

When he pulled his mouth away, it was only to kiss her cheeks, her temples, her eyes, and to whisper to her the remaining meanings. "Orange and safflower symbolize marriage; safflower also means welcome. Euonymus means 'your charms are engraved upon my heart.' "

He unlaced one hand from hers, used it to cup the back of her head against his palm. Keeping his lips against hers, he angled his head and took the kiss from leisurely to ardent with the simple pressure of his mouth against hers. She opened for him, and he slipped in to explore the warm recesses of her mouth. Again the deep sense of rightness pervaded her. Ending the kiss only when they both lacked breath, Rose found herself lying against the headboard, pillows propping up her neck and shoulders.

It was a nice position from which to view Peter. "Oh, Rose, I love you," he said, deep and low. "Whatever happens tomorrow, will you remember that?"

She didn't answer because he took her mouth again, and she gave herself up to the kiss, to him, to the man she loved. He slipped her nightrail from her shoulders while his lips still moved on hers.

He bent to kiss her, his hands sliding from her shoulders to cup her breasts. When he leaned over her to kiss them, she slipped his queue ribbon from his hair, and thrust her hands into the thick mass. As Peter's mouth lovingly renewed acquaintance with her breasts, his hair brushed over the tops of her breasts, and her nipples hardened. Gentle nips from his teeth sent heat spiraling to her lower body, and with a low laugh, he swept the covers from her waist down, using his hands to pull her nightrail down the rest of the way. His mouth returned to her breasts over and over, although his tongue also made forays to her rib cage, her waist, and navel.

"You've been dressed for far too long," she whispered to him. Peter was dressed in dark trousers and a simple white shirt, much as he might have been at home. He had long since discarded the cloak. Rose pulled his shirt from his trousers, thrilled to feel his rippling muscles smooth and taut under his shirt, and she probed the male nipples that pebbled under her touch.

"Help me with this," she demanded as she reached the buttons of his trousers.

Chapter Twenty-two

The ruling passion, be it what it will,
The ruling passion conquers reason still.
      —Alexander Pope, *Moral Essays*, 1732

"Impatient, aren't you?" he asked.

"It has been too long," she said.

Almost on the same breath, he answered, "I agree." He pulled his boots off, then his trousers, and as he pulled the last wisp of muslin from her body, he stepped out of his own remaining clothes.

When Peter covered her and she felt the warmth of his long, strong body pressed everywhere along hers, it was the most satisfying feeling she had ever known.

She gave a long, luxuriant sigh, and as she stretched, Peter slid between her thighs.

"Did one of those flowers mean welcome?" she asked. "Because you certainly are."

"Safflower," he murmured, positioning himself so that his entry was but an inch away.

"Welcome," she said, "oh, welcome, love." His slow, gliding entry was so exquisite that she found herself holding her breath. When she released it, it was on a sigh of rapture. Peter held himself still and deep so she could experience it fully.

It was enough, to hold him that way deep within her, to savor the feel of him, and then suddenly it was no longer enough. Desire grew, until she begged him to move, and he laughingly accommodated. Neither of them had much endurance after so long apart; after a few deep thrusts, they climaxed together, Peter's face buried against her neck, his hands in her hair.

When it was over, and they had sagged against the pillows, she raised her legs around him. "I won't be sore," she said, and his slow beguiling smile was one she had longed to see since she had first known him.

"That's good," he said, "because I want you so much, I wasn't going to be a gentleman about it. Keep your legs just as they are," he directed. "Hold on now, love."

He rolled them, gently gripping her arms, until he lay on his back, smiling up at her, and she was atop him. She put her hands down to balance herself on his chest, and realized that he was still hard inside her, and had just flexed.

Her eyes widened with surprise, and she moved a little, finding she could adjust the depth of him inside her. "I take it you like that?" he asked impudently.

"How did you guess?" she asked.

"The way you're holding me," he said. Rose looked down—her palms were flat on the planes of his chest.

"What do you mean?"

He flexed. She contracted around him instinctively.

"That," Peter said, his eyes sparkling in the candlelight.

Her surprised "oh" turned into a long moan of delight as he held her hips and gently thrust up. When he did it again, and she climaxed, he said, "That was for you, love."

Then he rolled them back to their original positions. Rising above her, he thrust deep, and then began to move in long, deep, rhythmic strokes that had her clinging to him helplessly. She felt the contractions rippling through her, taking her in their path, arching her back and tightening the muscles in her legs.

Her contractions caught him as well and tossed him into the swirling tide of pleasure. Peter sealed their mouths together, and as he spent himself inside her, their cries stayed within the enclosing circle of their mouths, their bodies, and their hearts.

"I love you," Rose said as her arms slipped from around him at last, sweet lassitude stealing over her.

"Remember that I love you," were the last words she heard from Peter as he slid from her, only to enfold her again in his arms, tight against his thundering heart. She never heard the rhythm slow and become steady, because she had already fallen asleep, soft and trustingly as a child.

Despite the night just past, Rose was up betimes, neither surprised nor concerned to find herself alone. After all, Peter had said he'd see her today. He had also said he loved her. She possessed more energy this morning than she'd felt in a long time. Even the disappearance of yesterday's glorious weather and the advent of a more typical English rainy day could not dampen her spirits.

But she made certain to school her expression before entering the breakfast room. Bertram sat at the head of the table, sunk in glowering misery. Rose decided to take a tray in her room, but Bertram fixed her with a vicious glare.

"Sit down," he barked.

She dropped into a chair. "How in blue blazes did you manage to sabotage my auction?" he said accusingly.

"How indeed? I didn't know anything about what happened yesterday. Don't be ridiculous, Bertram."

"How did you do it, Rose? Did you sneak out to see that bloody American?"

Surely Bertram didn't know about last night. No, of course not, Rose told herself, but she felt her heart skip a beat.

"You must have had the news confirmed by now," she said, signaling the footman to pour her tea. "Other people on the ship or ships that arrived yesterday must have told the same tale."

"I don't want you there," he said again.

Rose lifted two broiled tomato halves onto her

plate, and added toast. "Actually, Bertram, you need me more than ever," she said confidently.

"Oh? And why is that?"

"Because I am still the only one who knows what the plantation is worth, and how much weight to place on one season's ruined crops. There will be some who will think to bid you down. You don't have to do that."

Bertram made a few more derogatory remarks, but in the end, gave up. They set out a few hours later—in the carriage, since the rain had not let up.

Only half of the men who were there yesterday had returned, and one or two of them had sent their men of affairs instead of coming in person. Yesterday's news had indeed damaged the prospects for Bertram's sale, but he insisted it had to go on. There was a particularly large debt coming due, and he did not think waiting and letting the news spread would do him any good. Some creditors might close in on him even more tightly if they thought he'd lost assets.

There was no reasoning with him and Rose didn't bother to try. She took a seat much closer to the front this time, and Bertram shot her an evil glance, but did not object.

The opening bids were half of what Bertram had expected. Although he made his displeasure known, even threatening to cancel the auction, the men present sensed that the advantage was theirs.

The door at the back of the salon opened and Rose knew without even looking around that Peter was there. Peter seated himself while his barrister approached Bertram's and the two put their heads together.

A low cry of dismay came from the Fairchild family's lawyer, who began shaking his head violently. Peter's man walked back to his place beside Peter and sat down.

Rose looked at Peter, who was sitting a few rows back. His arms were folded impassively, but when he caught Rose's regard, he smiled with an intimacy that she knew in every warm place in her body was meant for her alone.

The man at Peter's side tapped his arm, and when the green eyes had glanced away and down to the man sitting next to him, Rose felt almost bereft.

Just then, Bertram exclaimed, "Bloody hell, no." He began to scowl while his barrister continued to whisper urgently in his ear. What on earth was going on?

Peter looked at Rose once more, gave her a conspiratorial wink, then rose from his seat. He strode to the front of the room, confidence limning every line of his tall frame.

Bertram had jumped to his feet as if he would block Peter's way. "I don't believe it, you backwater Colonial bastard. Where is your proof? Where is your proof, God damn it?"

Several of the men spoke up. "What's going on, Lansdale?"

"By God, this is damned irregular," another man exclaimed. No one seemed to notice Rose was there, or apologized for the rough language. She didn't care; she was fascinated by whatever drama was about to play out before her.

"Gentlemen, I beg your indulgence," Peter

began. "This auction is effectively at an end, although you are welcome to stay to hear the explanation."

"Over? How can it be over? If Lansdale has sold you that land outside the terms of this auction, I won't bloody allow it," one of the men cried.

"Gentlemen," Peter began again. "The land is no longer for sale. Lord Lansdale has no say over its disposition. I own the property and I am not disposed to sell it."

"No!" Bertram screamed, his face purple with rage. "So your man said, but I don't believe it. Ralph didn't do anything with that property while he was whoring and drinking himself to death. It's mine."

Peter had turned his head to look at Bertram. "Lord Lansdale, your father executed a contract with me, after I had contacted him about the property, before his death."

"Why didn't I know about this before? Why didn't you say something when you first came to London? What sort of game have you been playing, sniffing about my sister's skirts?"

Peter strode over to Bertram in two steps, seized his coat by its collar, and spoke quietly. Nevertheless his voice carried, for the room was not that large. Rose heard every word.

"Say one more disrespectful word about your sister, Lord Lansdale, and I will toss you out into the street like a common thug. This business of the property concerns you and me. In actual point of fact, it no longer concerns you, but I am trying to explain the circumstances because they are rather unusual."

Peter pushed Bertram down into a chair. "Now,

are you going to allow me to explain, or shall we just end this right now?"

Bertram sullenly nodded yes. Peter stepped away from Bertram, turning to face the fascinated crowd. "In addition to the news about Willow Oaks that arrived by ship yesterday, I received an additional bit of news. And a contract.

"Lady Rose's father," and Peter turned and formally acknowledged her presence in the room with a bow, "had entered into correspondence with me prior to his death. I offered to buy Willow Oaks and told him of my plans for the property. Perhaps he knew his sons wouldn't want it, or he approved the use I planned to make of the land. In any case, he agreed to sell me the property before his death."

"But he died, and Ralph inherited, and then I did," Bertram broke in resentfully. "That contract is no good. I supersede it as Earl."

Peter waited until Bertram stopped speaking, then resumed in a strong, even voice. "The contract was sent to America aboard a ship that encountered a storm. The *Constance* was considered lost at sea. What, in fact, happened was that, as a result of the storm, the ship drifted off course, making landfall finally in Haiti. From there, the survivors made their way north. The packet of documents was in the purser's safe and he did not survive the journey. Since the key went to his watery grave with him, it took some time to find someone able to open the safe. At that point, the documents were recovered, sorted out, and finally sent on their way."

Peter's barrister stood and produced the contract from a sheaf of papers he carried in a folio.

He brought it to Bertram's barrister, who looked at it avidly.

"My brother-in-law Adam received the contract just after I'd left for England and sent it on a ship after me. I received it just yesterday."

One man spoke up. "Why doesn't he know about it?" he asked, indicating the barrister who stood at Bertram's shoulder.

Cranwell spoke. "The Fairchilds have changed legal counsel since the ninth Earl's death." Bertram nodded glumly.

Peter crossed one booted foot over the other, and leaned back against the wall, apparently unconcerned about the explosion he had just set off in the now-hushed room. "So I thank you for your time, gentlemen. Any further discussion will be between Lord Lansdale and myself. I give you good day."

Muttering, talking, shaking their heads, the men filed out of the room.

"Give me that," Bertram said, extending his hand toward his barrister, who was still examining the contract. The man bent over his shoulder and whispered urgently to him.

"Wait a moment, Walters," Bertram said. He looked at Rose. "Come here, Rose."

Rose stood up and went toward the men at the front of the room. She wondered why Bertram's tone had changed from frustration to something that sounded like satisfaction.

"You were so eager to gloat that you didn't read all of this, did you, Walters? Look at this clause. Am I right, Coverdell?" he asked, listening as the lawyer whispered into his ear once more.

"This contract says that any sale of the property

is contingent upon the approval of Lady Rose. Therefore, 'tis not valid.''

All eyes turned suddenly to Rose. "Papa did what?" she asked.

Bertram's lawyer spoke. "Your father stipulated that the sale of Willow Oaks had to receive your approval.''

"Then 'tisn't given. I am the Earl now," Bertram interjected.

Coverdell looked intensely uncomfortable. Peter's barrister spoke instead. "I'm afraid not, your lordship. Lady Rose is specified by name. You may not stand in her stead in this matter.''

Coverdell nodded, his Adam's apple taut on his narrow neck. "He is correct," he said, his lips pinched.

"But I own Willow Oaks and everything attached to that property, as well as all other properties under the Lansdale purview," Bertram insisted petulantly.

"You don't own me, Bertram," Rose spoke up.

"Then what? You'll give it all to this American?" Turning to Peter, without even waiting for Rose to answer, he said coldly, "And you'd better have the blunt to back this up. I'll hold you to that price, of course. This contract was made before the storm, so you'll get no discount for its current condition.''

"Nor have I asked for any, Lord Lansdale," Peter said, unmoved.

"Well, Rose?"

This was her dream, wasn't it? Rose thought to herself, then realized it wasn't. Her father had only given her the chance to approve the property, not to own it herself. He had, in effect, sold it to Peter. But what . . .

"What if I do not approve?" she asked, keeping her eyes off Peter, looking only at Coverdell.

"The sale is not valid unless you approve it."

"Then if she doesn't, it reverts to me?" Bertram said, exultant.

"Only until Lady Rose approves a sale."

"Don't do it, Rose. Devonbury is about to offer for you. I'll get him to buy it. You'd prefer that, wouldn't you? Walters only came here for the property anyway."

"Did you?" Rose asked, turning to Peter.

"That's something I intend to discuss with you privately, Lady Rose," Peter said. "Will you do me that honor?"

"Rose, what are you thinking?" Bertram said. "Has he asked you to marry him? And if he does now, don't you think it's for the property? What has he been doing in London all this time, if not waiting for that contract to turn up?"

He turned to Peter. "You contacted our old firm, and found my father's notes that the barrister kept of their dealings on this matter. Your man said as much to me just now. But you knew that wouldn't stand up in a court of law. So you hung about London, hoping to get enough to make your case."

Bertram sneered. "Then your ship came in. How fortuitous for you."

Peter continued to regard Rose steadily, as if they were the only two people in the world. He didn't speak, neither confirming nor denying anything that had been said.

She looked at him. "Peter?" she asked.

"I would like to speak to you alone, Rose."

"I forbid you, Rose. He'll compromise you, and

then you'll be forced to marry him. He'll have your consent, and the property."

At that, Rose pulled her gaze away from Peter, and smiled involuntarily, thinking of last night. Then she had to laugh, she really couldn't help it. The men regarded her, dumbfounded, except for Peter, who looked away, one side of his mouth twitching with suppressed laughter.

"Ah, Bertram, if you only knew." Rose shook her head.

She then looked at Peter, and held out her hand. "Come, let's talk."

"You're not going anywhere with that blackguard." Bertram continued to sputter.

Peter stepped forward, but didn't take her hand. "Your pardon, Lady Rose. This needs taking care of first." He moved back toward Bertram's chair. In an easy motion, he put his hands on Bertram's shoulders and hauled him bodily from the chair.

"This is for your treatment of your sister." He paused a moment, letting his posture and his intent sink in. Bertram didn't move. "Put up your fists, Bertram," Peter said in a soft, deadly voice.

"You wouldn't dare," Bertram said.

"I only give warning once."

"You wouldn't dare," he said again.

Peter said nothing else. He drove his fist into Bertram's stomach, and when Bertram doubled over, Peter clipped him on the jaw. Bertram toppled heavily to the floor.

Rose clapped a hand over her mouth, not sure whether to laugh or cry. Her choices were narrowing. She didn't want Peter to take them away from her any more than Bertram already had, even if Peter acted from a motivation wholly unlike Bertram's.

While the other men rushed to Bertram's side, Rose turned to Peter.

"What was that for?"

"For slighting your honor, for doubting that you knew your own mind, and . . . for taking you away."

"Away from you?" she asked, tucking her hand into the crook of Peter's elbow.

"Away from what you loved."

With that enigmatic statement, Peter escorted Rose from the salon. Neither of them looked behind them as they left.

Chapter Twenty-three

For nothing this wide universe I call,
Save thou, my rose; in it thou art my all.
                              —William Shakespeare
                              Sonnet 109, 1609

It had stopped raining. Rose didn't want to be confined inside a carriage anyway, and the ground did not seem too wet. As they walked, Rose went over the scene at the auction in her mind. Something about it bothered her. They entered Hyde Park.

Just as they approached a bench, the rain began again, and they hastened back into the street to hire a hackney.

"Where to, Rose?" Peter asked. "You want to ask

me something." Along with his new more tender mood seemed to have come a remarkable sensitivity to her thoughts and feelings. Briefly, she thought this must have been what Peter was like before Joanna had altered the course of his life and destroyed his trust in women.

But she did not want to become distracted. "Were you going to tell me about the clause in my father's contract?" she asked.

"Of course." Peter leaned out to speak to the driver. Rose didn't really care where they went, at least not until they worked matters out between them. He indicated with a circular motion that they should just keep driving.

"Then why didn't you tell me sooner?"

"You heard me say I didn't know until yesterday that the contract had been signed by your father. Although Cranwell had learned of its existence, without the actual contract, I stood no chance of pressing my case."

"But why didn't you tell me last night?" She blushed at the memories, but stubbornly kept her gaze on him.

"I wanted you to know that I loved you."

"Is that what you came to London for, or for the sale?"

"Do you doubt me, Rose?" His gaze was searching and intent.

"I hate to say my brother is right about anything, but you have been here for some time and not declared yourself to me."

"But I did, nearly two weeks ago."

She looked at him, puzzled. "I haven't seen you since that night I refused . . . since the night I was, um, unable to dance with you."

He reached out a fingertip to stroke the tip of her nose. "Don't turn all stiff and proper on me now, dear one."

"Did you think to play Devonbury against me?" he asked softly, clasping her hand between his.

He wasn't angry, she saw. He truly only wanted to understand. She had already lost her heart to Peter, but this only made her love him more.

"No. But if he was my only chance to get away from my family, I—I don't know what I would have done."

She saw him acknowledge the hard truth of what she had said. "I understand. I can't blame you if you thought you had no choice." He took her chin with his hand, tipped her head up to him. "But you didn't love him."

She shook her head. He leaned forward to kiss the tip of her nose. Then he began to speak again.

"I did come to London for you, dearest Rose. I came to see if Bertram had taken you away from Willow Oaks by force, but when I saw you, you looked fine. I couldn't cause a scene, and I knew I wouldn't be allowed to court you, so I tried to see you at the social events of this ghastly marriage mart." She smiled ruefully, and reached up a hand to smooth back his hair.

"Seeing you with Devonbury made me realize how much I loved you. I didn't think that words were enough, seeing that there had been harsh words between us before. So I started sending you the carvings."

"Yes, I know you told me of their meanings last night, but they were not so easy to figure out."

"Didn't you read them?"

"Read them?" She frowned with concentration,

and then looked at him. "I don't know what you mean."

"Rose, what is your address?" Peter asked. "I have to show you."

"But you've been there."

"That was coming from a different part of London, and at night. We need to go to your home."

"Why?" She still didn't understand.

"I don't think you're going to believe me until I show you. I want there to be nothing but trust between us, now and forever." He leaned out again and told the driver her address.

"But I love you, Peter, you know that."

"Aye, and 'tis the most precious gift I have ever been given. You, Rose. Just you. But I don't blame you for having some doubt, given what you learned today."

"What are the carvings going to show me that I don't already know?" She laced the fingers of one hand through his, and he clasped them tightly in return.

"There's something more, something I thought you would see. I guess I haven't done this courtship business very well."

"It has been rather . . . unorthodox," Rose said with a smile.

" 'Unorthodox' might well be your middle name," he teased.

They arrived at the Lansdale family town home soon thereafter. Rose's mother was out making calls, so there were only servants home when Rose brought Peter in.

"Let me fetch the carvings," she said, preparing to go up the stairs.

"I don't want to let you out of my sight." During

the rest of the carriage ride, she had told him how
Bertram had drugged her and stolen her away from
Willow Oaks. Peter said that, in that case, he only
wished that he had hit Bertram harder.

"This would be most irregular, Peter, for you to
come upstairs," she said, making one last stab at
propriety as he began to follow her.

"You forget, I've been there," Peter said, wag-
gling his eyebrows in a mock leer.

Eunice, peering around a corner after hearing
an unexpected male voice, was the only one to see
them both go up.

"Show me, Peter," Rose said. When they entered
her room, he picked up the frame and emptied
out the pieces. Adam's way would probably have
been a better one, he reflected, but he'd wanted
to do things his own way, so he had no one but
himself to blame. And if it was his way to make it
harder on himself, well, perhaps he had learned
something. Or a few things.

Turning the pieces over, he inserted them with
the flower names up. "Look now."

She looked down, began to read. "Myrtle, um,
this is mimosa, ranun . . ."

Peter jammed his hands in his pockets. He
couldn't rush this, much as he might want to. It
was too important that she understand. "The Latin
name is acacia."

"Mmm, all right. Ranunculus, rosemary . . ."

Damn, she didn't understand. This wasn't going
well. "Rose, read the first letter of each flower
name," he said desperately.

"M, M, R, R . . ."

He took her hand, made her look up at him. "It's acacia, love, A. Please start over."

"Peter, I know you began sending me these two weeks ago, long before you knew of the contract my father sent you, but I still don't understand."

He seated her on the bed, went to one knee so their eyes were almost level. "One more time, darling."

She was beginning to look exasperated, but obediently bent her head and started again. Peter slipped one hand into his pocket, touching the two tiles that rested there. "M, M . . . ah, A instead, R, R, Y, M, E, R, O, S, S."

"Euonymous is the Latin name for spindle. See, that's what I carved there."

"All right, um, O, S, E."

So much for subtlety. He took her hand. "Here is how we signaled in the Navy. Short bursts, then stop for the end of words or punctuation. Follow me." He took her hand, traced out the first five tiles.

"M, A, R, R, Y. Stop." He moved her finger to the next set. "M, E. Stop." She looked at him, understanding dawning in her beautiful blue eyes. He did not release her fingers, though.

He said the last letters softly. "R, O, S, E. Stop." He reached into his pocket and slipped the last two pieces into the frame.

"P, W," Rose read on the last two tiles. "Primrose and wisteria. What do the flowers on the other side mean, Peter?" she asked. "The ones that represent your initials?"

"Primrose is for hope," he said slowly. "It also means 'I can't live without you.' "

"And the W?

" 'I cling to thee,' " he recited softly. Then he placed both his hands over hers, enclosing her hands and his over the circle of wood he had created to tell her of his love.

"And will you?" he asked. "Will you marry me, Rose?"

She bent her head down to his so their foreheads touched. The completed puzzle slid from her lap onto his knees. "Yes, my love. I understand. Yes." She straightened. "Now, when can we leave?"

"In a hurry?" he asked teasingly.

Suddenly they heard shouting, a man's deep angry tone, and a piercing woman's voice.

"I think we're both in a hurry now," she just had time to say, because suddenly Eunice burst in. "Miss Rose. Ooh, Master Peter!" she exclaimed. "The two of you had best be leaving now. Master Bertram is here and he met his mum on the way home."

"We can get out through here," Peter said, indicating the terrace doors through which he had entered last night. I'll show you how I climbed up the wall to get in. We can get down the same way."

"Is there anything of particular value to you?" he asked Rose, looking around the room. She picked the puzzle up from the floor where it had slipped when she and Peter stood up.

"Only this," she said, holding it in one hand. "And you." She stepped into Peter's arms. He hugged her hard, quickly, before setting her a little away from him.

Peter turned to Eunice. He named the inn where he had first stopped when he came to London. "Meet us there tonight. I'll have booked passage for America. I don't need to tell you not to say anything about where we are."

"Of course not, Master Peter. And me 'n' Malcolm, we'll name our first child after you, Master Peter. Or you, Miss Rose."

They both turned to stare at her in amusement. "Aren't you getting ahead of yourselves a bit?" Rose asked.

The little maid twisted her hands in her apron. "He asked me just before Master Bertram came."

"And you came anyway? How dear of you, Eunice," Rose exclaimed.

The shouting on the stairs grew louder.

"We'll see you tonight, then, Eunice."

"Oh, indeed you shall, mistress. Go on now, I'll tell them that you weren't 'ere. That I didn't see you. Go on."

Go they did, but Peter could not help smiling when he saw Lady Dalby's carriage turning into Rose's street as they left by the back garden. What timing she had.

Peter found a hackney that took them from west London to the Strand. Peter installed them at the inn and, with a quick hard kiss for Rose, went out to look for a ship.

While Peter searched for a ship to take them to America, Rose sat and marveled over the puzzle he had created for her, the beauty of it, the meanings he had chosen, and the message he had created.

They came within sight of Willow Oaks on the heat of an August day much like the day Rose remembered when she had arrived in America the year before.

This time she had a husband at her side, new life growing within her conceived from their love, and her loyal servant who had also found her heart in America.

As they came up the drive, Rose drank in the sight of the late-summer flowers that blossomed all around them, the deep green of the leaves and foliage, the drone of bees, and the flitting of butterflies from one plant to the next, pollinating and spreading future life everywhere they landed.

She saw evidence of the storm in the downed trees and trampled fields, but it did not look as bad as she had feared. She knew that people had been working for weeks, though, to clean it up. But she had no doubt that they would be able to restore the plantation to order and undo the damage eventually.

Then Rose gasped and sat up straighter on the seat of the carriage bringing them home. "Peter, what's that?" she asked and pointed. A bit of white gleamed off to one side near the water. Peter had brought the carriage in at an angle off the main drive, and she had wondered why.

"Why, what does it look like, Mistress Walters?" Peter asked. Rose loved this relaxed and charming Peter, the one that had emerged when he was sure of her, and sure that his love was returned. She had loved him before, but had lost her heart again—and again—to him in the weeks they had been traveling. Wouldn't Lily be thrilled to see Peter's happiness restored?

"Are you listening, fair Rose?" he asked. "What do you see?"

"I see a gazebo in the center of my knot garden. Oh, Peter, where did it come from?"

"I asked Adam to have it built for you before I left. I regret only that I was not here to do it myself."

"Oh, thank you, thank you," she said, reaching over to hug him. "You did know how much this meant to me."

"Remember, we have company," he admonished her playfully as she planted a kiss on his ear.

"Eunice won't mind. Besides, I think we are about to drop her at the stables, aren't we?"

"You can just let me off here, Master Peter," Eunice sang out from behind them. Peter slowed the carriage. Eunice gathered up her skirts and jumped down.

"I'll be up to the house later," she said.

"No hurry," Peter and Rose said almost simultaneously. Eunice smiled and waved as they drove away.

"We have to go to Oak Grove," Rose said. "Don't you want to see your new nephew?"

"Not as much as I want to see my beautiful wife in daylight in a bed that doesn't move, rock, or sway." Rose blushed.

"You can stop that now, love, we are married," Peter said with a grin. " 'Tis all perfectly legal."

"We were married by a ship's captain!" Rose said.

"I know you'll want a proper wedding and Lily will be more than happy to help you arrange it. But we weren't going to spend all those weeks apart."

"No, you're right, of course, my lord husband," Rose said demurely. "But I do think we should hold it sooner rather than later."

"What are you saying, Rose?" Peter asked, while his heart filled with joy.

" 'Twould be better to have an early marriage than to risk embarrassment and scandal."

"We haven't caused enough of that already?"

"But that was on the other side of the Atlantic," she said, laughing. "We have a clean slate here."

"Most of your flowers were spring flowers in your garden, Rose, were they not? Now that I have lifted the scales from my eyes, will you tell me what they were?"

"The azalea is for first love. White heather is for 'wishes that come true.' Phlox means—"

"Wait, I know that one. I had to choose between the primrose and the phlox for the puzzle I made you. Phlox means 'our souls are united,' does it not?"

"Very good," Rose said approvingly. "The tulips both have meanings of love. The red is a declaration of love, while the yellow stands for hopeless love. I wasn't feeling all that hopeful at the time I planted some of these."

"I know," Peter said softly, reaching out to clasp her fingers. "I know."

He pulled the carriage to a stop at the end of the circular drive.

"This day would be complete if I could see Lily and Adam and the children. Oh, and her new baby," Rose said, putting out her hand to Peter for him to help her down from the carriage.

Peter bent and swept her up beneath her knees. "Even though we've been married several weeks now, carrying you across the threshold of a cabin isn't terribly romantic."

"Peter, don't, I'm too heavy."

"You weren't before, and you aren't now. Or at least you won't be for several more months."

Peter carried her up the steps to the entranceway. Holding her with one arm, precariously balanced, he quickly reached out to open the door. He bent his head to join his mouth to hers as he stepped over the threshold.

Rose felt the familiar warmth rise within her, and twined her arms around his neck, giving herself up to the kiss.

Several voices called out, "Welcome back!" Peter nearly dropped her in surprise.

But remembering her delicate condition, he was able to ease Rose to her feet and make sure she was standing before three sturdy little bodies ran into him, jumping in their excitement to be picked up and hugged.

"Mama says you're our aunt now," a voice observed from the vicinity of Rose's waist.

"Violet!" she exclaimed, delighted. "I didn't think you would be here." She hugged the little girl and gave her a big kiss.

"Daddy's gots spies," she said in a loud, dramatic whisper, "and we knew when you docked because somebody was sent to watch for you."

Peter was working to extricate himself from his nephews' death grip on his knees so he could hug Lily as she came forward with the new baby in her arms.

"Everything all right?" he asked as he hugged her and the baby both. "He looks wonderful. And so do you."

Lily smiled. "Are you two married or do I have to take my children away from this scandal?" she asked in a low voice accompanied by an expectant look.

"Legal, Lily, it's all legal," Peter said.

"Hmmph," Rose put in, "if you call a five-minute ceremony on the deck of a ship a proper wedding."

"Well, we can fix that," Lily said. "But in the meantime, congratulations, Rose," she said.

Leaning forward for Rose to admire the baby and in a low voice that only Rose could hear, Lily murmured, "I owe you a greater debt than you can know. You've brought my brother back to me."

"Oh, no, Lily, he saved *me*, and brought me back." Rose cast a loving glance at Peter, whose back was being heartily thumped by Adam.

"I mean that loving you has restored Peter to the man he was before."

"Do you really think so?" Rose asked, touching the baby's feather-soft cheek with one finger. He opened his eyes, which were already a deep blue-green, and gave a yawn from his tiny rosebud mouth.

"I know so," Lily said. "He has Adam's eyes, doesn't he?"

"Yes, he does, although their eyes often change a few months after birth."

"What are you going to name him?"

"We'd like to name him Peter. And we would like you to be his godparents."

Peter had come up to Rose, and put one arm around her waist. "We'd be honored, Lily."

Lily looked around. "Why don't you two go upstairs to freshen up from the road. I'll have Adam round up the Bedlamites here. He can take them to the stables for a ride. I'll just nurse the baby, and he'll nod off. Then I can get something together in the kitchen for you. Mistress Steele sent over Virginia ham, some staples, and a lot of fresh fruit."

"Oh no, Lily, you needn't do all that," Rose protested. "Besides, I think the stables might not be the best place for the children just now."

"Why not? Adam took care of the horses while you were away, along with Malcolm."

"Well, that's just the problem, you see. Malcolm and Eunice, well, Malcolm and Eunice," and Rose waved one hand in the air helplessly, blushing.

Peter smiled wickedly. "Rarely have I seen you at a loss for words, my love." He bent to whisper in Lily's ear.

Just then, Eunice entered the room, tying her apron. "Malcolm and Eunice are getting married, I'll have you know, and there's nothing going on down at the stables that you can't take the children to see. The very idea," she sniffed in mock indignation.

But as she walked past them to consult with Rose about what she wanted Cook to make, Peter reached out and plucked a wisp of straw from her hair.

Eunice's composure didn't waver. "I didn't never say there weren't no greeting between us, now did I?" But she, too, blushed while Peter twirled the straw between his fingers, his smile broadening. Lily took Eunice aside to confer while Adam promised the children a ride from Aunt Rose's horses.

"Here we are, love, alone again. Or at least as much as can be managed under the circumstances." He swept her up in his arms again and proceeded to take the stairs two at a time.

When he pushed open the door to her bedchamber, Rose, who had been kissing Peter's chin, his neck, whatever she could reach, opened her eyes. "What is that scent?" she asked, while Peter let her slide down his body slowly. So slowly that when she stood again, she and Peter were molded together from breast to thigh, and she had absolutely no doubt about his intentions.

"No, Peter, not here."

"If not here, where?" he asked, laughing. "Do you want to go out to the gazebo?"

"Oh yes, but not right now."

"When?" he asked, running his hands up and down her back, then bringing them around to the front to unlace her gown.

"Stop, you're distracting me," she said, pushing his hands away playfully. "Where are the flowers?"

"What flowers?" he asked, feigning an innocent look.

Rose saw a single, perfect rose, standing in a narrow crystal vase on the window that overlooked the gazebo. "All this scent can't be coming from that one rose," she said, still trapped within the loving circle of Peter's arms.

"All right, all right, I'll kiss you," she said, Peter's mouth having claimed everything but her mouth as she looked around. His touch, his taste, and his passionate exploration of her mouth—as if it were the first time every time, she thought dazedly—effectively shut off thought.

Instead, there was only Peter, his warm touch, his strength, his own masculine scent, filling all her senses. He walked her backward to the bed, peeling off layers of clothes as he went.

"Close your eyes," he said, kissing each eyelid to make her comply. Then, holding her in his arms, he bent her back. She heard the counterpane being lifted off the bed, then she felt it against her back, and the last of her dress and petticoats were swept down her arms and off her body.

Peter followed her down, but they bumped heads as Rose suddenly sat bolt upright. "Ouch," he complained. She twisted around to look down.

"The bed is covered in rose petals," she said.

"Aye," Peter affirmed, smiling broadly.

"But how could anyone have known when we would arrive?" she asked.

"I worked this out with Adam and Lily before I left. I knew I was coming back with you, Rose," he said. "One way or the other. Now, will you lie down so I can make love to you?"

The petals scattered thickly over the bed under the counterpane were velvety soft. The scent filled her head with perfume.

"You are my perfect Rose," he whispered. Despite the wonderful scent of roses that proclaimed his love for her, nothing matched the velvet softness of Peter's mouth, and no fragrance was equal to the masculine scent that was Peter's own. She was truly home, home at Willow Oaks, home with Peter. Home was anywhere that Peter was, but how glad she was that it was at Willow Oaks.